DEVIL HEIR

USA TODAY BESTSELLING AUTHOR

RACHEL LEIGH

USA TODAY BESTSELLING AUTHOR

RACHEL LEIGH

IT SEEMS TO ME, THAT LOVE COULD BE LABELED
POISON AND WE'D DRINK IT ANYWAYS.
-ATTICUS

For Carolina,
I couldn't do this without you.

PLAYLIST

Part of Me—Afterlife
Unbreakable,—Kingdom Collapse
All I Feel Is You—The Broken View
Fix You—Coldplay
I Will—Matchbox 20
The Thunder Rolls—State of Mine
Enough—From Ashes to New
Dream Away—Keith Wallen
Light Up The Sky—From Ashes to New
Leave—Matchbox 20
It's Been Awhile—Staind

Listen Now
https://bit.ly/devilheirplaylist

PROLOGUE

FOURTEEN YEARS OLD

IT'S TOO SOON. How can someone who claimed to be madly in love with another person, marry someone else only six months later? Not to mention, making that hellish boy a part of our family. He breathes fire and I swear his eyes change from brown to as black as coal when he's angry. He scares me, he really does.

Now, I'm supposed to live in this monstrosity of a mansion with him? I've got no idea what Mom is thinking. Sure, my new stepdad is loaded, but that's about all he is. His son is his spawn and these men are a different breed of human. They lack empathy and knowledge of personal space.

Part of me thought my parents would be together forever. Even if I heard the arguments and the desperation for a better marriage in their voices. I'm starting to feel naive to think that happily ever afters exist. Then again, I'm only fourteen, so what do I know?

"Penelope," Mom hollers from down the long stretch of hallway. My door is cracked open just enough to let her words flow into the room.

"Coming," I yell back. I set my brush down on the new vanity that Richard, my soon-to-be stepdad, bought me. He purchased everything in this room. Everything is brand new. Pink and white walls, matching bedding, and wall art. Nothing like the room I had back in Portland. I'd give it all up to be back there with Dad—to have my family whole again. My insides prick with pain at the realization that we will never go back to that happy place, because none of us are the same people we were back then.

They'll tell me it's not my fault. People fall out of love, blah, blah, blah. It doesn't make me feel any better, though.

One last look in the mirror, and I'm ready to go to the church where my mom will take a new last name, and I'll be the outcast in this family.

Just as I step away from the vanity, my door flies open. At first I expect to see Mom, but since it's not her, I backstep, almost tripping over the stool behind me. "Go away!" I shout at Blaise. He stands there silent but rooted to the spot, like he just came in here to try and scare me again. He's got wide eyes and a blank expression. "I'm not scared of you," I tell him, hoping he doesn't see through the lie.

Slow, but heavy steps bring him in front of me. Face to face with my new brother. "You should be." He smiles devilishly. There's something so dark about this boy.

"Why aren't you dressed for the wedding?" I ask, gripping the sides of my peach-colored dress. Mom picked it out to match all the other girls in the wedding. She said I'm too old to be a flower girl, but the perfect age to be a junior bridesmaid. Blaise and I are set to walk together, since we're the same age. I begged Mom not to make me, but she brushed away my pleas and told me to suck it up.

"Because I don't want to. And I only do what I want."

I swear, the devil lives inside of Blaise. My body shivers every time I'm near him. He even visits me in my dreams and turns them into the worst nightmares. One night, I woke up to a loud bang in my room, and I swear he was in there watching me sleep. Another time, he lit my math textbook on fire because he didn't like that I was in the same class as him and his friends. Just grinned at me, opened it up, and took the flame of a lighter to it. Then he laughed. Who does that?

I turn on my white heels to walk away, but Blaise grabs my arm. "Let me go." I try to jerk away, but it does no good. He grabs a fistful of my perfectly curled hair and pulls. When I go to scream, he slaps a hand over my mouth.

"If you don't stop this wedding, you'll live to regret it. I don't want a stupid sister."

With the little space between his hand and my mouth, I open, then push forward and bite down on the skin of his thumb.

Blaise screeches, then shoves me aside like a ragdoll. I trip over the stool of my vanity and fall on the floor, bumping my head on the footboard of my new bed on the way down.

"Don't say I didn't warn you," Blaise threatens before walking out.

I'm left lying there with a gash on my head that's sure to leave a scar and a small rip in the side of my new dress. Tears stream down my cheeks as I push myself off the floor.

I know I can't stop the wedding. But, I also know that Blaise meant what he said. He's going to make sure I live to regret this day.

FIFTEEN YEARS OLD

Gathered around the dinner table, my stepdad stands up. "Blaise, Penelope, thank you for agreeing to have dinner with us tonight. I know this is out of the ordinary, considering you are busy teens that prefer to eat in your rooms while you watch those YouTube videos on your phones."

YouTube videos? He obviously has no idea what we really do on our phones. For example, five minutes before we came down here, Blaise had posted on the school page, "*Get your masks ready. Tonight, we raise hell. We, as in everyone but my skanky stepsister. Keep your smelly ass home, Penny."*

The comments were cruel. Some laughed, some said much worse. Lilith, the most popular girl in the freshman class, referred to me as Carrie the Freak. Maybe one day I will snap. Maybe one day I should.

I stopped reading the replies after that one.

Richard continues as he looks down on all of us sitting at the table. His eyes stop on me. Something shifts and I can feel him practically undress me with his eyes.

"Richard, go on." Mom nudges him from her seat as if she notices where his attention has gone.

Blaise slams his hands on the table, rattling the silver spoons against the china. "Yeah, Richard. Go on."

"Right," he looks away, "Ana and I didn't want to say anything until we had answers as to what was going on, but I haven't been feeling well lately. After a week's worth of tests, it's been confirmed that the cancer has returned. The good news is, it's contained to just a few spots and hasn't spread to any organs."

When Richard and my mom started dating, she said that he was sick. I don't know all the details, but he had a cancerous tumor in his stomach. The tumor was removed before the cancer had spread and we all assumed that was the end of it.

Blaise drops his fork to his plate with a clank. "And the bad news?"

"The bad news? Well, treatment will make me weak. I might need to take some time off work for a bit."

"That's the bad news?" Blaise blows out an airy breath. "That you'll have to miss work?" His chair slides back and he gets to his feet. "What a fucking shame that you'll have to miss a few days doing what you love the most."

It's apparent that Blaise has some resentment for his dad's busy work schedule. But he doesn't seem to complain at all when he's spending his father's money. I'm not a fan of Richard, by any means, but the guy just announced he has cancer. Again. Even if it isn't wide-spread, Blaise could have shown a little compassion. But that's beneath Blaise. He's making this all about him, like he always does.

We finish dinner in silence. The cook made a delicious honey-glazed salmon with a side of steamed broccoli and white rice. I practically force myself to eat as Richard gawks at me across the table, running his finger over the rim of his wine glass and licking his lips. He's always making these grotesque gestures that make me think he's flirting with me. Mom slops some rice on his plate forcefully, stealing his attention from me.

I push my full plate away, having had enough of Richard's attention.

"Penelope, don't be wasteful." Mom pushes my plate back in front of me.

I snarl as I look back at Richard who sits like a king in his chair with his bottom lip between his teeth.

"I've lost my appetite."

Mom huffs. "Fine. Go. But don't even think about coming down here in the middle of the night and dirtying up dishes for Jules to wash."

"Wouldn't dream of it." God, my mother is the worst. I get up, stop, and turn back around. "Sorry about your results, Richard." I might not like the guy, but I wouldn't wish cancer on my worst enemy.

He doesn't say anything, just lets Mom take his hand as she gawks at him with googly eyes. Sometimes I'm not sure if it's love or obsession she feels toward him. Sometimes I'm not sure if it's toward him or his money.

As I'm walking upstairs to my room, Blaise meets me halfway. "What are you doing up here?" I notice his hands are behind his back. "What do you have?" Blaise's room is in the basement. He never comes up here unless it's to taunt me.

"Move it, chicken legs. I've got shit to do. Ya know, 'cause I've got friends and a life."

I step to the side and let him pass, just so he lets his guard down. Once he does, I grab him from behind. "Show me what you're hiding!" I'm practically riding him piggyback as he continues down the steps. "Show me, Blaise."

Once we reach the bottom, he shakes me off and I fall to the floor. "Make me."

"Mom," I holler from the bottom of the stairs. My arms cross over my chest and I scowl back at Blaise.

He barks out a laugh. "Good luck with that. Even if she did hear you, she'd pretend she didn't."

Blaise walks past me, and being the fricken pushover that I am, I don't even try to stop him. What's the point? He does what he wants, when he wants. Hopefully whatever he was hiding wasn't mine, because if it was, it means he's up to something.

☠

IT'S ten o'clock on my birthday, the night before Halloween. Everyone is having the time of their lives while I'm sitting here scrolling through Facebook and watching Emery, my best friend, read a book. "What do you think they're doing right now?"

"Who?" She peers at me over her paperback.

"Everyone. Everyone who is not us."

Emery closes her book and sets it beside her. "Oh, probably getting drunk, breaking car windows, dancing in the woods with all those strings of neon lights they hang. Some are probably having sex on the ground."

"Sex? You think so?"

"Umm, yes. We're in high school now. Of course our classmates are having sex."

"You think Lilith's done it?"

6

"Lilith most definitely has. In fact, I heard she lost her V-card to your brother."

There's a pang in my chest. Blaise isn't a virgin anymore? Of course he's not. It's Blaise. Most popular guy in the school, even as a freshman. I'll never understand why, but people bow to him. He could get any girl he wants. Even Lilith James.

Emery seems to be deep in thought. "Em, what's wrong?" I grab her attention. She lifts her head and looks at me. "Nothing. Just thinking." Her legs uncross and she stands up. "We should go. They all wear those masks anyways. No one will even know it's us."

My eyebrows hit my forehead. "Are you insane? They'd toss us in the fire without a second thought. Actually, they'd toss me in the fire. You'd be sacrificed."

"Well, if they hate you, then they might as well hate me, too."

"You're the best, Em." She really is. Emery is my only friend and ever since I've arrived in Skull Creek, she's had my back. Even when she gets caught in the crossfire.

"That's what friends are for, right? You know what else friends are for? Crashing parties." She grumbles, "Come on. We can just stand back and watch. Aren't you the least bit curious about what it's like?"

"I'm sorry. I just can't do it."

Emery gets up, eating the space between us. Her hands rest on either side of my shoulders. "Fine then. How about a promise?"

I side-eye her. "A promise?"

"Uh-huh. I promise that one day, I will get us invited to one. Hell, I'll do you one better. One day, we will be with the in-crowd. We will *be* the in-crowd."

I laugh at her attempt at making me feel better. "So, you agree we shouldn't go?"

"I guess." She sighs heavily.

I'm glad she agrees. We'd just be asking for trouble by showing up there. Lilith would fry us. Blaise might even try to kill me.

I drop back down on the bed and reopen the Facebook app. For the hell of it, I click on Lilith's page, curious to see if she has posted anything about Blaise. That's when I see it.

Something that I can never unsee.

I tap Play on the video of Lilith standing next to the fire. Her mask is tipped up as she grips my diary in both of her hands.

"Read it. Read it," is being chanted continuously by the entire student body of Skull Creek High as they prance around in their masks.

Lilith stares the camera dead in the eye as if she's reading directly to me. "Last night, Lucifer came into my room when I was sleeping. He stood over me while I pinched my eyes shut. He was only there for a few minutes, but I think he was pleasuring himself while he watched me. Last week, he tried to get in the bathroom when I was taking a shower. I'm starting to get scared of him." Everyone gasps and giggles in the background. My heart sinks deep into the pit of my stomach. Lilith flips the page. "I followed Blaise last night. He went to that old barn off Highway 88. He's been going there a lot lately just to think. He didn't see me, but I watched him through the side window. He laid there peacefully on some bales of hay and just stared at the ceiling deep in thought."

Blaise enters the frame, trying to snatch the diary away from Lilith as she laughs manically. "All right, you've had your fun. Give it back to me." Lilith puts up a fight, but Blaise wins.

Blaise did this. He stole my diary, and I bet Lilith put him up to it. But, he did it, nonetheless.

A part of me died of humiliation in that moment.

Later that night, as the tears fell, the rest of me wished I could just disappear.

SIXTEEN YEARS OLD

It's never going to stop. *He* is never going to stop. I swing my backpack over my shoulder, ready to face another day in hell at Skull Creek High. It's my birthday today, which is sure to get me some unwanted, "special" treatment.

With my head hanging low, I step off the bus. My eyes skim the school grounds, looking for Emery. She always meets me at the bus.

The only thing worse than walking through this school, is walking through it alone.

When I reach the doors, Mr. Grady holds it open for me. "Thanks," I say to him.

Holding tight to the straps of my backpack, I head straight for my locker, but I'm caught off guard by the whispers and giggles amongst my classmates. I look around, taking notice of them all watching me.

My shoes match, my clothes are all on, and I don't have toilet paper dragging behind me. *What the hell is going on?*

As I approach my locker, my stomach unsettles. There's a crowd gathered and as soon as they see me, the whispers grow louder. "She's here." "Move." "This is gonna be fucking epic."

There's a big part of me that thinks I should turn around and walk out of this school right now. Save myself from the pain I'm about to feel. I have no idea what it is, and I don't want to know. All I want is to be left alone.

Holding my breath, I squeeze my straps and slide through the crowd. A lump rises up my esophagus, tears pooling in the corners of my eyes. Written in red marker down the length of my locker are the words, "You should have never been born." A few kids stand by with their phones raised, recording me—waiting for me to break down, but I won't. I refuse to give them the satisfaction.

"Move," I tell Lilith, who's blocking my path now. My

entire body itches at the unwanted stares coming from my classmates.

"Make me, bitch." She goes to shove me. I glower, trying to go around her, but she steps back in front of me. "What's the matter, birthday girl? Mad that your own family doesn't even acknowledge the day you were born?"

With a scowl, I snap back. "You don't even know what you're talking about, Lilith. Just get out of my way so I can go to class."

Lilith's words don't hurt me. The words on my locker don't even hurt. It's the laughs and the jokes made at my expense from people who just want to be accepted by this moronic clique that is formed out of pure evil.

Half the people in it don't even like each other.

Lilith and Blaise haven't got along since they had sex freshman year and he spread it around town that Lilith practically raped him.

Then there's Wade, who tries to be good, but still follows them. He doesn't take part in their antics but he's always in their shadows.

Chase is just a perv and looks at girls like they are objects.

But, Lilith and her group of mean girls, they are out for blood. They ridicule anyone they think is beneath them—which is everyone—but, I'm at the top of that list. If I had to guess, it's because she has a thing for Blaise and she's jealous of our close living quarters.

Blaise is a bully but most of his cruelty is saved just for me. This entire school bows to these people and I have no idea why.

I spot Emery walking up, and a sweep of relief passes over me. At least I've got one person on my side.

"I said move!" I shove Lilith back, suddenly feeling fearless and powerful with backup nearby. Not that I'd expect Emery to fight my battles, but of course she'd defend me.

Forget my locker. I start toward Emery, but she tucks

herself into the crowd. "Emery," I holler. "Wait up." I go to walk through the maze of students to find her, but she's gone.

"I'm not done with you, birthday girl." Lilith fists a chunk of my hair from behind me and jerks so hard that my follicles feel like they're on fire.

"Let go of me!" I screech.

She doesn't. She just pulls harder.

My backpack slides down my arm, hanging between us as my head is whipped back and forth. Everyone just stands there. Some laughing, some recording. No one even tries to get this crazy girl off me.

"Enough!" I hear Blaise shout.

Lilith loses her grip but doesn't let up.

"Get lost." Lilith snarls at Blaise, before spinning me around and slamming me against my locker.

"I said, enough!" Blaise bares his teeth, fists balled at his sides. Would he really hit a girl? Would he really hit someone to help me? "You know the rules. Now back the fuck off."

Lilith's hands skate down to my throat, wrapping around it and squeezing, but not with enough force to cut off my air supply. "Get off me, you fucking bitch," I howl. Tears stream down my face, but I don't even care. My heart is pounding so hard and nothing matters right now. No one matters. Screw them all.

Lilith gets right in my face. The scent of her mint gum lingering between us. "What did you just call me?"

"You heard me."

I don't even see it coming when her hand smacks me across my cheek. The sting only fuels the fire inside of me. I bring one hand up between us and grab hold of her face, palming it and squeezing so hard that my nails dig into the skin of her forehead and her cheek. Then, I drag my fingers down, clawing and dragging skin beneath my nails. Blood begins to surface as Lilith takes a step back. "My face! You scratched my fucking face." She leans in and breathes fire down my neck. "You're gonna fucking die. On the day of your birth, of all days."

Lilith parts the crowd as she walks away, her minions following behind her.

Blaise towers over me, pinning me with a scathing glare. "You done fucked up, Penny."

My stomach somersaults. I think he's right. Fighting back against Lilith James is a mistake. But, I don't regret it. Not even a little bit.

The students begin to scramble, heading to class before the bell rings. My heart rate begins to settle down with my nerves, although it's still beating kind of rapidly. "Why are you still standing there?" I ask Blaise, who's looking at me with that same death glare. My shoulders shrug. "Are you waiting for me to thank you for trying to stop Lilith?"

"Don't thank me. Lilith might've made a threat because you're an easy target and a fun toy, but if it ever comes to it, I'll be the one to carry it out. That's a promise. You see, Penny, I know what you've been doing. You act all innocent, even though you're nothing but a little whore, just like your mama."

Blaise finally stops looking at me and grabs a girl walking by. I'm not even sure who she is. I think she might be a senior cheerleader. She giggles as he grabs her by the ass and walks behind her, whispering something in her ear over her shoulder.

Once he's done breathing down her neck, he looks back at me and winks.

He's a damn sociopath. And I've got to live with him.

☠

ALL DAY LONG, all I've been able to think about are Blaise's words. Not the threat—that doesn't even faze me because I've heard so many of them—but the name he called me. A whore. Just like my mama. How can a virgin be a whore and what could I have possibly done to claim that title?

I try to brush it away for the umpteenth time, but it lingers.

"Happy birthday to my very best friend," Emery says, skipping to my side as I walk to my locker that is now only partially covered. The janitor tried to scrub it clean, but it seems the permanent marker is pretty indestructible. The principal said that since there were no witnesses, there would be no punishment and they'd have it painted by Monday morning. It's the end of the school day, and Friday, so hopefully when school resumes after the weekend, it'll be gone.

I'm still pissed that Emery dipped out when I could have used someone on my side. So, I don't say anything to her as I grab my bag and slam my locker shut.

"Hey, are you mad at me?"

I look over at her with knitted eyebrows. Then back in front of me as we walk side by side to the exit. Emery always gives me a ride home now that she has her driver's license. I almost caught the bus but don't want to deal with people more than I have to. So, I'm sucking up just for the ride.

"What the hell did I do?"

Giving her the same look, I stop walking. "You didn't even try to help me. I was being pulled and dragged by my hair and you just hid."

Emery places a hand on my arm. "I'm sorry, Pen. She scared me, too."

"Yeah right," I huff, "you're obsessed with Lilith and her crew."

"Wanting to fit in and being obsessed are two different things. Don't you want to fit in? Or do you prefer to live in the shadows of everyone else while getting trampled on?"

"I would never be friends with that girl. Ever. She's pure evil."

"Yet, you live with the devil himself."

"You're right, I do. But not by choice," I add.

"Well," Emery snickers, waggling her brows, "what if I told you that I had a way to make it up to you?"

"I'd probably think you're up to something, in which case, I'd say forget about it."

I start walking toward the doors again, but Emery grabs my arm with excitement dripping from her touch. "We got invited!"

"To…a birthday party…for me…at your mom's house?"

"No." She chuckles. "The Devil's Night Party."

My head instantly shakes no. "Not a chance." I start walking again, this time picking up my pace.

"Pen, please. We have to go. There's this guy; he's a senior, he plays football, and he asked me to come. I said only if you could go too, and he eventually gave in. He just said not to tell Blaise that he was the one who said it was okay. But, we can go."

"No," I draw out. "You can go. That's clearly not an invitation for me. I prefer to stay alive, at least for tonight."

We reach the parking lot and as soon as I spot him, my stomach twists in knots. "What in the world?"

"Holy shit, Pen. Is that for you?" Emery beams as she jogs up to my side.

"I've got no idea what's going on." We walk closer to where Blaise stands with his ass propped up on the hood of a silver BMW with a giant bow on top of it.

"Umm, call me crazy, but I think that's yours." Emery keeps talking, but I don't hear a word she says as we approach Blaise.

"What is this?" I wave my hands at the car he sits on top of. It's most definitely not a gift from him; otherwise, he wouldn't look like he wants to toss me in the trunk and drive it off a cliff.

"It's a gift. From your dear old stepdad." He hops down

and eats up the space between us. "He asked me to wait out here with it since he and your bitch of a mom had to go on a business trip."

"But, why? Why would Richard buy me something so expensive?"

Blaise leans in, his lips flush to my ear. "I'm sure you know exactly why. After all, you are his little whore." Blaise tosses the keys at me, then walks toward his own car.

"What?" I mutter under my breath, looking down at the keys in my hand.

Does he think I'm having sex with his dad?

"Girl, this thing is fucking amazing," Emery hollers from the driver's seat, where she's checking out the interior.

"Get out of there. I'm not taking this thing." I walk over to where she sits and pull her out by her arm. I will never accept anything from Richard. He's a pig, and even though he has never touched me, I know he wants to.

The guy gives me the creeps. And, apparently, Blaise has already made the assumption that I have been having sex with his dad. "I feel sick," I tell Emery. "Please, just take me home."

I need to clear the air and set Blaise straight.

☠

AFTER PRYING Emery off the car, I finally convinced her that I wasn't taking it and we went to her house, leaving the car sitting in the school parking lot. "I still think you're insane for not accepting the gift. It's your birthday. Everyone gets presents."

"Not those kinds of presents, and not from people like Richard." I didn't tell her about Blaise's accusations. Just the thought makes bile climb up my throat.

Blaise is already gone, probably helping set up at the party spot in the woods. I really need to talk to him tonight.

15

"Okay," I spit out on impulse. "One hour. That's it."

"You're lying?" Emery jumps off the bed and stares at me like I just bought her a damn BMW.

"We disguise ourselves, and when I say it's time to go, we go."

"I fucking love you." She throws herself into my arms and I smile, knowing that this is making her extremely happy. This is all Emery has ever wanted. To fit in. To be somebody instead of nobody.

I just hope I don't live to regret it.

CHAPTER 1
PENELOPE

Two years later

MY SWEATY PALMS white-knuckle the steering wheel. I never wanted to come back to this town—the town that I once called home. I never once looked back. Nor did I ever miss the place. I can count on one hand the number of friends I made when I was here and I haven't spoken to any of them since I left. Not even the one I considered my best friend— Emery. In that regard, she's better off. All I did was drag her down.

I can also count on one hand the number of times that my mom has come to visit me—exactly once. She treats me as if I just up and left her for no reason at all. The truth is, I left for a good reason; she just didn't hear my cries. Either that, or, she chose to ignore them.

It doesn't matter. I'm living a good life in Portland. I've got real friends and a family that love me. I might not have all the luxuries I did at my mom's house in Skull Creek, but I never wanted those *things* anyway. This town holds my mom's dreams, not mine. For me, it's a black hole of harrowing memories and a mountain of regret.

I got out, though. And even if I'm back, it's only tempo-
rary. One week and I'll return home. Hopefully, my body will
still be intact and my heart will still be viable. You just never
know what to expect when you cross paths with Blaise Hale
—aka, my stepbrother.

As I turn onto my mom's road, my heart begins galloping
in my chest. I creep slowly, very slowly down the street, until
a car comes flying up behind me, laying on the horn. I pick up
my speed and glance back at it in my rearview mirror. It's a
small, black sports car with tinted windows. It's also loud, but
I assume it's meant to be.

I continue to accelerate, but the car behind me doesn't let
up as they ride my ass. It only adds to my anxiety as I draw
closer to the Hale estate. "Get off my ass!" I howl, staring
back at the driver through the mirror, even though I can't see
him or her, and they can't hear me either. In one minute, I'll
turn off this road and they can continue on their merry way,
while I enter hell, as I like to call it.

With a flick of the blinker, I tap my brakes, hoping this
asshole lays off a bit and doesn't rear-end me.

Granted, I know my car is nothing fancy, but I bought it
with my own money—hard-earned money at that. I can't say
the same for most of the kids in this rich town. Richard
bought me a car for my sixteenth birthday and I never even
started it. He would have bought me anything I wanted.
Money was no object to him, but allowance meant acceptance,
and I refused to accept the screwed-up lives these people live.
Well, used to live. Richard passed away last week. That's why
I'm here. Don't get me wrong, I'm not the least bit sad. I
suppose when you disengage from the life that another
person is living, you also turn off all empathy toward that
person.

Richard wasn't home often, but when he was, he made it
known. He was creepy. Always making disgusting comments
and undressing me with his eyes. He never touched me, but

I'm sure he would have if I'd allowed it. Mom was always a bit envious of the attention Richard gave me—as if she thought I was the only one in the world who could steal him away from her. Even if it was just his attention I was taking. Not that I wanted it. I couldn't stand the guy.

Richard traveled a lot for work, even as his cancer progressed, and Mom often traveled with him, leaving me here with his spawn, the devil. Part of me will always resent her for that. For turning a blind eye to the hell I was living in. It's not so much the hell Blaise put me through, it's the fact that I followed him down and allowed it to happen. I was a doormat—a weak and pitiful doormat.

Blaise made it known to the entire school that I was off-limits. Not to be looked at, befriended, or bullied. No, the bullying was left to him and him alone. Some listened. Some did not. Lilith James being one of those who went against everything he said and added to the misery that was my life. She was the female version of Blaise.

None of that matters, though. I've changed and I dare him or Lilith to try and pull that shit on me again.

At least, I hope I have. I guess time will tell.

My entire body shivers when I realize the car behind me has turned down the driveway to the house. Now that we're stopped at the gate, I'm able to feel the vibration of the heavy metal music blasting through the speakers of his car.

It has to be him. I can feel it in my bones.

Rolling down my window, I stretch my hand out and tap the buzzer to have the gate opened. I will not let Blaise give me entrance. I refuse to engage with him.

Dammit, I shouldn't have come here. Nothing good can come of being back in Blaise's space.

I'm only here for Mom, I remind myself, yet again. No matter how many excuses I made up in my head to get out of this, none of them seemed good enough to use. I really think in some sick way, she loved Richard. Even if it did all start because she was after his money. She doesn't know I know her motives, but I do. I know Mom better than anyone. She's always desired expensive things and wanted to live like a Kennedy. Well, she did and now she's bathing in millions because her husband died, leaving her every penny he owned. Wonder how Blaise feels about that? Chills skate down my spine at the thought. His horns probably grew six inches when he got that news.

The wrought iron gate begins to open for me, and I didn't even have to introduce myself. My guess is, Mom told them I was coming. Probably said, *"Don't call the cops if you see a rusted-out, old white Ford at the gate, it's just Penelope."*

My entire body jumps when the asshole behind me begins laying on his horn again. I snap myself out of my thoughts and realize that I've just been sitting here with the gate wide open. That's sure to earn me a few sly remarks, maybe even a bucket of pig's blood over my head while I'm showering. Yes, he did that. It was the day of my first period. Mom decided to run her mouth and Blaise thought it would be a good opportunity to be a jerk. I showered for three hours to make sure it was all off me.

I'm rolling down the driveway at a leisurely pace—deep breath in, deep breath out—when Blaise revs the engine of his car and swerves to the side of me. His passenger door is almost touching my driver's side when I glance over at him. The windows are pitch-black, but there is no doubt he can see me. As long as he can't see the pool of sweat beneath my hands or hear the pounding of my heart, I'll be okay. Blaise has always had an insatiable hunger for my fear.

I go to raise my hand to flip him off, but he accelerates and pulls in front of me, forcing me to slam on my brakes, so I'm not the one rear-ending him. "Asshole!" I shout, knowing that, once again, he did not hear me.

He's probably laughing his ass off right now as my blood is boiling.

I will not let him get to me.

Finally, I make it down the long driveway, stopping in the roundabout, unsure where I should park. I've never driven here. I was sixteen and without a car when I left and never once came to visit. It's just as I remember it, though. A big-ass house full of nothing. Nine bedrooms, six bathrooms, and a basement big enough to bury a thousand bodies beneath it, and a shitload of *things*. That's all it has. Things that mean nothing to me but everything to people who live here because they are shiny and expensive.

I hate this house. I hate the memories inside of it. All the feelings I pushed away and swore I'd never feel again come rushing back as I shift the car into park. Blaise hasn't got out yet. His music is still bumping, in what I assume to be his parking space right in front of the four-stall garage. I'm hoping he stays put—at least until I get to my room and lock the door. Maybe I can get away with just staying in there for the entire week. Aside from my attendance at the funeral, I'm not sure why I can't.

Deep breath in, drawn-out exhale. My fingers slide as I grip the door handle from the massive amount of sweat my body is producing. It's October in Washington, I should not be this hot.

Without wasting any more time, I push the door open, then lift the lever above the floorboard to pop open my trunk. Gently, I close my door, trying not to draw attention to myself. I hurry to the back, grab my black suitcase and drag it behind me as I head for the pillar of cement stairs. Being in front of this huge house makes me feel extremely small. My home in Portland is a little three-bedroom ranch style. One story, one bathroom.

Giving the suitcase a lift, I make it up the first couple stairs, but this thing is so damn heavy that it weighs me down and makes the climb difficult.

A car door slams behind me, and I don't even look over

my shoulder. I know who it is. If I make eye contact, his antics will begin. Sweat dribbles between my breasts and I'm already out of breath by the time I make it halfway up the stairs.

Dammit. I know they have a butler that could come out here and help me so I can make my grand escape.

Like a ghost, I feel his presence draw near. The hairs on my neck stand up and the sensation of tiny prickles trails down my entire body.

There is no need to turn around and look; I know he's there. "Sorry about your dad," I say, hoping to start things off on the right note.

He doesn't even acknowledge my words. Just keeps walking until he's bypassed me on the stairs. He's taller. At least six-foot-two now. His hair is lighter, with natural high-lights softening the dark brown—it's also longer than the buzz cut he wore two years ago. There's length on the top that's flipped over to one side with a close shave around the bottom half.

"I see those muscles haven't grown much, Penny." His words scratch at my skin. He walks at an amble pace as I tug and pull the suitcase up the stairs. Being the utter jackass that he is, he doesn't even offer to help. "It's been awhile, sis."

I let out a howling breath. That title makes me cringe. *Sister and brother?* Is that what we are? Sure as hell doesn't feel like it. Not then, not now. There is no love between us. The only thing I feel for Blaise is pure hatred.

"Just a heads-up, we had to move your room. You'll be next to me for the time being." He waves a hand and jogs up the stairs while I drag a hundred pounds of luggage behind me. "Come on, I'll show you the way."

That almost sounded…nice. But Blaise doesn't do nice. He opens the door and steps inside, leaving it open for me. I was fully expecting it to slam in my face. "What do you mean my room has changed?" I holler as he continues walking.

He doesn't respond. Just keeps moving, expecting me to follow behind him like a little puppy. I stop in the foyer, taking it all in. The sights, the smells, the quiet. It's exactly the same. The white furniture still sits unblemished in the sitting room. A polished chandelier, that costs more than my home in Portland, hangs freely from the vaulted ceiling above me.

Blaise stops walking, turns around, and glares at me with bloodshot eyes. He's probably high. "I ain't got all day. If you'd like to get to your room, then hurry your ass up."

Do not engage. Do not react.

I decide to dump the suitcase and find my room before I drag this thing all through the house. Setting it against the wall, I follow behind Blaise. I still remember every crack and crevice of this place. I'm not sure I'll ever forget.

We walk down the narrow hall and bypass the staircase. "Wait," I say, stopping my movements and nodding my head to the staircase. "Bedrooms are up there. Where are we going?"

He doesn't turn around as he speaks. "Your old room was up there. You're downstairs for the week. We had to make a few changes."

A rumble climbs up my throat. "That doesn't make any sense. There are now only four people living here. You, my mom, Jules, and Benjamin—the butler." Jules is the live-in maid who has been here since long before I came into the picture. "There are nine bedrooms. What kind of changes would possibly need to be made to fill all those rooms?"

Blaise stops in front of the downstairs door that sits off to the side of the kitchen. His fingers grip the door handle and he quizzes me with a sinister smile on his face. "Changes that don't involve you sleeping upstairs."

With a huff, I spin on my heels and turn back around. "I'll just talk to my mom and she'll fix this. There is no way that I'm sleeping in the room downstairs next to you. Not to mention, the hangout room you and all your gross friends inhabit."

I know what he's doing. This is proof that Blaise has not changed one bit. I've been here five minutes and he's already trying to dictate my stay so that he has access to make me miserable.

"We're remodeling," he says, point-blankly.

"Bullshit."

"Would I lie to you?" He steps closer, walking with a slow swag that has my stomach turning.

I'm not the same girl I was back then, and it's time he knows it. I stand my ground. I don't turn and walk away. Staring back at his golden eyes, I cross my arms over my chest. "You would most definitely lie to me. In fact, I don't believe a damn word that comes out of your mouth."

The corner of his lip tugs up in an egotistical sneer that sends a rush of heat to my palpitating chest. "We're not sixteen anymore, Penny. People change. I see you've changed. Was that your first swear word?"

"Fuck off!" I grumble, not at the comment, but at the nickname he's plagued me with. He knows how much I hate it when he calls me Penny.

"Oh, shit. She does it again."

We're face to face and although my entire body might as well be in flames, I plant two sweaty palms to his chest and shove him back. "Just leave me alone, Blaise. I'm only here for a week, then I'll be gone and we can go on with our lives, just like we have for the past two years."

As if he's completely ignoring my offer of peace for the week, his eyes trail down my body, making me feel exposed. Even though I am wearing a hoodie and sweatpants. "You've grown up, Penny. You've grown up a lot."

I feel sick.

"Whatever." I sweep the air with my hand. "I'm going up to *my* room. See you at the funeral."

I know damn well they aren't remodeling upstairs. This house is still practically brand new and there's no way Mom would want any remodeling done, especially with everything going on this week.

Leaving my bag in the foyer, I jog up the hardwood stairs. My fingers trail along the banister and a rush of emotions hits me like a tidal wave. When I was fourteen, I slipped and fell down these stairs and cut my outer thigh. I had just gotten out of the pool and was trying to hurry to my room before Blaise and all his friends caught a glimpse of me in my bikini. Not only did they see me, they also bore witness to my tears. I ended up getting six stitches and still have a nasty scar. Wade, the decent one of the bunch, sat with me while the driver pulled the car around, so Jules could take me to the hospital. Blaise was furious with him for being nice to me. But Wade didn't care. He was Blaise's only friend to ever stand up to him, and it was usually in my defense.

The smile I didn't even realize I was wearing immediately drops when I reach the top of the stairs and see plastic along the floor and in front of a few of the rooms. "No way!"

He wasn't lying. They seem to be painting all the walls in the hall. With my sneakers still on, I pad across the plastic, crinkling it beneath my feet. I reach my old room at the end of the hall and sure as shit, all my stuff is gone. When I moved, my furniture stayed. I knew I'd never come back to visit, but Mom and Richard didn't know that. They kept my room intact for me, the one decent thing they've done over the last couple years. Or so I thought. Apparently, Mom moved me down to the devil's lair.

"You can apologize later for calling me a liar."

My breath hitches when Blaise's words roll onto the back of my neck.

"Doesn't change anything. I'm still not sleeping in your dungeon."

"Then I guess you can have the couch."

Not a chance. That couch is not the least bit comfortable. It's apparent that it was only bought for the looks. The comfortable couch is exactly where I don't want to be—the basement. It's where Blaise would always hang out and play video games with his friends. There's a pool table down there, a pinball machine, surround sound, and a huge sectional with a massive television. At least, there was two years ago. It's also where Blaise's room is. There are two bedrooms down there with an adjoined bathroom.

The thought makes my skin crawl.

My shoulders shrug and I smirk. "I'll just sleep with my mom then."

Blaise lets out a roaring laugh. "The ice queen? Good luck."

He's right. My mom is not exactly the cuddling type. She never quite grasped the whole mothering thing. She's cold and disconnected and we have absolutely no relationship. When she asked me to come to the funeral, her exact words were, *"It would be terrible for our image if you didn't attend."*

With a huff, I pout like a toddler and walk with heavy steps over the plastic. "Fine. But, the minute you start your shit, I'm out. I'll get a hotel if I have to."

Blaise holds up his hands in surrender. "Wouldn't dream of starting shit with you, Penny. After all, we're family."

I pinch my eyes shut. *Family.* That word's just as bad as *sis.* Bile rises in my throat. So much for escaping the memories of my past life. All at once, they're hitting me head-on and I wish they'd just knock me out because I don't want to remember.

Not the tormenting, not the pranks, and most definitely not the temptation.

CHAPTER 2
PENELOPE

NOTHING HAS CHANGED. Not even the basement. It still reeks of testosterone mixed with expensive cologne and a hint of pot. The cologne at least smells pretty good—like birch and black currant.

Benjamin, the butler, brought my suitcase down for me, which was helpful, even though I felt bad because he's like seventy years old. He seemed to struggle almost as much as I did. Blaise was right, I still have no muscles. I'm puny and underweight with the same body I had when I was fourteen. My boobs have grown a little, but not much. My hair is shorter, much shorter. Mom never let me cut it. When I moved, it reached the top of my ass. The next day, I got it cut to my chin. Now, it's shoulder-length and I also took the plunge on my virgin locks and got it lightened with caramel-colored highlights. It's still brown, but not as dark as it was before I left.

The basement door slams shut, startling me.

"Son of a bitch!" I hear Blaise yell. His steps are thunderous and echo throughout the room I'm in. It's the smaller of the two down here and everything out there can be heard in here. I don't need anything big, so this works. I've got a full-size bed, a dresser, and a tv mounted on the wall. I just wish there was more distance between Blaise and me. Being this close to him is unsettling.

It's not the memories of everything he did to me that haunt me or even pushed me away. It's the memories of what we did together. Just thinking about it makes me feel so gross that I need to shower.

I stand up and grab my suitcase then flip it on the bed. Once it's unzipped, I take out a pair of black sweatpants, a long-sleeved t-shirt—Ryan's orange basketball shirt from last year—and some clean underwear. I sleep in Ryan's shirt when I miss him the most. Right now, I really miss him. Clutching the shirt, I smile. Ryan and I have been together for almost a year. It's not exactly the best relationship. We fight, break up, and get back together much too often, but we make it work. I doubt we'll be together forever, but I have no interest in being with anyone else right now.

Crossing the room, I reach for the handle on the bathroom door, hoping like hell Blaise isn't in there. Another thing that's unsettling—sharing a bathroom with him. He has access to me whenever he wants it. I'm really hoping that he's matured over the last couple years and doesn't still pull the gruesome pranks he did back then. There's a lock, but Blaise is smart. If he wants to get to me, he'll find a way.

I breathe a sigh of relief when I see that the bathroom is empty. The first thing I do is lock the door that leads to Blaise's room. I can hear some shuffling around in there, but unless he picks the lock, my privacy is safe. No way he'd go that far. I really need to chill out and quit worrying. It was bad, but it wasn't *that* bad. Okay. It was that bad, but we're older now. Besides, my last night here, Blaise was different, gentle, even somewhat normal. I left the next morning and never said goodbye. It wasn't necessary. Two hours prior to his change in behavior, he had pulled me out of a burning barn. A barn that was burning because of him and his friends.

They had to have known I was in there. So, the only thing I can come up with is, they wanted to kill me.

I wasn't in the right state of mind when Blaise swept me into his arms and carried me away. Fear had taken over and I couldn't think straight. That's why I let things go as far as they did. That's what I keep telling myself. That's what I'll always tell myself. If I'd known then what I found out the next morning, I would have pushed him back inside that barn and let him burn.

Blaise and I stayed in an abandoned farmhouse all night while firefighters battled the barn fire. The next morning, my soul felt charred and I was humiliated that I let things go as far as I did. For years I've tried to make excuses. We were young teens. I was traumatized from the fire. The truth is, for the first time ever, I felt connected to Blaise that night. The look in his eyes when he pulled me out of the burning barn spoke volumes to me. He didn't want me to die.

Although, a part of me did die that night.

With a hesitation gnawing at me, I slowly pull my sweat-shirt over my head and drop it to the floor. I wait a minute, just to see if he's going to try and open the door before I finish undressing. Completely naked, I reach into the stand-up shower and turn the water on. Fortunately, I brought my own toiletries, because all that's inside the shower is Blaise's body wash and shampoo. After all, this is his bathroom. Has been forever. Long before I even knew him.

Once I have everything I need lined up on the shower shelf, I step inside. I wonder how Blaise feels about me invading his space. It's no secret that he's never liked me. When I first met him, I thought it was just typical brother/sister behavior. Even if we'd only met a couple months prior to our parents' wedding. It began with harmless pranks, but those pranks became dangerous. I begged my mom to let me go live with my dad countless times, but she refused. Even after he threatened to take her to court, she didn't budge. He never did because he couldn't afford to battle it out with her. She'd win without a doubt. It was more about winning for her and I was the prize that she kept from my dad.

The final straw came after the barn fiasco. I could have died that night. My fingers run over the scar that covers my forearm. It's hideous and a constant reminder of that night. I never told her, or anyone, what happened. But, for some reason, she just let me go. Never batted an eye as I walked out those doors.

My nails dig into my scalp as I scrub my hair, trying to think about something else. *Ryan.* My saving grace. He's everything that Blaise is not. He's funny, smart, and good-looking. He's an all-star athlete with a bright future that doesn't involve living off a trust fund—not that Blaise will be doing that. I wonder if he knows that he wasn't left an inheritance. I can't imagine he does; otherwise, he'd be raising hell and probably wouldn't be staying here anymore. He's eighteen, which means he can go wherever he wants.

I'm guessing there was some sort of stipulation in Richard's will that allowed him to stay here until he graduates. There has to be because there is nothing but bad blood between my mom and Blaise. He hates her with a passion and I'm sure the feeling is mutual.

A knock at the door has my body jolting, which causes my feet to slip on the suds beneath me. I grab a hold of the handle on the shower door and save myself from falling on my ass. "Hurry up in there. I need to take a piss," Blaise says between knocks at the door.

"One sec," I holler, trying to steady my heart rate from my *almost* fall.

There are plenty of other bathrooms in this house and he can't go use one of them? God, he's insufferable.

I grab my razor on the shower ledge and pop the top off, dropping it on the floor, but not bothering to pick it up. A couple swipes under each armpit and I set it back on the ledge. A quick rinse and I'm calling this five-minute shower good, all because my wonderful stepbrother needs to piss.

"Any second now, Penny." His voice is so close that he might as well be standing next to me. Though he's on the other side of the door, he's still only inches away, while I stand here naked and dripping. Water falls off me onto the cream-colored bath rug I'm standing on as I look around for a towel. I pull open the cupboards beneath the sink, hoping to find them, but no luck.

"I'm trying. Hey," I raise my voice, "where are the towels?"

A menacing laugh creeps through the crack beneath the door and my body freezes. "Seriously, Blaise. No towels?"

"Oh, I have towels, Penny. But, they're in the linen closet…out here."

You've got to be kidding me!

Slamming the cupboard doors shut, I snatch the hand towel that's hanging on a hook by the sink. I pat myself dry the best I can, then click the lock on the door to the room I'm staying in and open it. Once it's closed, I holler, "It's all yours."

Ryan's shirt is still sitting on top of my open suitcase on the bed so I grab it and throw it on. I'm still soaked, with water falling down my back, but at least I'm covered up. I wait a second until I hear the bathroom door close before going out into the living room.

Holding the door handle for dear life, I look around and find a closet about six feet away to the left. I can make it there and back before Blaise comes out.

Not wasting any time, I tiptoe over to the linen closet. Just as I pull it open, the bathroom door opens up, and take a deep breath.

Dammit. I've always put myself in these awkward situations. I set myself up for this, but he knew it. He knew I'd need a towel. Blaise is smart, and I don't just mean book smart. He thinks ahead. Ever since our parents got married, he's been three steps ahead of me. Right now, he's three inches behind me with his breath rolling down my back, chasing the beads of water that spill down my spine.

It's just my luck that I opened the door to the furnace room—not the linen closet.

"Towels aren't in there, Penny." His fingers sweep my soaking wet hair to the side and I swallow hard when the heat of his touch radiates through my shivering body.

Like an idiot, I just stand there. Allowing him to taunt me with his touch. That's what he's doing, after all. He's trying to get a reaction out of me. Unlucky for him, I won't react.

In one swift motion, I spin around. With my eyes dead-bolted on his and the corner of my lip curled, I walk past him, nudging him with my shoulder. I'm glad Ryan is on the taller and bulkier side because if he weren't, my ass would be hanging out right now.

"Ya know, I could have grabbed you one. You didn't have to come out here and flaunt your ass."

Scoffing, I spin back around to face him. My eyes stay down, not wanting to look at him, but against my better judgment, I do. Blaise is tall, much taller than me. When we're face to face, I have to look up, but oftentimes, I try not to. Looking into his eyes is dangerous. They're golden brown right now. They're not holding that black ring around them that usually surfaces when he's angry. A look I've become accustomed to.

My heart flip-flops and I wanna rip it out and tell it to quit betraying me. "*Flaunt* my ass? If that's what you think I'm doing, you're delusional." God, he's infuriating. Only Blaise would think that me coming out for a towel was some kind of ploy to get him to notice me.

His shoulders rise and fall in an egotistical manner. "Wouldn't be the first time."

Clenching my teeth, I fight the urge to lash out. In the

past, I would have. I would have let him wriggle under my skin. Not anymore. "Think what you want, Blaise. Doesn't matter. One week and I'll be out of your hair."

"Running away already?" he mutters under his breath, but I hear him loud and clear.

"Running away isn't what I'm doing. More like, leaving the past where it belongs."

The ring around his eyes darkens as his gaze falls to my mouth. His Adam's apple bobs as he swallows. Fingertips begin trailing featherlike over my bare shoulders. "The past is never as far as you think, Penny."

Before I can react, his lips collide with mine like a head-on train wreck. Hard, forced, and painful. I keep my lips pressed tightly together as his hand cups the back of my head, bunching my hair and pulling me so close that his lips slide between my clenched ones and our teeth clank together. "Quit fighting it," Blaise grumbles into my mouth. Why is he doing this? Does he want me to be powerless beneath him? I won't do it. I won't give him the satisfaction.

I try to free myself, but he only fights harder to coerce his tongue into my mouth. So hard that I can feel the sting on my bottom lip from busting open. A metallic taste seeps into my mouth and I'm sure he tastes it, too.

His growing bulge in his shorts hits my hip bone and I'm sickened for getting aroused by it. I stop pushing so hard, then I become butter in his hands. His tongue slides into my mouth, tangling with mine in a sharp, igniting kiss. My legs begin to shake as my sex throbs in dire need for attention.

Blaise's phone chirps and his eyes open until we're staring back at each other, our mouths still connected. His hands still tangled in the mess of my hair. I break the kiss and whisper, "You shouldn't have done that. I have a boyfriend."

In an instant, he lets go and steps back, his fists clenched at his sides. His jaw clamps down as he gnashes, "Who?"

I'm not telling him any more details than he needs to

know. My life back home is not his business. All I know is that I messed up. I gave in to temptation. Temptation that shouldn't even be there.

I sweep the back of my hand across my mouth and look down at the blood from my lip. Blaise grabs my hand, takes one look at the streak of blood, and runs his thumb over it. "Sucks for him. Next time, maybe you'll be a little more compliant."

I breathe an audible sigh. "There won't be a next time."

His lips twitch with humor, brows raised. "Keep telling yourself that."

Why do I feel like I'm under some sort of spell? Being near him, in this house, it's mind-altering. I hate Blaise. So why do I melt at his feet?

Blaise drops my hand and shifts his attention to his phone on the end table beside him. He picks it up, takes one look at the screen, and that devilish look he wears so well returns. "Might wanna put something on, Penny. We've got company."

Great. His douchebag friends are coming over; I need to get out of here. The perfect excuse to go upstairs and make something to eat. Not only am I starving after the long drive, I also plan to avoid his crew at all costs. I turn around and pull open the door to the linen closet, getting it right this time. As I reach for a towel, the basement door opens.

My eyes widen. It's not one of the guys, it's Emery coming down the stairs. The flopping of my heart stops and it begins beating rapidly.

I clench the towel in my hands and look over my shoulder. "Emery? What are you doing here?"

She looks different. Her frizzy whitish-blonde hair is now straight and long. Braces are gone. Her boobs have really filled out, like *really* filled out. She's tan, tall, and beyond gorgeous.

"Holy shit! Penelope?" She eats up the space between us

and literally throws herself at me. I just stand there, stiff as a board. Emery takes a step back and studies me. "I can't believe you're here. It's been, what, like three years?"

I force a smile on my face as a million thoughts run rampant through my head. "Two years this weekend. But, yeah. Here I am."

Emery swats playfully at Blaise's arm. "You didn't tell me your sister was coming home."

I wanna scream at her that I'm not Blaise's sister. I wish people would stop referring to us as siblings. We are not brother and sister. My stomach churns again. "I should probably go get dressed." I look from her to Blaise who is wearing a shit-eating grin.

"Yes. Go get dressed then come back and hang out with me. I'll just be watching Blaise play video games." She fakes a gag and I fake another smile.

Why, though? Why is she just going to sit here and watch Blaise play video games?

I don't ask that, though. Instead, I walk back to my room. Once I reach the door, I glance over my shoulder. My chest aches when I see Emery's arms around Blaise's waist. He's looking down at her the same way he looked at me only moments ago.

I guess I got the answer. They're together. Blaise is dating my former best friend—and he just kissed me—and I kissed him back.

CHAPTER 3
BLAISE

MY GAZE DARTS to the door as Penny goes to close it. Just before she does, she glowers at me. I roll my eyes and look back down at Emery. I smile inwardly when she slams it shut. That's what she gets for coming back here. She should have known I wouldn't make her return a peaceful one.

"I missed you," Emery says, pressing her lips to my bare shoulder.

I step around her, knowing that the guilt trip is coming. She should know by now that shit doesn't work on me. "Yeah. I've been busy." I drop down on the couch and grab the tv remote.

"Where were you earlier today? I stopped by and you weren't home."

Slamming the remote on the couch, I lean forward and lock my eyes on hers. "What did I tell you about that shit? Don't come here unannounced. Ever!"

With a pout, Emery rounds the couch and sits down on my lap. "I've been worried about you. You won't talk to me about your dad and—"

"Dammit, Emery!" I spit, pushing her off my lap. She falls onto the floor dramatically. "I told you I don't wanna talk about him." I'm on my feet, pacing the room as if I'm searching for something. Although, I don't have a clue what I'm looking for. I just need her to lay off. This girl is always on my ass about everything. *Why didn't you return my call? Where were you? Are you mad at me?*

Penny's bedroom door opens up and I stop walking. She's wearing an oversized shirt that says *Hallstone High Football.* The ends of her hair have started to dry but leave a damp spot on the shoulders of the shirt. I can't tell if she's wearing anything underneath it because it's so long. But, knowing Penny, she most definitely is. The old Penny would have been wearing shorts that touched her knees. This Penny is unpredictable. She's feisty, older—beautiful, but in a way that makes me all the more certain I have to stay away from her.

We all exchange a quiet glance until Penny breaks the silence, "I'm just gonna go get something to eat. You two have fun." She shoots her thumb over her shoulder.

"What? No," Emery huffs in her direction. "We have so much to catch up on."

Penny raises a shoulder. "It was a really long drive. I'd rather just eat something and go to bed. Rain check?"

"Sure. I guess that'll be okay."

"Great. I'll see you later then." Penny blinks from Emery to me.

Why is this girl always so nice? And to people who don't deserve it. Emery was Penny's best friend when she lived in Skull Creek. They did everything together. When Penny left, Emery attached herself to Penny's archenemy and bully, Lilith —they practically celebrated Penny's departure. Lilith pushed Penny around for years. After gym class in seventh grade, she stole all of Penny's clothes while she was showering and put them in the boys' locker room. Now, Emery and Lilith are still best friends and the queen bees of Skull Creek High, and Penny is none the wiser. Emery has always dreamt of being in the "in-crowd," so it's really no surprise to anyone that she's Lilith's little bitch now.

Once the door to the basement closes, Emery begins tracing her fingers down my arm. "How long is she here for?"

"She said a week."

"Wonderful," she grins, "Lilith is going to have a field day with this."

"You two *will* leave her alone. You hear me?"

Her nose wrinkles and she leans back and reads my expression. "Since when do you care what happens to that girl?"

"Since when is she just *that girl*? Last time I saw you two together, you were joined at the hip."

"Maybe you're not the only one who was affected when she left without saying goodbye. Am I not allowed to be angry, too?"

"I wasn't affected." I look past her, not allowing her to see the lie behind my words. "I don't give a fuck about that girl."

"When she left, you got into two fights, suspended from school, and lashed out at everyone who tried to talk to you. And that was just the first week. Don't try and act like you weren't affected."

"Drop it," I deadpan. This girl talks too damn much. And how the hell does she even know this shit about me? We weren't friends then. Hell, I'm not even sure we are now. She's just a nice distraction and a piece of fine ass, but that's as far as this thing goes.

"Fine. Are we really gonna just hang out down here while you play video games?" Emery runs her fingers down my arm. "I can think of something much more exciting than that." Her brows rise, causing mine to do the same.

Piquing my interest, I grab her by the waist and give her a swift jerk, crushing our bodies together. "Oh yeah? What's that?"

She bites the corner of her lip with her perfect white teeth. Her blue eyes dance around mine. "Let's go in your room and I'll show you."

"Uhh-uhh," I shake my head, "Couch. Now."

Her raised brows droop. "The couch? But why? What if Penelope comes back down here?"

"Well, I guess she'll learn that this is my space. She's just borrowing it." The thought of Penny walking in on us is oddly satisfying. I brush Emery's long hair over her shoulder. "Besides, my bitch of a stepmother is coming home soon so she'll be hung up with her for a while. We've got plenty of time."

"Blaise," Emery drags my name out in four different syllables, "it's been two years. You're not still hung up on that chick, are you?"

My neck cranes as I look down at her, unsure of what she's implying. "What the fuck is that supposed to mean?"

"Oh, come on." She giggles. "I know all the shit you pulled on her back then. Let's not forget that I *was* her best friend. You wanted to hurt her, and you succeeded by making her life hell."

"'Was' is the operative word. And I was never *hung* up on her. She was just a fun little toy to play with. You both were." My fingertips clench her ass cheeks and I hoist her up as her legs wrap around me. "Now, quit talking about my sister and show me this excitement you promised."

"Never said I cared if you did hurt her." Emery presses her lips to mine and I carry her around the sectional until we're on the long stretch of the couch. I set her down and she grabs my hand, cupping my fingers and pushing them against her crotch beneath her mini skirt.

If I wasn't sure before, I am now. Emery is the same bitch she became when Penny left. If anyone wants Penny to get hurt, it would be her. The shadow of Lilith James, who wants to shine on her own but never will because she will always be a follower. I pull my hand back and place it on Emery's head, pushing her down. Her doe eyes peer up at me and I rush things along. "We don't have much time."

She scowls but doesn't dare argue with me. I pop the button on my jeans and let her slide them down, taking my boxers with them. Once they're dangling around my ankles, I kick them free and drop down on the couch with my cut-off t-shirt still on.

Emery stays kneeled like an obedient girl waiting for instruction. My fingers wrap around my dick and I grip her hair before stuffing her mouth. She opens wide and takes the shallow end and I move my hand out of her way. My head falls back and my arms spread at my sides.

With my eyes closed, I try to focus on the warmth of her mouth. The flick of her tongue on my under shaft. I try to focus on anything but Penny. I knew her return would rattle up shit inside my head. The last time I saw her, my dad was still here. He was alive and well. She knew he was sick, but she never once checked in on the man who was supporting her mother.

I draw in a deep breath. *Quit thinking about this shit.* I've got a hot-ass girl sucking my cock right now and all I'm thinking about is my stepsister who ditched and dismissed me the minute things got intense. Okay, that's a lie. Things were always intense. I never wanted the girl in my life. She and her mom came in like wrecking balls and chased my mom away. I should hate her. I should hate her sea-green eyes and the cluster of freckles on her nose. Her brown hair, now considerably shorter, that still has the slightest wave to it at the ends. Her petite frame, and tits that are now mounds instead of pebbles. Her new sailor mouth that leads me to believe she grew a backbone. I should hate it all.

When I realize that Emery is no longer sucking me off, I lift my head. "What the hell? Why'd ya stop?"

Her eyes are wide with discomfort. "Umm. Is everything

okay?" She glances at my cock and I follow her gaze, seeing my soft member resting on my thigh.

I'm as surprised as she is. This has never happened. My cheeks flush with heat and the longer she watches me, the angrier I become. "I've got a lot on my mind. Keep sucking."

"Maybe we should talk about—"

"I said keep sucking," I huff, feeling frustrated and slightly humiliated at the same time.

Her shoulders shrug and she begins stroking my length and licking my head, but she doesn't take her eyes off me.

Just as I try to relax again, I hear footsteps coming down the stairs. Before I can even look up, it's confirmed that Penny has caught us. "Oh, gosh. I'm sorry." She turns and hustles back up the stairs with resounding steps.

When I look at Emery, she's just staring at me, holding my limp cock in her hands. "You know what, fuck it. It's obvious you have no idea what you're doing." I lean forward to fish for my boxers on the floor.

"Blaise, what's gotten into you?"

"Nothing," I say bluntly. Standing, I pull my boxers out of my jeans and step into them. "It's been a crazy week. Maybe you should just go. I'll call ya tomorrow."

Emery snatches her purse off the arm of the couch. "You know what? Fuck you, Blaise."

"Fuck me? Fuck you!" My eyes roll. "Actually, you probably wouldn't get that right either." I snap the waistband of my boxers.

Emery storms off, and I let her. The truth is, Emery wasn't the problem. At least, not tonight. She's a needy chick with a ton of emotional baggage, which is exactly why she and I will never be an item, but my lack of desire is due to my traitorous stepsister invading my fucking head again.

CHAPTER 4
PENELOPE

MY FEET SLIP against the freshly waxed hardwood floor as I walk back and forth, biting the tip of my thumbnail. I reach the end of the kitchen island, and pivot around, only to walk back again. Why did I let him kiss me? That was probably the dumbest thing I've done since the first time I allowed it to happen two years ago.

And why did I go back down there? I should have known better. It's Blaise. Of course he was in the middle of getting a blow job. Wasn't the first time I walked in on him and another girl. *But, Emery?*

Why am I here? Why did I fucking come back to this hellhole?

I stop at the end of the island, gripping the corner and stare out the large French doors that overlook the mountains. The picturesque view of the sunset dipping behind the point offers me a sense of calm. This house really does have the most beautiful view.

One week. *I can do this.*

My head snaps away from the view when the basement door flies open. Emery seems pissed as she slams the door shut. "Oh, hey, Penelope. I didn't realize you were here." Her words come out in an airy huff.

"Just waiting for my pizza to finish cooking." I glance behind me at the timer on the oven. Three more minutes.

"Pizza? Like a frozen one?" She curls her fingers and admires her freshly-painted nails. "Why didn't you just order out or have that cook guy make you something?"

I almost forgot that I'm surrounded by the rich and unable. I chuckle as I pick up a hot pad from the center island. "Cook guy?"

"Henderson. Or whatever the hell his name is."

"Henry," I correct her. "And, it's no big deal. I don't need anyone to make my food for me."

"Right. You always did prefer to do things yourself, didn't you?" My response is a subtle nod.

Emery pulls out a barstool on the other side of the island and sits down. She's changed. Nothing like the quiet girl I left behind. It seems time has changed us all—everyone except Blaise. I, too, am no longer the pushover I used to be. Let's just hope that my time here doesn't reveal otherwise.

"So, you're only in town for a week, right?" Her shoulders draw back and her chest puffs out like she's showing me that her boobs have tripled in size. They're quite stunning, really. Perky with just the right amount of cleavage peeking through her white, see-through V-neck. "They're real," she says, pulling my attention away from her chest.

I look up at her with wide eyes, realizing that she caught me staring. "I'm sorry. I guess I just pictured you as you were when I left."

"Don't be." Emery cups her breasts and gives them a jiggle that has me blushing for reasons unknown to me. I'm not into girls, but I'm also not used to being around girls who are so outspoken and carry so much confidence—especially a girl who was convinced she'd be wearing thick padding in her bras until she was old enough for a boob job. "It's the pill.

Started taking it two years ago and suddenly, I filled out." She beams. "Wanna touch them?"

My brows hit my forehead. "Touch them?"

"Sure. Why not?"

I can feel my cheeks flush with heat as I turn back to the oven. "No, thanks. The pill, huh? I'm assuming that means—"

"Mmhmm. Better safe than sorry. Then again, I'm not sorry at all. It gives me a nice rack to show off and ensures I won't be getting knocked up by any of the jerks in this town."

I can think of another way to ensure that doesn't happen. Like possibly not sleeping with said jerks. But I don't say it.

I am slightly envious, though. I can't even force a cleavage with duct tape.

"Come on, Penelope." She chuckles. "We're not kids anymore. Aren't we all having sex?" She chuckles again with this condescending tone that is all too familiar. She sounds like Lilith—the female version of Blaise, only worse. So much worse.

"Yeah. I guess so." I won't elaborate. In fact, we need to get off this subject before Emery begins asking questions about my sex life. "Yes. One week," I spit out, answering her question from earlier. "I'm here for one week. Once the funeral is over, I'll be on the fast track back to Portland."

Emery straightens her back on the stool. "Wait. That means you'll be here for the annual D-Day Party." She begins clapping her hands together in excitement. "And, it's your birthday! I almost forgot. You'll be what, like, eighteen?"

Like, eighteen? Has she forgotten that we are the same age? Her being exactly two months older. "Yeah, I'll be eighteen. And no, I will not be at the party."

"Oh, come on. It'll be fun. Everyone will be so happy to see you back."

"Doubtful. I'm sure the memories of me have since faded.

No one even knows who I am anymore. Besides, those parties and that scene were always your endgame, not mine."

The timer on the oven goes off, so I hit the button to shut it off. With the hot pad in my hand, I pull the oven door open and slide my pizza out, setting it on two hot pads on the island before I begin cutting the pizza in triangles.

"You're right." She scoots her stool back and stands up. "But, you should still come. You left so abruptly. Maybe you need to give the town something to remember you by." Emery winks before her fingers dip underneath a slice of pizza. She lifts it up and takes a nibble at the end of the triangle. "Ooh, that's hot." She spins on her heels. "See ya around, Penny."

I stand there dumbfounded. Who the hell even was that girl? And since when does she call me Penny? No one calls me that except for Blaise.

Shaking it off, I open the glass cupboard door and pull out a piece of fine china, also known as a plate that's probably worth more than my entire outfit. Scratch that—*is* worth more than my entire outfit. The Hales do not believe in paper plates. Well, at least my mom doesn't. She thinks they are wasteful. All this coming from a woman who would skin a rabbit to make a coat.

With my plate in one hand and a glass of water in the other—because bottled water is also frowned upon here—I head into the sitting room that houses furniture with the same comfort level as the hardwood floor.

There is no television because everyone that lives here watches tv in their own rooms. It's crazy that this was my life at one time. Living with my dad, we have family movie night at least once a week. Popcorn, blankets, and a comfy couch with worn leather and water spots. It's lived on and I'd much rather have that than this home where everything is for show.

Just as I sit down, I hear the door to the mudroom off the

kitchen close and the clanking of heels on the hardwood come closer.

"Penelope," Mom says in a soft tone. I look over as she walks toward me, but she stops. "Oh honey, don't eat pizza on the couch. You'll make a mess." She digs into her purse and pulls out her phone then takes a call. Apparently, it was ringing. Didn't even hear it. She gives me her backside as she walks away.

"Good to see you too, Mom," I murmur. It's been almost a year since I've seen her and I knew better than to expect a warm greeting. Honestly, I didn't want one. My mom has never shown me affection or anything that resembled love. I'm actually really surprised she wanted me at the funeral so badly. She begged continuously. I got calls, day in and day out, until I finally caved. Then again, I shouldn't be surprised at that either. She said it herself that it would be frowned upon by her social circle if I wasn't there.

As I eat my pizza, I scroll through old pictures from Portland. I stop when I get to one of me and Ryan. Staring at it for a long minute, I wonder if I'll ever love him. I wonder if I'll ever *be* loved by him. I wish my feelings for Ryan were stronger, but my heart feels chained, unable to let anyone in.

I send him a message, just to see how he's doing.

Me: Hey. How's everything going?

A few seconds later, a response comes through.

Ryan: Good. Just hanging with the guys. How's everything there? I miss you.

Me: I miss you, too. I can't wait to come home. Who's all there?

Ryan: Mikey, me, Greg, and Lana.

Mikey is a friend of ours, but also the twin brother of Ryan's ex, Erica. I tend to get a little jealous for the simple fact that he cheated on me with her a few months ago. Yeah. Our relationship is not butterflies and rainbows. In fact, it's more like dark clouds and rainstorms.

Me: And Erica?

I ask because Lana is Erica's best friend. Mikey is her brother. Of course she's there.

Ryan: I mean she's around.

Me: Real nice, Ryan. I leave and you're back to hanging out with her.

Ryan: Calm down. Nothing's going on.

I close out of my message and slam the phone on the couch beside me.

"What's got you all fired up?" My body jolts as Blaise's words hit my ears. With his arms crossed on the back of the couch, he leans in so close that I can smell Emery's perfume on his shirt.

My eyes roll. "None of your business." I take another bite of my pizza and drop the crust back on the plate. He's still there, breathing down my neck like he's always done. "You can go now."

"Oh, it's gonna be like that, is it?" His arm comes over my shoulder as he reaches down and grabs the crust off my plate.

I snarl in disgust when I hear him begin chewing on my leftovers. "You're so gross."

"And you're wasting my pizza. Besides, the crust is the best part."

My eyes roll. "In case you've forgotten, this is my mom's house now, so that food in the freezer belongs to her."

Blaise lets out a roaring laugh then stops suddenly. I blink and find him in front of me. He adjusts his pants and kneels in front of where I sit with my legs crossed like a pretzel. "Oh, Penny. Your mom's been feeding you lies again?"

I grab my next slice and bite off the end with a curled lip. "Truth hurts, does it?" I say with a mouthful. I'm pretty ballsy for talking to Blaise like this, but he's going to learn one way or another that I'm not a doormat to anyone anymore.

His eyes narrow and his jaw clenches. "You're in for quite a treat, Penny Pie."

My stomach twists into knots at the nickname. The only time he ever called me that was the night of the fire. I don't even eat pie because of it. Every time I look at the round dessert, I swear I can feel the heat of the flames.

"Don't call me that," I spit out in a rage. It didn't sound that angry in my head, but it was enough to grab his attention. I drop my pizza on my plate with a clank of the golden-brown crust. "In case you've forgotten, my name is Penelope." My legs uncross and I kick them out in front of me, my feet hitting Blaise's gut. He gasps then grabs the coffee table behind him to stop from falling backward but doesn't say a word when I stand up and walk out of the room.

Is that really all it took for him to shut the hell up? Me standing up for myself?

☠

I'M LYING in my room with my eyes shut, listening to an audiobook with buds in my ears when I hear loud voices coming from outside the room. I pull one of the earbuds out, the voices ring much louder. Not just any voices, Blaise's and Mother Dearest's. Kicking my feet over the side of the bed, I get up.

"You know better than to come down here, Ana," Blaise shouts so loudly that his words reverberate through me.

"I just want to talk to Penelope. See how she's doing. That's all." Mom's voice is much softer, almost as if she's pleading with Blaise.

"Like you care! You don't give a damn about Penny. Now go back upstairs and pretend she doesn't exist like you always have."

There's a pang in my chest. Not because of what he said, but because there is so much truth to it, and it hurts.

There's a brief silence before the door to the basement slams shut. I walk closer to the door, listening intently to figure out what Blaise is doing out there. Something jostles inside of me. Like coldness and warmth colliding. My hand grips the door handle and I give it a turn, then jerk it open suddenly. As if he knew I'd be there, Blaise is standing directly in front of me with his palms pressed to either side of the doorframe.

I swallow hard. "Why'd you make her leave?"

"Because she's a bitch," he says, simply put.

"She's my mom."

He raises a brow, "Okay. Your *mom* is a bitch."

I bite back a smile. Most people would lash out when their mom is called such a name. Not me, because I know it's true. I love my mom, but I hate that she dragged me down to lift herself up.

"Regardless, she obviously had something to say to me. I should hear her out." For her to come down here, knowing that Blaise has forbidden her to, means that it had to be something important. Most people would probably send a text message or make a call, but not her. Even in the two years I've been gone, she's only called me a handful of times and it was usually just to boast about herself.

"If it's that important to you, then go upstairs and talk to her. I don't want her in my space. I've already allowed her…"

His words trail off, and I'm curious why. "Allowed her to do what?"

"Forget it." He moves out of the way and waves me past.

With one earbud still in and the other dangling around my neck, I pop the loose one back in and turn around to go back to my bed. I could go upstairs, but honestly, I don't really care what she has to say. She's had years to talk to me and chose not to.

Blaise grabs the handle and closes the door, so I lie back down in bed. I don't know why my mom sounded so fearful of Blaise. It's not like her. She has never groveled to anyone. She's headstrong and one of the bluntest people I know. Richard is the only person in the entire world who I've ever seen her suck-up to. Suck-up is too weak of a word—she kissed his ass and probably wiped it for him, too. She lived to please him. Like the time he bought me a car for my birthday.

Just as my eyes begin to close, ready to chase away the day and drift into a dreamless sleep, my bedroom door flies open. "Penelope Jane! You get your behind out of that bed and go thank Richard for the generous birthday gift that you will be accepting."

I roll over to face the door, blanket tucked up over my shoulders. "I don't want it, Mom."

"Do you have any idea how much money that car cost?" Her voice is stern and forthright. She continues to stand in the doorway, the light from the hallway protruding into the dark room.

"I'll buy my own car. Tell him I said thanks, but no thanks."

Anger spills from her pores. I didn't intentionally try to piss her off, but I'm not sorry.

"When did you become such an ungrateful little brat?"

Ungrateful? Is that what I am? All because I won't let my mom's new husband buy me shiny new things that he'll eventually make me pay for in the form of sexual favors. No thanks.

"Richard asked me not to say anything until this whole birthday mess blew over, but he was planning on asking you to take his last name, so you can be a Hale like the rest of us. That's how much he loves you."

I chuckle, unknowingly. "I will never be a Hale. I'm a Briar and until I'm married, I will remain a Briar."

"Briars are weak, Penelope. Your father is proof of that. Briars run when things get hard."

"Hard? Is that what you having an affair is called? And correct me if I'm wrong, but you're the one who ran away, you just took me with you."

Mom squeezes the door handle so hard that I fear she'll break it off. "You're right. I did take you with me because that man can't even afford to take care of himself. I won and he lost."

There she goes again referring to me as a prize in her divorce. Mom only keeps me here because she couldn't handle the thought of my dad feeling like I chose him. I do choose him; she just won't let me go. Unfortunately, my dad can't afford to fight her in court and she's threatened to prove him to be unfit if I made the choice to leave on my own. I don't stay for her. I stay for him.

"He's not some deadbeat. Dad is a good man and makes enough money to support himself. He's always earned his way in life, unlike you. You just take and spend."

Mom loosens her grip on the door and softens her tone. "Richard can take care of us forever, Penny. One day, this will all be ours. Just accept his gifts and do what he wants. It will all be worth it. I promise."

My phone begins ringing, pulling me out of the wretched memory.

"Hi, Dad," I say into the speaker of the phone.

"Hey, sweetheart. How have things been going at your mom's?"

"Like I never left," I say with sarcasm in my tone.

"And your friends? Have you got out to see them?"

I could tell him I have no friends. Emery feels more like a stranger now then she did the first day I met her, but I don't tell him that. "Yeah. It's been a blast." I lie.

"Look, Pen. You know I love having you here, but don't ever feel like you have to stay on my account. I know you've got a life back there in Skull Creek."

I want to gag. "My life is in Portland. I won't be staying here a day longer than necessary."

"Glad to hear it. Love ya, Pen."

"Love you, too, Dad."

We end the call and I smile to myself. I've got a good life there. I wouldn't trade that life for this one for anything in the world.

CHAPTER 5
PENELOPE

IT'S BEEN two days since I've arrived. It's also rained for those two days, forcing me to stay inside this house of misery. Not that I have anywhere to go or anyone to see. It's my birthday today and Emery asked, scratch that, Emery begged me to meet her for lunch at the pizza joint downtown. As with everything I'm invited to, I tried to get out of it. And like every other time, I gave in. It'll be fine. For years, I was invisible in this town; I doubt anyone even remembers the events of my last night here. Who am I kidding? Of course, they do.

Thirty acres caught fire that night. I was engulfed in flames even as I hid away with Blaise, who claims he was trying to protect me. That night I was reminded of what I already knew—Blaise is a liar.

Stop it, Penelope. Don't overthink this. It's just lunch. No one cares about what happened two years ago—exactly.

It was two years ago today that I spent my last night in Skull Creek. My birthday, nonetheless. At an age where I should have been crushing on boys, getting drunk for the first time, and learning to do my makeup. Instead, I was sworn away from boys by Blaise and spent my days looking over my shoulder to make sure no one was out to get me.

"Happy birthday, sweetheart," Mom says as she presses a chaste kiss to my cheek, leaving behind a film of waxy residue and the overwhelming stench of coffee. She sets her mug on the kitchen counter that's rimmed with bright red lipstick. The same color that is probably stained on my cheek.

With a rub of my fingertips, I try to remove it. "Thanks, Mom."

"Plans today?" She taps away at her phone as she asks me the question.

"Probably going to a party. Getting drunk. Might bring back a few guys. Hope that's okay?"

"Sounds like a wonderful time," she responds coyly, without even lifting her head to acknowledge what I said. There's no use in telling her what I'm really doing. Which is just lunch and back here to spend my birthday in bed.

Once she finishes whatever she was doing on her phone, she tucks it into the pocket of her cream-colored dress pants. "I'll be out most of the day. Henry will be picking up a cake later today. We will celebrate around...six o'clock? Dinner and cake sound good?"

"Yeah, Mom. That sounds great." I smile. A real, genuine smile because I'm actually very surprised that she remembered, let alone planned dinner and dessert.

Maybe today won't be so bad, after all.

My phone begins flopping around on the counter as it vibrates. Mom picks it up before I do, checks the screen, then examines me like I did something wrong. "Emery? Really, Penelope? That girl is nothing but trouble."

I hold my hand out to her, but she holds back on giving me my phone. "Why in the world would you say that? You used to love Emery."

Mom gets serious. "Used to. She and that Lilith James girl have been raising hell ever since you left. Graffiti, fights, parties, skipping school. You name it and these girls were likely behind it. Along with that destructive brother of yours."

In all of what she said, I took away one thing—brother. "Blaise is *not* my brother! God, I wish everyone would quit calling him that."

"But, he is your brother, Penelope. Just because you haven't been around, doesn't mean—"

"He is not!" I spit out, snatching my phone from her and storming off like she just said the most offensive thing imaginable. I really need to quit reacting that way, but I wish everyone would stop referring to him as family. He's not family. Family doesn't do what we did. Family doesn't feel what I felt.

☠

EMERY LEFT a message to meet her at Poppy's Pizza Joint at two o'clock. After rifling through my suitcase, tossing everything onto the floor and sulking for twenty minutes because I have nothing to wear, my finger hovers over the screen, ready to send a text message to Emery telling her I can't make it. I take a deep breath, suck it up, and close out of the message, then grab a pair of black leggings and an oversized knitted, cream-colored sweater to wear.

Once I'm dressed, I dab on some light makeup, consisting of concealer, mascara and clear lip gloss. With my hair down and a hair tie around my wrist, I leave the bathroom.

Just as I walk out the door leading to the living room, I stop when I see Blaise on the couch. His elbows pressed to his knees, head in his hands. Something must be wrong.

I should check on him.

No, I shouldn't.

Whatever he's going through isn't my business. Tiptoeing out of the bathroom, my plan is to just go up the stairs and leave, but Blaise lifts his head. "Where the hell are you going?"

"Umm. Meeting up with Emery." I cross the strap of my small black purse over my chest and drop my phone inside it.

"She never told me that. Where are you meeting her?"

"Not that it's any of your business, but we're getting lunch at Poppy's…for my birthday." I say it as a reminder that it is, in fact, my birthday. Maybe he'll chill out on the asshole attitude if he's made aware.

Blaise pushes himself up and levels his eyes with mine. "She's not the same girl, Penny. You're in for some disappointment if you think your best friend is still in there somewhere."

Mom mentioned Emery had changed. Unlucky for her and Blaise, I'm a 'see for myself' kinda girl. Emery has been kind to me since I returned. I have no reason to think she's this terrible person they're making her out to be.

"I'll be fine." I shift slowly toward the stairs, hoping he's done.

"Don't care if you're not. Just thought you should know."

I reach the stairs and go up, exiting through the mudroom and out to the side of the house. There's a stone atrium above that leads to the garage or to the paved driveway. My car isn't in the garage, though. I'm still parked out front. My little white Ford Focus looks so sad and out of place in front of this house.

With a click of the button, I unlock the doors, but as I get closer, something isn't right.

Dammit! My back tire is flat.

I go over to get a closer look and it's not just flat, it was definitely sliced with something sharp—a knife, maybe? I walk to the other side and see that the driver's side tire is flat as well. Crouching down, I run my fingers over the gash. *Who would do this?*

I stand up and look around but don't see anything suspicious. No one is here except for the groundskeepers and… "Blaise!" I shout so loudly that his name echoes off the house. With rage in my steps, I stomp back the way I came, tear the door open to the mudroom, not even bothering to shut it. "Blaise!" I shout again, knowing he won't hear me, but the turbulent anger I feel does not care. When I'm at the basement door, I rip it open and slam it against the door stopper, causing it to bounce back at me.

Jogging down the stairs, I'm met with Blaise three-quarters of the way down. Ripping my purse over my shoulder, I chuck it at him, but miss when he ducks out of the way. So I give him a shove, causing him to fall back the three steps he just came up. It's a soft landing, so, unfortunately, he'll be fine. "Really, Blaise? You're still doing this shit? How old are we now?" So much for him taking it easy on me on my birthday. I go down the rest of the way and push him again as he begins to get up. He falls back down and laughs. He actually laughs and it only fuels the fire inside of me.

When he goes to get back up, I give him another push against his shoulder. His coy expression fades and the softness in his eyes is replaced with that black ring of anger. "What the fuck is your problem?" He grabs me by the ankle, jerking hard enough to bring me down with him. I land in his lap and squirm to get away, but he locks his arms around my chest, barricading me against him.

"Don't play dumb! You slashed my tires. Did you really expect me not to react?" My feet kick at his legs as I try to free myself.

"Calm your ass down, would ya? I didn't slash your damn tires."

"Like I believe anything you say to me."

"Why in the world would I do that? Huh? What would I gain by destroying your tires?"

I stop squirming because I won't get up until he lets me.

There's no use in wasting my energy. "You'd keep me here. Keep me away from people. Just like you used to do."

"You say you've changed. Maybe I have too."

"You're incapable. You'll always be the same pompous, possessive jerk you've always been." My breaths become ragged as I relax my body against his, feeling depleted.

"And you'll always be a timid mouse who lets everyone walk all over her."

Tensing up again, I try to stretch my arms to unlock his, but it does no good. "I was timid and I did let people push me around, but not anymore. I'm stronger and I've grown a back-bone," I spit out in a shaky breath.

"Oh yeah? Prove it. For starters, get off me."

I nudge, twist, and pull, trying to get free, but he doesn't budge. "Let go of me and I will."

"You say you're stronger. Fight me." His chin rests on my shoulder as his legs fall open to the side. I'm situated on my ass between them and my heart begins pounding against my chest cavity. "Unless…you don't want to." I close my eyes and pinch my lips together as I try harder. "I don't think you've changed as much as you think you have."

I might not have the physical strength needed to fight Blaise off, but I've returned with determination. He will not belittle me anymore. I will not let him dictate my life. "You want the truth? I do want you to let me up. Because I hate you, Blaise. More than I've ever hated anyone. You kept me at arm's reach when we were younger. Pushed me around. Pulled horrible pranks on me. Then, you sucked me in and spit me out. You tricked me. For that, I will never forgive you. I'm here for a week and when I leave, I'll go back to forgetting you ever existed."

"You could never forget me, Penny." His clipped exhale hits my neck and my head tilts instinctively, relishing in the warmth that runs down my body. "I know that to be true, because you'll always have the memory of your first time…

with me." The tips of his fingers graze softly against my stomach. Goosebumps cascade downward, but I just sit there motionless. "Those memories are tucked away inside of you, but every now and then, they rear their ugly head, don't they? You hate yourself for what you did with me?"

I swallow in an audible gulp. "I do hate myself for it."

"But there's part of you that wants it to happen again, isn't there?" His fingers rim the waistband of my leggings, dipping beneath them.

"What? No! Never!"

A rumble climbs up Blaise's throat. "It's just us here. You don't have to lie to me." His hand slides down farther and I'm fearful of how he'll react when he finds that I'm soaking wet. I don't want to be. But my body is reacting to the soft, warm touch. Even if it's coming from the fingers of a cold, heartless guy.

My stomach somersaults when I notice the growing bulge against my tailbone. "I'd die before I had sex with you again. It never should have happened. You started that fire. You pulled me out and pretended to be the hero and took advantage of the moment."

"You're bare. Why? Who you fucking, Penny?"

He pushes his hand down even farther and we continue to talk as if we're both ignoring what's really happening right now. Ignoring his question, I push about the fire. "The proof was everywhere. You and your stupid friends tried to kill me." My neck bends downward as I look at my arm, though the rough patch of leather is covered with weaves of soft cotton from my sweater. I try to keep it covered as much as I can. It's hideous. Every now and then, I can feel the fire eating away at my flesh. Then I see Blaise's eyes as he swept in to rescue me. Fearful, desolate eyes. I'll never understand the events of that night. Mainly because Blaise will never give me a reason to.

"Seems we're both liars then. You don't believe me, and I

don't believe you." Two fingers rub circles around my clit and the sensation that shoots through me is unnerving. I shouldn't feel this way, not with him.

I can't sit here anymore. My heart jumps into an irregular beat, sweat rolling down my chest into my bra. "Whatever. Just let me up, please."

Blaise curls his fingers and slides one inside of me. I let out a gasp. "Is that really what you want?"

Yes. No. I don't know. I love this and hate it at the same time. My body is betraying me again, and I want to let it.

Blaise dips another finger inside. "You're dripping wet, Penny. I don't think you want me to stop as much as you think you do."

My hips flex upward when he begins drumming his fingers at my G-spot. I hate that he's witnessing how good he's making me feel.

I don't say anything as he continues to pump his finger. Every now and then, he hits a spot that causes my body to jolt, but I fight back the urge to cry out in pleasure. I lose that fight, though, when my entire body fills with an insatiable need for release. My insides close in around his fingers and I clench my thighs.

"Don't fight it, Penny. Just give in to the pleasure. Come for me."

My mouth gapes and my eyes close as my heart jackhammers in my chest. My back arches as my hips rise and fall. Blaise picks up his pace and his breaths become rapid and unfulfilled in my ear, as if he's enjoying this as much as I am. "Oh, God," I cry out. My arousal drips into the palm of his hand.

"Holy fuck, you liked that, didn't you?" I'm slightly embarrassed because I'm not sure if it's normal to have that much fluid come out during an orgasm.

This is only the second time I've ever had one and the first was during sex with Blaise. He's the only guy I've ever done anything with.

"Okay. Let me up now, please."

Blaise licks the lobe of my ear, sending another wave of shivers down my spine. His hand is still down my pants.

"I'll let you up if you answer my question."

"What question?"

"Have you fucked him?"

My back steels against his chest. "Who?"

"Your boyfriend."

"That's not your business." I grab his hand and pull it out of my pants.

"Does he make you come the way I do?"

My cheeks flush with heat and I don't respond.

"I'll take that as a no. Fine. Let me give you a ride to Poppy's and I'll let you up."

"Why? Why would you want to give me a ride? And what makes you think I'd let you?"

"You wanna get up, don't you? Accept the generous offer and we can be on our way."

I've got no choice. I'm already late meeting Emery. Mom's driver is out. I've got no choice. "Fine."

Blaise gives me a firm squeeze. "Happy birthday, Penny." His lips press to my hair on the back of my head and chills shimmy through my entire body, causing me to clench my pulsating thighs.

God, I hate him. But I hate my body more for reacting to him like this.

When I'm finally free, I jump up so fast you'd think someone poured gasoline on us and struck a match. Bending down, I pick up my purse and hurry to my room to change before Blaise gives me another reason to stay out there.

Never again. I will never let myself fall for Blaise again. I just can't. He's a terrible person, not to mention, he's my…stepbrother.

CHAPTER 6
PENELOPE

AGAINST MY BETTER JUDGMENT, I got in Blaise's luxurious car. My plan is to just accept the ride and not talk at all. I'll be kind and thank him when he drops me off, and leave it at that. I'm trying really hard not to beat myself up over what happened downstairs.

Blaise's car is really nice and I'm fascinated by all the lights and shiny features. My fingers run over the neon glow on the dash.

"You like it? Just got this baby a couple weeks ago."

"It's all right. Must've cost a fortune."

"Few hundred grand. Not bad for this gem."

My eyes pop wide open. "A few hundred grand?"

I wonder if he'll even get to keep this once the estate is finalized and everything is turned over to my mom. Knowing her, she won't let him keep it. She will take every last penny that belongs to her. I'm not even sure Blaise knows that he's not getting anything. I almost feel bad for him. His whole life he's been given everything. He doesn't have a working bone in his body. Now that I think of it, he probably won't even be able to afford college.

"Did you ever find your mom?" The words come out

before I can put any thought behind them, and when Blaise pins me with a hard stare, I regret even asking.

Blaise returns his eyes to the front windshield and shifts into reverse without a word. Once the garage is completely opened, he hammers his foot to the gas pedal with so much force you'd think he had a hundred pounds of lead in his shoes. Without even coming to a complete stop, he slams into drive and whips around in a circle, taking us down the paved drive.

My timing is impeccable. Waiting until we are in this confined space to ask him a question that's sure to send him to a dark place.

When my mom and Blaise's dad started dating, Blaise's mom just sort of disappeared. I didn't think much of it. No one ever really talked about it, so I assumed that she just moved away to start over. Turns out, she never told anyone where she was going. I once overheard Blaise and his dad talking about a dead end with the private investigator they hired to track her down.

My last night in Skull Creek, I got the courage to ask Blaise about her. It was the first time I'd ever brought her up. He gave me the same silent treatment he is now, but after a few minutes of silence, he told me he thinks his dad sent her away. He left it at that, not wanting to go further into detail.

I have to get his mind off that, so I opt for an easier question. "What's with the remodel? The upstairs was perfect before."

Blaise doesn't look at me, but he squeezes the steering wheel so aggressively that the blood drains from his knuckles. "It was my dad's stupid idea. Some ridiculous attempt at trying to get you to come back."

I scratch the back of my neck. I've got no idea what he's talking about. "Why would he think I'd come back if he demolished my bedroom? And when did anyone plan on telling me this?"

With his eyes on the road, Blaise talks, slowly relaxing his vise grip on the steering wheel. "He put the plan in motion a couple months ago when he was still feeling good. Apparently, he thought if you had your own living space, like the basement, you'd move back in." He pierces me with raised brows, as if he's questioning the truth in that statement.

"I wouldn't have," I spit out.

"Yeah. Well, you know Richard; he at least wanted to try. Too bad he kicked the can before he tried to lure you back just so he could have one last Hail Mary at getting you to milk his cock."

"Oh my God, Blaise!" My lip curls in disgust. "We've been over this. I have never, nor would I ever, have sex with that dirty old man."

"No shit. He's dead," Blaise deadpans, piercing me with a hard stare before his eyes shift back to the road.

It's no surprise that Blaise isn't even affected by his dad's passing. For one, he had plenty of time to prepare for it. And two, he never liked the guy either. I'm not even sure he loved him. Which is odd, considering we are born loving our parents.

There was a time that Blaise thought something was going on between Richard and me. But, we put that to rest the night of the fire. Apparently, Richard was still trying to find ways to get me back to the house.

"So, what now? Is my mom finishing the remodel or just leaving it partially finished up there?"

"Your mom isn't doing a damn thing. Once the dust settles after the funeral, the carpenters will resume finishing it. But, it won't be for you. That's for damn sure."

I nod in agreement. No hasty words. No smug reply. I don't even want a bedroom here anymore, let alone an entire living space.

The rest of the ride is quiet, aside from the power of this expensive as hell car. Blaise takes a sharp turn into the back parking lot of Poppy's, swerves into a space and comes to an abrupt stop. With my fingers teetering on the handle, I look at him. "Thanks for the ride."

He doesn't even look back, just kills the engine and swings his door open.

"Hey! What are you doing?" I open the door and close it behind me, jogging to catch up to Blaise as he walks to the back entrance. "Wait," I grab his arm, "you're not seriously going in there, are you?"

With a swift jerk, he pulls away and runs his tongue over his bottom lip. "What? I'm not invited…sis?"

My nostrils flare. "No, actually, you were not invited. So, if you wouldn't mind turning around and going back home. That would be great. Thanks." I pick up my pace, walking in front of him and hoping like hell he leaves.

At some point, he catches up to me, throwing an arm over my shoulder, then snickers, "And how would you get home, Penny? You think your *friends* are going to give you a ride?"

I toss him back the same sinister look he threw at me. "Maybe I'll ask Wade for a ride." It's not entirely true, but I knew I'd get a reaction out of it.

Only, it's far more of a reaction than I expected when Blaise grips my forearm and spins me around to face him. "What did you just say?" His eyes burn into me with the same wrath as his fingertips that pinch my skin.

I swallow hard, wishing I'd just left well enough alone. But, what's done is done. "You heard me."

Tugging me closer, I get a whiff of his cologne as a gust of wind sweeps by us. "Listen up, Penny." He enunciates my name as if I don't already know it. "You can walk around with your nose stuck in the air acting like you've changed, but I know deep down you're the same scared girl you've always been. I feel your pulse racing under my fingertips. I can see the fear in your eyes. Don't push me because you know what it feels like when I push back."

He doesn't give me a chance to respond as he tosses my arm away like it's garbage and struts into Poppy's like he owns the place.

Giving myself a few minutes to slow my racing heart, I collect my thoughts in the parking lot. Here I thought that maybe Blaise was softening a bit, but I keep getting these reminders that he's still the same jerk he was back then. Looks like I'm deemed an outcast again. The girl who everyone avoids because Blaise told them to. Even Wade—especially Wade. I'm not sure why it's always bothered him that Wade was nice to me. Guess it's because Wade was told not to be and he was anyway. They're best friends, though—him, Chase, and Wade—yet, Blaise still acts superior to them. I never would have done that to Emery, or any of my friends back home.

Feeling a bit anxious, I start walking again. The closer I get to the door, the more I second-guess being here. I'm walking into Blaise's territory now that he's here. If he weren't, I would have felt more wanted.

I'm not sure when Emery became so popular. Hanging at Poppy's, going to parties. I guess it was the life she always wanted, and now she's living it.

I've got no idea what I'm walking in on, but ready or not, here I come.

CHAPTER 7
BLAISE

"YOU," I point to Emery as she sits on top of the table giggling with *my* friends. "Bathroom. Now."

Her pleased look instantly falls and she drops down onto her feet. Her three-inch heels click-clack across the floor as she follows behind me. The place is packed, as per usual for a Friday evening. Not to mention, the night every student in this town waits all year for—Devil's Night.

As soon as I reach the ladies' restroom, I palm the door and push it open, holding it in place until Emery walks in with her tail between her legs. There are two girls gawking at the mirror, touching up their crayon-colored faces. I grab a compact mirror out of one of the girl's hands, Nikki, I think is her name. I close it with one hand and hand it back to her. "You're done. Get out."

The girls share a look, then leave as they were instructed. Once the door closes, my arms cross over my chest. Biceps bulging, veins protruding.

Emery slides up closely, but I don't touch her. I look down on her with a dark stare. "I see you've missed me." Her hands snake up the back of my shirt, the overpowering stench of whiskey rolling off her tongue.

"Not even a little bit." I take a step back, opening the space between us. "I wanna know why the fuck you invited her here and didn't so much as mention it to me."

Emery sniggers. "Come on, Blaise. It's her birthday. We just wanted to have a little fun with her."

"We?"

"Don't act like you haven't done the exact same thing. Lilith told me this day was always dedicated to making her miserable. And in case you've forgotten, I was also on the receiving end of your jokes, even though I know they weren't directed at me. Ex-best friends ring a bell?"

"So, you plan on...what? Spitting in her pizza? Maybe loosen a leg on her chair?" My voice rises. "What the hell is her plan, Emery?" Her, as in Lilith. The fucking succubus that she is.

Her shoulders shrug as she bats her fake lashes. "Guess you'll have to wait and see." She goes to turn away, thinking that it will be that easy.

Grabbing her by the waist, I pull her into me until her back is flush with my chest. Leaning close, lips ghosting her ear, I grit through my teeth, "Don't you ever go behind my back again. You hear me? Lilith might have made you, but I will fucking break you. Mark my words."

I can feel her body tense under my grasp. Giving her a shove away from me, she takes a few steps forward, glances over her shoulder, and gives me the look I've been waiting for —proof that she's scared.

The corner of my lip tugs up, pleased with myself.

Emery should fear me. I've got so much shit on that girl, I could destroy her coveted reputation in two seconds flat. All it would take is the swipe of a thumb on my phone and proof of her whored ways will be shared with the entire student body of Skull Creek High.

Following behind Emery, I catch her scared eyes glancing over her shoulder. I waggle my brows and she turns back around. Stupid girl would normally take it as an invitation to spread her legs. I think we both know that we're not on that playing level anymore. She's going too far, planning shit behind my back and taking Lilith's side over mine. I knew the two were close, but Emery and I had an understanding. In fact, everyone knows that you're either at my side or you're behind me—those with Lilith are always behind me.

Lilith gets away with what she does for a reason. The others, they will not betray me and get away with it.

As soon as I round the corner and look back at the table where everyone is gathered, my entire body floods with a rage. Fists clenched at my sides, I bite down so hard that I can hear the grinding of my molars. My boots move across the laminate floors rapidly with thunderous steps that vibrate in my clouded head.

One of Lilith's groupies nudges her. Once her eyes find me, the entire crowd does the same. Chase's expression of pure happiness drops immediately. Penny is finally able to free herself from his grip and slides away from Chase, not even bothering to look in my direction. Even though, my presence is the only thing that saved her ass from a moment of humiliation and sexual harassment. She'll never acknowledge it, though. She'll assume I'm responsible because I'm still making the world stay an arm's length away from her. Maybe I am, and I didn't even have to lay down the rules since she'd returned.

Silence engulfs this section of the restaurant. But because the music from the jukebox is so loud, the rest of the guests are none the wiser.

"What's going on over here?" I pop my ass cheek on the corner of the booth. I see a few girls Lilith runs around with. Emery is sitting quietly at a table with Wade and Cory—a guy who thinks he's our friend but really just rides our coattails. Chase has resorted to texting on his phone to avoid a confrontation with me. Smart guy. And Penny, well, she's a ball of nerves with her hands tucked in the sleeves of her sweater. Is that what people do just to be accepted? They put up with groping, cat calls, and shady-ass remarks just so that they can remain seated with the in-crowd?

Pathetic.

All these assholes need to grow a backbone.

"Well, don't end your fun on my account. Chase, you were in the middle of feeling Penelope up as she repeatedly told you to stop. Lilith, you were laughing your ass off, along with all your followers. What's changed?"

When no one answers, I look at Penny. "Did you like it?"

Her lips press together in a thin line and her cheeks flush pink.

"You told me yourself that you're tougher. Why'd ya let him do it?"

"Dude," Wade chimes in, "you're embarrassing the girl. Drop it."

I spin around to face him at the table he's sitting at. "Was I talking to you?"

Penny slides out from her space behind the booth, everyone watching—waiting. She goes to walk past me—to run and hide like she always does, but I grab her by the arm. "Let me go, Blaise."

"Chase. Apologize to my sister."

Penny watches her feet and shakes her head. "Stop it. Please," she whispers.

"Now, Chase."

"I'm sorry, Penelope. Didn't hear you ask me to stop. In fact, you were laughing."

She laughs when she's nervous. I don't tell him that, though. It's a sound I've picked up on and actually kinda like. But no one should be making her nervous except for me.

"It's okay, Chase." Penny lifts her head and tacks me with a glare. "I've gotta use the restroom." She jerks her arm away from me and keeps walking.

Emery slides out of her seat and chases after her. I don't stop her because Penny trusts Emery. For some unknown fucked-up reason, she just does. She's got no idea what her former bestie has warped herself into just to be popular. She won't listen to me, so it's time she learns for herself.

CHAPTER 8
PENELOPE

I WILL NOT BREAK DOWN. "DAMMIT." I slap my hand against the stall door in the bathroom. It ricochets back, practically laughing at me. Just like everything and everyone does when I try to stand my ground.

"Whoa, girl. Calm down," Emery says. I didn't even know she came in. I couldn't hear anything outside of my internal thoughts screaming at me.

"Easy for you to say." I walk over to the sink, slam my purse down, and press my palms against the cold vanity. I lean over and take a deep breath. My head twists and I look at Emery. "Why are you even hanging out with these guys?"

"Come on now. It's what we always wanted. To be one of them. Well, I got us in, so just go with it."

I shake my head, no. "I never wanted this. You did. They're still the same people they were freshman and sophomore year, Emery. They're using you for their own gain."

"That's not true. Lilith has actually been a really good friend to me. Unlike my best friend who left me high and dry without so much as a goodbye."

There's a pang in my chest. She's right. Emery doesn't know why I left, though. No one can ever know the reasons I felt so disgusted with myself that I had to run away and never look back. It wasn't just the fire that almost took my life; it was the fire that burned inside of me. One I had to put out before the flames swallowed me whole.

I lift my head, feeling the sorrow trickle at the corners of my eyes. "You're right. I wasn't a good friend. I'm sorry, Em."

"Prove it. Come with me tonight. For old times' sake."

"The Devil's Night Party? No." My fingers slide up and down my arms as I stare past her. "For as long as I live, I will never attend one of those parties again."

I only went once. One night that started off fun—a celebration of the holiday and my birthday rolled into one. Against my better judgment, I had a few drinks and let loose. I got a glimpse of everything I'd always been so curious about. *What happens at these elusive parties?* It's what every outsider always wanted to know.

Chaos. That's what happens.

Emery takes my hand in hers, holding it gently like I'm a toddler that needs coddling. "It's been two years, Penny. Things are different now. These guys aren't as bad as they seem."

"Oh yeah? If I remember right, I was instantly back to being the butt of their jokes after only five minutes of being in their presence." I jerk my hand away. "And thanks for standing up for me, *friend*."

Emery's warm gaze turns to a glare. "I'm just trying to help, but it seems you're still sour about shit from the past." She storms past me and out the bathroom door.

With my back to the bathroom wall, I slide down until I'm sitting on the cold, hard floor. I rifle through my purse, looking for my phone, but it's not there. Dammit. It must have fallen out when I threw it at Blaise. So much for calling an Uber.

What Emery said was uncalled for, but she's right. I've

been living in my own world of pity for far too long. Bad stuff happened. Bad stuff happens all the time. She's also unaware of what happened that night. As far as the public know, they all think the fire was an accident. No one even knows I was inside. I didn't even seek medical attention out of fear the cops would be involved. At that time, I didn't plan on moving away from Skull Creek. It wasn't until the next morning, as regret ran through my veins, that I knew I had to leave for good.

That was the last night I saw Emery until my return three days ago. It was at the Devil's Night Party. It was our first year in attendance and it was everything I'd hoped it would be. Everything I was missing out on. At least, it was for a little while.

Everyone wore a mask. You could be whoever you wanted to be. For me, it was perfect. I didn't have to be Penelope Briar—sworn off by Blaise's commands, belittled by my peers. It didn't matter that I wore no makeup. I was as beautiful as Lilith, with Roxanne, the head cheerleader's smile. I wore confidence like it was a winter jacket. I strolled through the parted forest, lit with a neon glow, with my head held high. I felt unstoppable.

Until I was stopped.

Emery had wandered off into the woods after having a little too much to drink. I went looking for her, thinking maybe I'd find her pressed up against a tree, taking a few minutes to herself. Instead, I was met by the rulers of Skull Creek. All lined up in a row, stretched far enough to make me walk a few yards to try and go around them, and likely summoned by the devil himself.

All eyes were on me—glowing like embers through the sockets of their masks. There was no sense in trying to get away. They had me right where they wanted me.

I had on the prettiest mask there. It was a plastic shell with a strap that wrapped around my head. All black with red roses covering it and a thick white outline around my mouth. I was wearing a pair of blue jeans and my usual pink, worn *Converse* slip-on shoes. That's likely how they picked me out of the crowd.

"This isn't funny, guys. Just let me go find my friend." I shuffle a few steps, hoping to part the two smaller ones in the middle, thinking maybe they'll let me through.

"Your friend is gone. You get us now." A familiar voice comes through the opening of the neon green mask with white slashes across the cheek. It's Chase. Which instantly alarms me. When Chase does something, it's usually because Blaise puts him up to it.

With my heart in my throat, I turn around to go back out the way I came in. I can still see the lights in the distance, though I'm out pretty far into the woods. It's a straight shot; if I have to run, I can probably make it.

My feet move quickly, but until I have reason to pick up my pace, I'll just leave them thinking I'm unaffected. They all feed off fear. It brings them some sort of sick happiness. Bullies—that's what they are.

I make one wrong move, glancing over my shoulder, and I trip over a stupid branch in my path. I crash down on the ground, roughing up my jeans and scraping my hands, but I get myself up and push my mask on the top of my head, so I can see clearly.

They're not chasing after me. They gave up.

As soon as I start walking back to the party, my body crashes into a six-foot Chase. His mask is still on but I know it's him. "What are you scared of, Penelope? I don't bite…hard." He laughs in this sinister way that alarms every cell in my body.

Before I can even react, a circle has gathered around me.

"Toss the bitch over your shoulder and let's fucking go!" It's not a guy this time—it's Lilith.

Blaise orchestrating destruction is dangerous, but having Lilith join his side and taking a part in it is deadly. She has no mercy. She has no soul. She's vicious, and I wouldn't put it past her to go as far as letting these guys strip me of my clothes and gangbang me. All while she stands there with a smile beneath her Day of the Dead mask.

Bile rises up in my throat, but I swallow it down. "Let me go right now or I'll call the cops." I step around a guy I don't recognize, but he throws an arm out.

"Oooh," the guy mocks me. "She's gonna call the cops. Should we let her go, guys?"

"No." "Hell no." "Not a chance." They all say in unison.

The circle closes in, everyone taking two steps toward me while an arm wraps around my waist from behind. "Don't fight it, baby. If you're a good girl, I might help you," Chase breathes in my ear.

Help me? I shouldn't believe him. But, right now, I'll take all the help I can get.

"Monster" by Kanye West plays in the distance. Everyone out there is having the time of their lives, disguised as someone else, blending in, laughing, drinking—relishing their teenage experiences. That was supposed to be me.

Instead, I'm here. Strong arms lift me up as my feet kick freely off the ground. "Stop!" I shout. My arms are restrained, tucked tightly against my stomach. "Please! Just put me down. I'll leave. I'll never come to your stupid parties ever again! I'll do anything. Just let me go." Tears prick the corners of my eyes, but no one cares. No one listens to the quiet girl who's begging for mercy. Willing to make a deal with the devil to save herself. Only this time, the devil doesn't want to barter; he just wants to see my pain.

I lift my head when the door to the bathroom opens. "Get your ass up. I'm taking you home," Blaise says from the doorway of the bathroom.

Swiping away tears I didn't know were there, I get up off the dirty floor. "I'll pass." I go over to the sink and turn on the cold water, letting it run over my hands.

Blaise comes up behind me, his angry expression offsetting my sad one. "It wasn't a question. I tried to warn you, Penny. But you didn't listen."

The ice-cold water burns my skin, riding up my arms,

hitting me in the chest like a zap of lightning. Something awakens inside of me. A fire is lit.

Pulling my hands back, I give them a shake then look at Blaise in the mirror. "Fuck you."

Maybe it's the memories flooding my mind, or maybe it's the fact that I've been made a mockery of for the last time. But, it ends tonight.

Blaise growls as he takes me by the arm and starts to pull me away from the sink. I yank my arm back and level my eyes with his. "I'm done being your little toy, Blaise. Go play with Emery, or your friend, Lilith." I grab my purse off the sink and step past him, pushing the door open. Hurried steps lead me down the hall to the back door that we came in. With two hands, I shove it open and let it close slowly behind me. I take in a deep breath of fresh air, ready to get the hell out of here.

CHAPTER 9
PENELOPE

MY FEET ACHE, I'm hungry, and I'm starting to regret turning down Blaise's offer for a ride home. Stubbornness tends to get the best of me and it isn't until I'm choking on my own pride that I realize it.

It's a ten-minute drive from Poppy's to the Hales' house. Which means, at least an hour walk. I'm halfway there when I hear the revving of an engine behind me. A glance over my shoulder has me turning back around immediately. It's not Blaise, but it's another one of those snazzy expensive rides, so it's safe to assume it's someone I don't want to encounter. Especially out here, alone.

The road is desolate, eerie almost. Weeping willow trees hang over the paved road, hiding the sun that's also cloaked by thick clouds.

As the car comes closer, my heart beats faster. The engine revs again, causing me to walk off the side of the road, hoping they just go around me. "Penelope," the driver shouts from behind me.

I turn around when I recognize the voice. "Wade?" My feet no longer move as I stand glued to the mossy grass on the side of the road.

The car door opens and his black boots hit the asphalt. With the door left open, he walks toward me—solemnness in his expression.

"What are you doing here?" I ask him, craning my neck to try and get a look in his car to see if he's alone.

"Blaise said you left on foot so I skipped out on lunch and figured I'd come give you a ride."

"But…why? Why leave your friends to help me?"

The corner of his mouth lifts. "I see you still ask a lot of questions."

Wade is an attractive guy. He's no Blaise Hale, but his kind demeanor makes him a thousand times more gorgeous. Sandy blond hair, blue eyes, and the body of a surfer. Though, he doesn't dress like one—at least not anymore. He's still got the baby face, but dresses like a punk in all black and has a sleeve of tattoos on his left arm. Tattoos he didn't have when I moved away from Skull Creek.

"I guess I just never know what to expect with you guys." I begin digging the toe of my shoe into the moss I'm standing in.

"You should know by now that I'm on your side. They're just a bunch of bored assholes."

"Then why hang out with them? If you think they're assholes, I mean?"

"Let me give you a ride. The birthday girl shouldn't be walking alone down dark roads by herself, especially tonight of all nights."

I want to tell him I'm not scared. That sometime in between pushing Blaise down the stairs and getting groped by Chase, I found the fight in myself that I've been looking for. But, it's probably best I keep that to myself.

"Did you mean it when you said you're on my side?"

"Of course," he angles his head toward his car, "come on."

I believe him. Maybe it's because he's never given me a

reason not to. I did some social media stalking a few weeks after I settled into my home in Portland, and as it turns out, Wade was at a cabin with his family the weekend of the fire. There were pictures to prove it. So, for now, I still trust the guy.

"All right. I'll accept the ride."

"Sweet. Buckle up, baby, because this thing has some serious power." His brows waggle and I laugh, even though I'm pretty nervous. If Blaise finds out that I let Wade give me a ride, he could quite possibly kill us both.

We get in the car and it's pretty similar to Blaise's, with a teal glow on the dash and black leather seats that you sort of melt into. Wade shifts into drive and when he burns out, I look behind us just to see the trail of smoke his tires kicked up. He beams with dancing eyebrows. "Relax. We'll get you home safely."

"I'd appreciate that," I tease. Wade doesn't scare me. Then again, I've never rode in a car with him. My hands fold in my lap as I look out the passenger car window. Wade turns the volume up as "Unbreakable" by Kingdom Collapse plays through the speakers surrounding us.

Aside from the music blasting, the silence between us is deafening. Even if I wanted to talk to Wade and catch up, he wouldn't be able to hear me over the bass shaking the seats.

As if he read my thoughts, Wade turns the volume down so that it's just a buzzing in my ear, instead of a bass drum thudding against my eardrum. "So, what do you do for fun over there in Portland?" Wade asks, gaze shifting back and forth from me to the road.

"I umm…actually do a lot now." It's true. I actually have a life there, unlike here. "I've got a boyfriend. He plays basketball and I've never missed a game. Bonfires and parties on the weekends."

"Whoa! You, Penelope Briar, go to parties? I don't believe it for a second."

"Why is that so hard to believe?" It's a question I'd like an answer to. It's not like I'm some sort of slug who's always left behind. I'm not hideous-looking. I've got a sense of humor. People actually enjoy my company.

"In the two years you lived in Skull Creek, I have never once seen you at a party."

"Wade," I look at him with a scowl, "I was sixteen when I left. That was two years ago. People grow a lot in two years. At least, when they live in a place that allows them to grow, they do."

Wade's eyes soften and his shoulders slouch as he drives with his wrist dangling over the steering wheel. "Maybe that's what I need then. Move away so I can just be myself."

Shifting to face him, I tuck one leg under the other. "What do you mean? You've got it made here. You're Blaise's best friend. Doesn't that make you some sort of king, or prince, or something?"

Wade chuckles. "Maybe that's the problem. I've been in Blaise's shadow my entire life. People just know me as his best friend. No one knows the real me. Not sure anyone even cares."

"I do."

Wade's eyes catch mine. There's something hiding behind them. It's like he wants to tell me something, but he won't.

"Ya know, you can tell me whatever's bothering you. I'm pretty good at keeping secrets." Lord knows I have many of my own.

"It's nothing." He shakes his head. "Just forget about it."

I won't force him to talk, but everyone needs someone to vent to. I'm sure it's not easy having friends who are assholes like Chase and Blaise. They have no compassion or depth. It's totally understandable that if Wade were feeling a certain way, he'd hold it in out of fear of judgment.

I get it. I've been there. I am there.

"You going to the party tonight?" I ask him out of curiosity.

"Nah. Not really my thing. I'll go to every weekend party, but this one I skip out on. Too much drama."

"I get that. I've heard they're pretty crazy."

"How about you?"

I feel like I can trust Wade. I'm not sure why. Maybe it's because he's never given me a reason not to. I know he's friends with Blaise and Chase, but he's nothing like them. He's a good person. "Actually, I think I am. Don't tell anyone, though. I sort of just want to go and see Emery. Maybe have some fun in this town for once."

"My lips are sealed."

We pull up to the Hale house and my stomach drops when I see Blaise out front next to my car. His back is pressed against the driver's door with his foot kicked up behind him. I'm not sure what's more unsettling, the fact that he's going to rip Wade a new one for giving me a ride, or the fact that I have to face him after what happened in the basement earlier.

Wade comes to a rolling stop. "And this is where I say goodbye and fly the fuck outta here."

"Yeah. You better go. He looks pretty pissed." I grab the door handle once Wade clicks the unlock button. "Thanks for the ride."

"No problem." He pauses for a beat. "Be careful at the party. Lots of crazies out there."

"Thanks, I'm actually thinking I'll disguise…" My words trail off when I notice Wade's looking over my shoulder with a leery expression.

I follow his gaze to my window and breathe out a heavy sigh when I see Blaise standing at the door. Before I can push it open, he gives it a pull. Drawing in a deep breath, I speak on the exhale. "What do you want?"

Blaise grabs me by the arm and pulls me up like I'm a rag

doll. With his fingers pinching my skin, he slouches down and glowers at Wade. "We'll talk about this later." Then he slams the car door closed and Wade burns out, leaving us standing in a cloud of smoke.

"Let go of me." I tug my arm back, but he only tightens his hold.

"What the fuck was that?" He walks, pulling me along with him.

"That was a ride from someone in this town who actually has a soul."

"He's also got a dick that he'd stick in your pussy the minute you let your guard down. Stay the fuck away from him." He keeps pulling me until we're standing by my car.

"My tires." I look up at Blaise. "Who filled them?"

"These should get you through the next couple years if you don't drive like an asshole like Wade."

Confusion is written all over my face as I crane my neck, looking at him for answers. "You bought me new tires?"

"Because I need you out of my fucking house and in that other state ASAP. Flat tires won't take your ass anywhere and we all know Daddy can't afford to buy them for you."

That's a lie. My dad might not be rich, but we're not poor. He would have got me a couple used tires and I would have been perfectly fine with that.

"I don't want them," I spit out on impulse, shifting my body away from his.

Blaise drops my arm and takes a step back to get a better look at my face. "Come again."

"I don't take handouts and I know you. Accepting these tires would mean I'm indebted to you. I won't do it." My arms cross over my chest as I stare past him.

"Jesus, you're a pain in the ass, Penny. Quit overanalyzing everything and accept the fucking gift."

Blaise walks past me, nudging my shoulder with his, all too aggressively. I turn around and watch him walk away. His head held high and his shoulders drawn back. Why is a guy like him toying with me? He's the epitome of perfection on the outside. He's the one every girl wants and every guy wants to be. So, why am I getting this special treatment? Not just his asshole tendencies. He kissed me a couple days ago. He fingered me earlier. The thought alone makes me blush with humiliation.

Better yet, why do I want more of this side of him? Why do I want him at all?

Shaking away all the questions I'll never have answers to, I walk back to the house. I need to find my phone. I'm hoping it fell out of my purse earlier in the basement; otherwise, I've got no idea where it is.

It's almost six o'clock, so we should be having my birthday dinner soon. I'm still surprised that Mom went to the trouble and actually planned something. Butterflies flutter through my stomach. Maybe she's changing for the better and we can start fixing our broken relationship.

Opening the basement door, I close it behind me and walk downstairs. To my surprise, my phone is lying right next to the couch on the floor. I bend down and pick it up, immediately noticing the notifications. Six missed calls from Ryan. One from Heidi, the closest friend I've got in Portland, and a dozen different text messages. *This is odd.*

"So," Blaise says, startling me from the couch. I walk closer and look down at him lying there with his eyes closed, ankles crossed, and arms folded under his head. "Did you decide to keep the tires on or do you plan to take them all off and burn 'em in the back yard?"

"I guess I'm gonna keep them. Even though, I'm still not sure why you did it." I open my text messages and begin reading them. Confusion sweeps through me as I read the message from Heidi.

"Told ya. I want you gone and you can't drive on rims alone."

Ignoring Blaise, I keep reading.

Heidi: Ryan is losing his fucking mind. Says you cheated on him. What in the world is going on?

Me: What are you talking about? Why would he think that?

I hit Send then move on to the messages from Ryan as I walk away from Blaise, pacing the length of the basement.

Ryan: What the fuck is this?

Ryan: Who is that?

Ryan: Who the hell is that, Penelope?

Ryan: We're done. Don't ever talk to me again.

It feels as if someone has reached into my chest and squeezed all the blood from my heart. I have no idea what's going on?

Me: I'm so confused, Ryan. I'm calling you.

As soon as I hit Send, I tap the Call icon. It rings, and rings, and rings.

"Hey, this is Ryan. Leave a message."

"Ryan, it's me. Please call me back. I have no idea what happened, but I didn't do anything. Call me. Please."

I hit the End button and look up. Blaise is now sitting, his eyes deadlocked on me. That's not what's disturbing, though. It's the pleased look on his face. The corner of his lips tugged up in a smug grin.

My phone vibrates. It's a text from Ryan. A video.

"No," I mumble, looking up with fire coursing through my veins.

It's a video that Blaise must have taken on my phone while he was fingering me on this very floor. He caught every second of it, from start to climax.

"You!" I harden my stare at Blaise. "You did this."

"What's the problem, Penny Pie?"

"I will never forgive you for this. Ever." I mean every word I say as the video plays in the background.

Tears threaten to fall, but I hold them back, choking down

the lump lodged in my throat. "I hate you. I hate you so fucking much."

I'm so tired of everyone in this town thinking they can dictate my life. Not anymore.

Once I'm away from that monster, I send Emery a message.

Me: How close are you and Lilith?

Emery: Not very. She's still the same bitch she's always been. Life is just easier this way, ya know?

Me: Perfect. I'll see you tonight. Our secret?

Emery: Absolutely!

CHAPTER 10
BLAISE

GOOD. She hates me. I guess my job here is done. It's what I wanted, right? For Penny to hate me with every fiber of her being? So much that she leaves and never comes back? I thought I succeeded the first time, yet here she is. Granted, it's for my dad's funeral and she's leaving again, but a day in this house with her is too long, let alone a week. Being so close. Feeling the temptation roll out from under her bedroom door like hot lava.

I fall back over the arm of the couch and lie down with my legs dangling over the side. Penny is in her room slamming stuff around, probably with that douchebag boyfriend of hers on redial. He was no good for her, anyway. I'm not sure if anyone she picks ever will be. Penny isn't exactly the best at making decisions for herself—our encounters are proof of that.

There's a gust of air as she jerks her bedroom door open. "Where's my damn lotion?" she huffs, still out of my sight as I lie here with my eyes closed.

"No clue what you're talking about."

"My jasmine-scented lotion. It was by the sink, and now it's gone."

"You're shit outta luck because I've got no idea where your lotion is. I guess next time you won't leave it in *my* bathroom."

When I feel her presence near—like a ghost hovering over me—I open one eye and lift my head. She's wearing a pair of black leggings and a long-sleeved black Thrasher t-shirt with a lightning bolt on it. It suits her dark and lonely state of mind.

Standing in front of my hanging feet with crimson cheeks and flared nostrils, her hands press to her hips.

"Look at you all fired up. It's kinda cute," I say with a suppressed laugh.

"No one else has been down here. I want my lotion. Now!"

"Calm down, Lucifer. I'll give you five bucks for a new bottle of lotion."

"Lucifer, huh? Seems a little hypocritical, considering you're the reason a good relationship ended today."

"Good relationship?" I spit with a hearty laugh. "Consider it a favor. The guy was fucking someone else anyway." My head drops back down, eyes closed.

"You're lying."

"Wish I was. Truth is, your fuck buddy has a new fuck buddy. Erin, Emily—"

"Erica?"

My eyes open and I snap my fingers in her direction. "That's it."

Straight-faced, she opens her phone, taps at it and then holds it up to me, showing me a picture. "This girl?"

"Could be." I scoot myself up with a sigh and grab my phone that's at my side. Once I find the pictures that the dumbass kid sent me, I turn the phone to face her. I was planning to hold on to these gems for a bit, but I'm pretty fucking tired right now and she's going to keep going with this.

Penny slaps a hand over her mouth. Her head shakes, battling disbelief.

"Truth hurts, huh?"

As tears begin to fall down her cheeks, it's obvious how much the truth does hurt. "Jesus, Penny. Don't cry. He's a fucking idiot." The last thing I want to do is console the girl, but the tears that fall because of someone else hit me differently than the ones that fall because of me.

Penny turns abruptly and hurries up the stairs. With a heavy breath, I fall back on the couch and shut my eyes.

When did life get so complicated? Since when do I feel grief when Penny is hurting? There are a few people that have any sort of effect on me in this world. I don't care enough to give most people a second thought. But, Penny lives rent-free in my head and I can't figure out why I let her.

She hates everything and everyone in this town because of me. She's also made it clear I'm not of importance in her life. She officially hates me and even if she didn't fight me off earlier today, she only lets things go that far because she doesn't know how to say no. Hell, she'd probably even let Chase put his fingers in her pussy.

The thought has me springing up off the couch because if I don't change my scenery and my thoughts right now, I'll dwell on that and it will drive me mad.

If I ever find out anyone I know has ever tried to fuck Penny, I'll kill 'em with my bare hands.

Somehow I end up upstairs where Penny is walking in and out of the room, hollering for her mom. When she comes back to the kitchen, she looks confused with her pink-tinged cheeks and nose. She stopped crying, but the proof of her heartbreak is visible. "Have you seen my mom?"

"No. Thank fuck."

Her emerald eyes roll. "Still an asshole I see."

"Always." I pull out a stool at the center island. "She's

probably out with her new boy toy getting an outfit for her dead husband's funeral."

"She said we were having dinner then cake at six o'clock." She taps her phone on the counter to check the time. "It's almost seven."

I laugh, unable to stop myself. "You actually believed her? You are a naive girl, Penny."

"Don't you have something to do? More relationships to destroy?" Penny slides her finger across the two-tier cake sitting on the counter. Once she's got a nice scoop of teal frosting, she sticks her finger in her mouth. I watch her with a slack jaw and she acknowledges my gawk with a scowl. "What?"

The girl might not have curves, or an ass, but her plump lips make up for it. I bet they'd wrap nicely around my cock.

"Nothing," I say with a wide-stretched smirk.

She sucks the last bit of frosting off with a puckered forehead as she watches me. "Why are you still sitting here? Isn't tonight your night to rain down fire and steal the souls from the helpless residents of Skull Creek?"

Taking a finger full of frosting for myself, I slide my finger in my mouth and suck it off. "Nope. Not going."

Taken aback, Penny drops her shoulders. "You're kidding, right? Isn't that like…your thing?"

"Not this year." I stretch my legs out in front of me and lock my ankles. "Looks like you're stuck with me, birthday girl."

I'm not really feeling the whole party vibe tonight. Most wouldn't the night before their dad's funeral. I'm actually surprised because I didn't even like the guy. I guess the closer it gets to finally laying his ass to rest, the more real it all becomes. He's not coming back. Mom's not coming back. At eighteen years old, I'm an orphan. I've got family members still alive but none that I've ever been close with. Doubt I'll ever even see any of them again unless they come knocking for a handout. In which case, I'll unkindly tell them to fuck off.

"I'd rather die a thousand times than spend another birthday stuck with you." Penny taps her phone again, likely checking the time.

"In that case, you'll be spending it alone because I think Mommy Dearest forgot about ya." I swipe the bottom layer of the cake again, getting another finger full.

For a brief moment, I see sadness sweep her eyes. "She's just running late. But, even if she did stand me up, I most definitely will not be stuck with you for another birthday. I'm going out."

With my finger mid-air, headed for my mouth, I stop, setting my wrist on the counter. "What do you mean you're heading out? Where are you going?"

She raises her chin. "Wherever you're not."

"If you plan on going to the party, you're asking for trouble."

"Why is that?"

"Simple. You weren't invited."

Penny chuckles. "Is anyone really ever invited to those things?"

"No. But people *are* uninvited and you were freshman year when the high school class took over. When *I* took over."

"You? Or Lilith?" Penny goes to walk away, but I throw my hand out, stopping her. Curling my arm, I pull her toward me. There's no way in hell I'm letting her go to that party. She will not destroy everything I've fought for.

"Me. Lilith might play the game, but I control the players."

To my surprise, Penny doesn't fight me off. She stands over me, looking down to where I sit on the stool. "Well,

Blaise," she enunciates my name with a newfound confidence that has my cock twitching, "I'm not playing anyone's game. I'm a lone wolf doing my own thing. And tonight, I'm doing what I want."

Who the fuck is this girl? Since when does she tell me what she's gonna do? "No, you're not. You're staying home."

"Like hell I am." This time, she pulls back, but I go with her.

Standing up, I tower over her. "You need to let go of this dream to fit in with this crowd."

Her back steels as she gapes at me. "Seriously?" She blows out a heedless breath. "First of all, I never said I was going to the party. Second, if you think I'd ever go because I have a dream of fitting in, then you don't know me at all."

I take a step closer, eating up the inches between us. "I know you better than you think I do." Biting the corner of my lip, I bring my hand up to her face, trailing her mouth with the frosting that's starting to dry. It crumbles as I wipe it across her lower lip. "You pretend to be this sweet and inno-cent girl, but you've got a wild side that begs to be unleashed."

Her tongue darts out, licking the sweet sugar as I push my finger inside her mouth. At first, she squirms, but when I lock my other hand around her head and force her to take it, her doe eyes dawn on me with curiosity as her mouth closes around me. I can hear the thoughts running rampant inside her head. *How far will he go if I don't stop him? Will he kiss me? Will I let him?*

Temptation has always been a bitch to me. I already know the answers to all the questions she likely has. I'll go as far as she lets me because her body is my weakness. I'll devour her mouth and leave her breathless. And, she will let me. Penny will never deny me. No matter how much she hates me, I am her kryptonite and she is mine.

I slide my finger out of her mouth and watch her lips as she licks the frosting. She misses a spot, so I sweep my finger across her upper lip and suck it off. "Mmm…sweet." Penny's chest heaves as the tension between us coils. I know she feels it as much as I do.

Screw it. It's a rarity that Penny even allows me to get this close to her. Might as well take advantage of the moment.

I grab her by the face, fingers pinching the skin of her cheeks as I pull her mouth flush with mine in a forced but rousing kiss. She fights it, at first. Lurching her head back, gripping my shoulders, and pushing, but there is no drive behind her shove.

My arm slides down and spoons her waist as I jerk her body closer. Penny completely lets her guard down, falling into the kiss. Our noses bump, hearts pounding in sync, while our tongues tangle together.

Everything intensifies when I suck her bottom lip between my teeth. Penny wraps her arms around my neck, coercing me. She tastes so sweet. Like sugar and sin. This thing between us is fire. Dangerous. Hot. You don't dare fall in, though, because you'll get burned. But, the thrill is too exciting to completely ignore.

I'm not sure when she became such a good kisser. I refuse to let my mind wander to where she might have learned. My hand slides to her stomach, lifting the corner of her shirt, grazing her bare skin. Penny shivers at my touch while she tugs at my hair by the fistful.

When my mouth moves to her neck and she tilts her head, I suck at the thin skin, working my way down to her collar-bone—kissing, biting, sucking.

"We should stop," she mutters.

I silence her with my mouth. My head shakes. Cupping her right breast in my hand, I squeeze. "There's no stopping this."

"What in God's name is going on here?" A voice comes from behind us. Not just any voice.

Penny pulls back, tensing up while all the color drains from her face. "Mom. I…umm, it was nothing. I just—"

"You just, what? Thought that maybe you could lure Blaise in by being a whore." She walks closer, slamming her purse down on the kitchen table.

I find it comical as I watch Penny fumble over her words. "No. It's not like that. It was—"

I press a finger to her lips, hushing her. "You don't have to answer to her. You're a big girl." I spin around to face my bitch of a stepmother. "Isn't that right, Ana?"

Ana's eyebrows unfurrow and she swallows hard, choking down the hateful words I know she wants to spit at me. "You're right. Penelope is eighteen years old now." Her hands fold in front of her as she stands tall, not letting her emotions get the better of her. "Did she throw herself at you?"

"Mom! Stop. Can you please just let this go?" It's as if Penny is worried I'll throw her under the bus and make her out to be the whore her mom thinks she is.

"No." I turn around to look at Penny. "She didn't throw herself at me. I kissed her because she was sad that she's spending her birthday home…alone. Because that's where she's staying tonight—home." I spin back to Ana, still wearing a scorned look. "But apparently she's not, because here you are. You two enjoy your cake." Feeling pleased with myself, I leave these two to rip into each other. If anything, it'll teach Penny to stick up for herself once in a while. She needs to learn somehow.

I think I made my point clear. She's not going anywhere tonight. She's a damn fool if she's even considering going to the party. I can only imagine what Lilith has planned for the night. Two more days and Penny will be gone. I just need to keep her ass in one piece for the next 48 hours, so I can send her back to where she belongs.

Shutting my bedroom door, I walk into my room. Once I'm in my closet, I draw in a deep breath before pulling down the shoe box full of pictures. I had one task for the funeral tomorrow and while I've been putting it off, time is running out.

CHAPTER 11
PENELOPE

I'M beyond mortified as my mom stands there staring at me like I'm a total stranger. The disgust on her face is apparent. Her eyes zero in on me as she takes slow steps toward me. "How dare you! You come back here for one week and think that you can just throw yourself at your brother. For what? Money? Newsflash, Penelope. He doesn't have any."

Feeling sheepish, I take a step back. I've never feared my mom before, but she's grown more and more ruthless over the years and to be honest, she scares me now. Her desperation for money is no longer there, considering she has millions now, but I'm worried that the money has changed her—given her the power she's always thirsted for.

"It's not like that, Mom. You know money means nothing to me."

"Then what are you doing?" she shouts, directly in my face. Morsels of spit hit my cheek and I sweep them away.

"Blaise told you. *He* kissed me." My voice cracks and I know she's feeding off my fear.

"And, you let him? He's your brother!"

Something snaps inside of me. Years of bottled-up emotions hit the surface as I scream back at her. "He's not my brother! He's Richard's son. Your stepson. He's nothing to me. Nothing!"

"How dare you talk to me with that tone." Her hand swings back then meets the side of my face before I can stop her. "You will respect me, Penelope."

My hand cups my cheek as I fight back the tears. I will not crumble at the hands of this horrid woman. "I hate you. I hate you more than I hate Richard, and more than I hate Blaise. I hate this whole family and I wish I'd never moved with you. I should have stayed with Dad from the start."

"Your father was a poor excuse for a man. Couldn't even afford to keep his family together. Yet, you worship the ground he walks on."

She's pure evil. If I didn't know it before, I'm sure now. "My dad is a good man. He works hard for the money he has and he loves me. Unlike you. I'm pretty positive you hate me as much as I hate you."

"You are such a foolish girl. Do you think your father's love will put a roof over your head and buy you nice things? You have the world in the palm of your hands, Penelope. Do you realize this? Do you have any idea what your life could be if you'd just accept it? No. You don't because you're too caught up in fairy tales and happily ever afters. A bit of advice, they don't exist, so quit chasing them."

I've got no idea what she's even talking about. Fairy tales and happy endings? She's officially lost her ever-loving mind.

"This can all be ours. Together."

"I don't want a cent of that man's money. Keep it for yourself. Lord knows you need it."

My mom rolls her eyes, turning away from me. She begins pacing the room while nibbling at her freshly painted thumbnail. "For some reason my husband loved you. He looked at you like you were this angel sent to him and he was distraught over the idea of losing you. He loved you as if you were his own child, probably even more than he loved his own son."

"Mom," I say, grabbing her attention. "Richard didn't love me. He was obsessed with me. He was a twisted man with some sick fetish."

"He was not obsessed. What is the matter with you?" Her voice rises. "You were his daughter. He wanted to take care of you."

"You're wrong." I walk out of the kitchen, holding my cheek in my hand. Richard didn't want to take care of me. He wanted to own me, just like his son does.

So much for dinner and cake. I'm not sure why I ever got my hopes up. She hasn't changed, and she never will.

Tears fall carelessly down my cheek as I go downstairs. By the time I reach the bottom, I'm full-on sobbing. I try to control it, but I can't stop my heart from breaking a little more each time I see my mom. She wasn't always like this. It wasn't until my dad lost his job and we lost our family home that she went off the deep end. Sometimes I think I'd rather she'd been this way my whole life, so I didn't have to live with the memories of how she used to be.

Fortunately, Blaise is in his room, so he won't get the chance to tease me for being weak and emotionally unstable. I go into the room I'm staying in and drop down on the bed. Lying on my stomach, I try to calm myself down, but the harder I try, the more enraged I become.

The people in this town are horrid. They all treat me as if I'm a waste of skin—even my own mother. I've been pushed down, pulled around, and tossed aside one too many times.

THE LONGER I laid in bed, the angrier I got. Being stuck in my thoughts did nothing for my sour mood. I've been gone for two years and I return only to be treated with the same animosity I got my first two years of high school.

Right now, I don't know who I'm more furious with, Blaise or myself. Why in the world did I let him kiss me like that? It was like no kiss ever shared between us. It was raw and passionate and made my stomach flutter. At that moment, I would have gladly given all of myself to him. I cannot let my guard down like that again. My mom and his dad are married, even if he is dead. As much as I try to deny that we are family, we sort of are. I think I just pretend we're not so I don't feel so dirty for what we've done—what we are still doing.

I'll never understand why Blaise is so cruel to me one minute then desires me the next. Easy access? Convenience from being in the same house? I know men are hornballs, but to lust over someone you loathe is pushing boundaries that I'm sure Blaise has set in place.

He could have any girl he wants; yet, he puts his hand down my pants and sticks his tongue in my mouth. I've heard him bash me when he didn't know I was there. One night during sophomore year, I overheard Chase talking about how he'd fuck me until he breaks me—barf. Then Blaise went on to say how I'm scrawny, basic, and weak.

Ugh. Thinking about it just fires me up more.

I'm going to that party tonight, come hell or high water. So what if I was *uninvited*. I just invited myself and it's time that Penelope Briar has a little fun of her own.

I tear the blanket off me and jump out of bed. Somehow, I need to get into Blaise's room and find his stash of masks. He's got a whole tote full of them that he always brings and leaves at the entrance to the party, because rules are, you have to wear one. Well, I don't have one. I used to, but it burned in the fire.

Guess I'm going to have to play nice for a few minutes. It's the only way to get what I need.

Instead of going through the shared bathroom, I go out of my room and knock on his bedroom door. "Blaise? Got a minute?"

He doesn't answer so I knock again.

Still nothing.

I press my ear to the door, trying to listen to what he might be doing, but it's silent. I turn the handle, and to my surprise, it's unlocked.

"Blaise," I say again as I slowly push the door open.

I look to the left and see him sitting on the floor with his back pressed against the side of his bed. "Blaise?" I tiptoe closer and that's when I see the AirPods in his ears. There are pictures scattered around in front of where he sits. But that's not what has me stopping in my tracks. It's the one in his hand—of me. I mailed it to my mom last year after going on a field trip to the botanical gardens. I was standing in front of a water fountain with my hands in the air. But, why does Blaise have it? Better yet, why is he looking at it?

I should leave. If he catches me standing here while he's got that picture in his hand, he's sure to lose his mind with embarrassment.

My eyes sweep the room, hoping to see the tote sitting out for the party. Even if Blaise isn't going, I'm sure someone is bringing all the spare masks.

"What the hell are you doing?" Blaise snaps, grabbing my attention. He pulls his ear buds out and tosses them on the floor beside him before he begins gathering all the pictures and tossing them back in a shoe box.

"I...umm. Wanted to talk to you about something."

"Jesus! Don't you know how to knock?"

"I did. You didn't answer and it was unlocked."

"What the fuck is that?" Blaise jumps up, fleeting to my side.

I look down at my clothes, trying to figure out what he's talking about. "What?"

The back of his hand grazes my cheek as his expression hardens. "Who did that? Did she hit you?"

"Oh. Yeah. I'm fine, though. She was just extra pissy today."

"Stay here," he barks before brushing against me to leave the room.

I grab him by the arm. "No. Please, don't say anything. It will just make things worse."

Blaise grips both sides of his head and begins pacing the room like an animal. "Who the fuck does that woman think she is?"

I've got no clue why he's so bothered by her slapping me. It's not like it was the first time. Two years ago, he watched her do it and stood there completely unaffected. In fact, I think I heard him laugh when he walked away.

"You said it yourself, she's a bitch."

He continues to walk the length of the room as he watches his feet. "She won't get away with this."

"Why do you even care?"

Stopping in his tracks, his eyes snap to mine. "Why do I care?" He mimics me. "Because your mother seems to think she can hurt whoever she wants to get what she wants. That's why."

Trying to get a better understanding, I push further. "And you're mad because she hurt me? You don't even like me, Blaise."

He takes a breath and settles down a bit. "You're right. I don't. So, what did you come in here for?"

Slow steps lead me to his bed and his eyes never leave me as I sit down. I've never sat on Blaise's bed. Now that I think of it, I've only been in his room once in all the years I've known him. It's not really important to me, but it makes for conversation, so I opt to ask about the inheritance. "Why would he leave everything to her? You're his son?"

With a side-eye, he scowls. "Why are you asking about my dad's will?"

"No." I shake my head, pushing away any suspicion that I'm after his dad's money. "It's not like that. I don't want anything from him or her. It's just that, my mom brought it up and I'm curious why he wouldn't leave anything to you."

Blaise walks over to his dresser, my gaze following him. "Hey," I spit out, springing from the bed. I reach past him and grab my lotion. "You said you didn't have it." I quirk a brow. "Why do you have it?" That's when I smell it. Not the bottle. No, it's stronger. I look down at Blaise's smooth hands and grab one of them, bringing it up to my nose. Inhaling deeply, I scoff. "Why would you use jasmine lotion?"

When he bites the corner of his lip in a wry smile, I drop his hand and wipe mine on my sweatpants. "Oh my God, Blaise. You didn't?"

"Sure did. You're welcome to inspect me for proof."

"Don't you have Vaseline or KY for that?" Oh my gosh, am I really talking to him about lubricant right now? I run my hands down my red face. Though, I'm not sure why I'm the one flustered. "Don't answer that."

Blaise yanks open a drawer and my cheeks flush even hotter. Lying inside are napkins, lotions, creams, condoms, and just about anything a guy would need to get off with or without a girl. I look down. Is that a dildo? "Oh my gosh." I slam the door shut. I wonder how many girls have used that communal wand.

"Why so flushed, Penny? It's not like you don't get yourself off. It's natural. It's normal."

"I know." I turn away so he doesn't see that I'm now even redder in the face. I hate that I wear my emotions for everyone to see.

"Whoa. Wait a minute." Blaise spins me around by my shoulder. "You *do* pleasure yourself, don't you?"

I don't say anything. If I lie, he'll see right through it.

Might as well plead the fifth. I shouldn't care what he thinks anyway.

"Holy shit." He laughs. "You haven't, have you? You've never once just rubbed your nub or stuck a finger inside you just to see what it feels like?

I need air.

"Don't be embarrassed. Just answer the question."

"Why are you even asking if you know the answer?"

"I just wanna hear you say it."

"You're sick, you know that? You don't even need my lotion or your hand. You get off on humiliating people and throwing their flaws in their face."

"Fine. Forget it. I got my answer. You should give it a try sometime, though. I hear some girls prefer to earn their own O's."

"Okay. Will you shut up about it? I was asking you about your dad's will." I open the top of my lotion and squirt some in my hand then sit back down on the bed and rub it in.

"Right. The will. I'm actually surprised he didn't leave it all to you. After all, you were his favorite show to watch."

My stomach turns at his words. Blaise knew about his dad's obsession, even if my mom failed to see it. Or maybe she did and she just didn't care because she had access to his money.

"Can I ask another question?"

Blaise's phone beeps on his bed with a text message, so he picks it up. Seconds later, he goes over to his open closet and pulls something out. The tote! "You're going to anyway."

My eyes stay glued to it as he lifts the lid and shuffles some masks around then puts the lid back on. I almost forgot the question now that I've found what I came in here for. "Where will you go once the estate is settled?"

Blaise lifts the tote and carries it over to the door then sets it down. "Here's a little life lesson, Penny Pie. You can't believe everything you hear."

Not even paying attention to what he says, I nod toward the tote. "I thought you said you weren't going to the party."

"I'm not. Chase is coming to pick it up. Which means, unless you wanna see him, you should probably hide out in your room for the rest of the night."

"I most definitely do not want to see him." I won't be staying in my room, though I don't tell him that. I need to get a mask before Chase comes. If I show up at the party without a mask, everyone will know I'm there and I would prefer to be a stranger at the party than a nobody.

"He's gonna be here in like five minutes. Are we finished? 'Cause I got shit to do," Blaise says, suddenly becoming annoyed with my presence in his room.

"I think my mom left again. It's my birthday and I'm spending another one alone."

"Guess you shoulda got some friends while you lived in Skull Creek, huh?"

Asshole.

"I tried. You wouldn't let anyone be my friend except for Emery."

"Yeah. Probably should've kept that bitch away, too."

Using the sympathy card, I play on the lonely birthday. "Will you have cake with me, please? I know it's silly, but it's not a birthday without cake and eating it alone is depressing."

"No," he deadpans, kicking around some clothes on the floor.

"Pretty please?" I fold my hands in prayer with a pouty lip. He's definitely getting annoyed with me and certainly does not want to waste ten minutes of his precious time eating cake with the likes of me, but I'm not giving up.

"Fucking A, Penny. You're serious?"

"Dead serious."

"I don't even like you."

"I don't like you either. But, beggars can't be choosers."

With a heavy breath, he picks up the tote. "Fine. But no small talk. I hate that shit." He kicks the door open wider to make room for him to walk out with the tote of masks.

I smile inwardly and follow behind him.

With my lotion in hand, we walk up the stairs and into the kitchen. "You can go put that in the mudroom for Chase. I'd rather not see him when he comes to pick it up."

"You do realize this isn't your home anymore and my friends are more welcome than you are, right?"

"Duly noted." I take a seat on the stool in front of the center island where the cake sits.

Blaise walks down the small hall to the mudroom and I'm officially proud of myself for my little manipulation tactic.

"Are you gonna cut that or do you plan on us using our hands?" He's so sarcastic, but his sarcasm at this moment is actually attractive. The last time we were in this kitchen, we couldn't keep our hands off one another. It was hot and I hate that I want it to happen again.

Don't go there, Penelope. Do. Not. Go. There.

"Why are you acting so weird?" Blaise asks as he pulls open the kitchen drawer and retrieves a large knife.

"I was just thinking." I stand up and push the stool back to the counter. "I left my e-reader in my car. Do you mind putting a slice on a plate for me? I'll be right back."

"Whatever." He waves the knife in the air. "Hurry your ass up. I'm only doing this because I know what it's like to spend birthdays alone."

My heart aches as I stop my steps toward the mudroom. Aside from his mom leaving and his dad dying, I thought his childhood was perfect. Not to mention, Blaise has never willingly said anything that might give anyone a reason to believe that he's been hurt or hasn't lived this perfect life. "You do?"

"My parents were assholes, too, Penny." The knife slices through the cake. He lifts and repeats.

"Yeah. I guess they were." I continue with my plan to get a mask. For a sliver of a second, Blaise and I had common ground as far as our childhood goes. Almost as if, we connected on a deeper level than just smart-ass comments, pranks, and belittlement.

I open the door to the mudroom then close it behind me. I flip on the light and hurry so I can get this over with.

Pulling the top off the tote, I rummage through it quickly. There are at least three dozen masks inside. I don't even care what it looks like, I just need one.

I pull one out and hold it up. It's black, with metallic scratches all over it. This'll work. I tuck it under my shirt and leave through the garage. The sun has almost completely set. There's a stillness in the air that feels eerie. Even though it's my birthday, this day of the year has always felt dreadful to me. Darkness is always looming. People are plotting chaos and destruction.

Emery's living the life she always wanted, fitting in instead of standing out. I do feel bad for leaving the way I did and not talking to her for two years. I was so ashamed of what I'd done with Blaise and my mind was tormented by the memories of the fire. Regardless, she's still my friend and I know, deep down, that she'd take my side over Lilith's. We've been through too much, shared too many secrets.

I pull open the passenger door and bend over to stick the mask snug under the seat. When I come back up, chills dance down my spine.

I'm not alone.

"What do you know, it's the birthday girl," Chase says from behind me. I don't even have to look at him. I'd know that voice anywhere. It's smooth but has this sarcastic bite to it.

Taking a couple steps back, I close the door then turn around. "Blaise is inside."

"I know. He's in that big house, ten yards away." His

fingers skate up my cheek over the handprint that's still sensitive to the touch. Stopping at my ear, he tucks a few strands of hair behind it. "He let you come out here all alone? I'm surprised, but also very pleased."

"Don't touch me." I swat at his hand.

He withdraws with a sneer. "Ooh. Someone's learned how to stick up for herself. Where was that bravery two years ago? I mean, I'm not complaining. I like that you took what was given to you. Felt good, too."

My stomach churns just thinking about it. It was one of my weaker moments. I ate out of the palm of Chase's hand that night. I was sucked in with compliments and attention, hanging on his every word.

"Don't remind me. I almost forgot how little your dick was right before you tried to burn me alive." I go to push past him, but he grabs me by the waist, scooping me up until my chest is pressed against his.

"You shut your fucking mouth. First of all, I didn't do shit. Quit spreading lies or you just might end up in another barn." He hisses the threat. "Maybe this time, I'll fuck you instead."

"Let me go." I squirm, trying to free myself.

"That's not what you said that night two years ago. You were practically begging for it." He glances over my shoulder and slowly loosens his grip on me. His tone shifts immediately. "I told you, Penelope. You're not my type. Geez, can't a chick take a hint?"

I turn around and see Blaise. He drops the tote on the pavement and starts walking toward us. "Get in the house, Penny."

Without even arguing, I leave while I have the chance. If Blaise seriously believes Chase, he's a damn idiot.

Even if he does, I know the truth.

Chase strokes my cheek, adoration in his eyes. "Ignore Lilith, Penelope. She's just jealous because Blaise put this protective armor around you. Not to mention, you're a knockout."

"Yeah. Okay." I blow out a sarcastic breath. "And, protective armor? More like a ring of fire. Blaise wants me to be miserable so I'll move away for good. He hates me."

"You know what I think?" Chase tucks a strand of hair behind my ear. "I think he secretly likes you."

"Not a chance. Trust me. He hates me. See this," I point to the scar on the side of my forehead, "pushed me down two years ago."

My body trembles when Chase presses his lips to the scar on my forehead. "I'll tell you what, beautiful. Take care of me and I'll take care of you. How's that sound?"

Drawing back, I try to look at him in the sliver of light from the full moon. "How could I possibly help you?"

The tip of his finger trails across my bottom lip as he stares back at me with hooded eyes. "I can think of a few things you could do for me."

Ugh. I'm gonna be sick. I go to push past him, knowing exactly what he means. "I'm not screwing you, Chase."

Before I can get to the door, he grabs me by the waist and pulls my back to his chest. His heavy breathing rolls down my neck. "I don't think you have much of a choice, birthday girl. You see, they're locking you in here, one way or another." He reaches into his pocket and pulls something out. "But I have the key."

Locking me in here? I attempt to jerk away, but I'm too weak in his hold. "Help," I shout. "Someone get me out of here."

"No one can hear you. It's just me and you now. So, what do you say?"

I swallow hard, pushing down the lump in my throat. Tears well in my eyes and I turn around slowly in his arms. I really don't want to do this, but it seems I have no choice. "I just wanna go home."

I don't say anything else as Chase pushes me onto my knees. I don't fight the inevitable. One way or another, Chase will get what he wants.

The sound of his zipper sliding down is unnerving. Like jail doors slamming shut. A final nail in a coffin. But it's nothing *compared to the taste of my tears on my tongue as they drip onto his cock and I suck them off. One by one.*

Chase never gave me the key. He pushed me down in the hay while my face wore his cum. Then he walked out, clicked the padlock and was gone—just like everyone else.

That's when I knew. I massively screwed up. Regret ate at me for days. I should have tried harder to get away. Chase never told anyone and neither did I. I'm pretty sure Blaise would have killed him for showing me any sort of attention.

CHAPTER 12
BLAISE

PENNY ISN'T EVEN BACK in the house when I grab Chase by his neatly pressed polo shirt. Gripping it by the collar, I level my eyes with his. "You touch her again and you will live to regret it."

Chase smiles as if this is some sort of joke to him. "She's only here for a couple more days. Let me have a little fun with her."

"Our ideas of fun are not the same. You wanna put road-kill on her front seat, go for it. But you touch her and I'll break every bone in your goddamn hand. Are we clear?"

His shoulder shrugs as he cocks his neck to the side. "Her tight pussy might be worth a couple broken bones. Maybe I'll take my chances."

My teeth grind so hard that a piece of molar chips. I turn my head, spit it out to the side, then clench my fist, ready to lay it on his cheek and break his jaw.

"Blaise," Penny hollers from the front of the garage, stealing my attention. "What are you doing?"

Chase mocks her. "Yeah, Blaise. What are you doing?"

I cut him a glare and shove him back a few steps. "Take what you came here for and get the hell outta here."

As I walk away, Chase hollers from behind me, "Couple more days, buddy. Everything can go back to normal."

We'll see about that.

If he thinks I'll forget about the way he's been trying to get in her pants, he's mistaken. Just because I've let shit go before, doesn't mean I've forgotten. Chase has been trying to get with Penny since sophomore year. Not because he likes her. He just has this fantasy of being with the shy virgin, the one nobody dares to touch because I'll murder them. What he doesn't know is Penny has already lost her virginity. I stole that from her two years ago.

Penny is standing in front of the closed garage door. Arms crossed over her chest, scowl on her face. "What was that all about?"

"What did he say to you?" I keep walking until I bump her chest with mine, pushing her up against the garage door. My hands plant on either side of her head. When she doesn't respond, I try again. "What did he say to you, Penny?"

She peers up at me with her innocent eyes. "I didn't come on to him if that's what you're thinking. I can't stand that prick."

"I believe you. But I wanna know what he was talking about when he said you were begging for it two years ago."

Penny gulps. "You heard that?"

I want to scream at her. I need all the answers. Instead, I play it cool. "Yes. Now tell me what he meant."

"Can you," she gestures at my arms nervously, "give me space and I'll tell you." My hands drop and she moves away from the garage.

"There. Now, talk."

She's silent for a few seconds before she speaks. "Do you remember the night of the fire?"

My shoulders rise. "Most of it, yeah."

She begins chewing on her thumb nail nervously and I want to slap it out of her mouth and make her get on with this conversation. "Chase is the one who dumped me in the barn while the others were outside. I thought they were just gonna lock me in and leave. I had no idea you guys planned on burning the place down."

I wave my hand in the air. "I know all that. Would you get on with it?"

"Fine." She stops walking and looks me in the eye. "Chase dragged me in the barn and everyone left, leaving him to lock it up with me inside. He made me… I gave him a blow job in the barn. At first he said he'd help me if I did it, but when I still didn't oblige, he forced me on my knees. I was left with no choice."

No. My head shakes as I fight to believe what she's saying. "You're lying."

"Needless to say, he didn't help me at all. Instead, he stole my dignity."

"What the fuck?" I spit out, pushing her by her shoulders until she's back up against the garage. "Chase? Really? You're lying. You have to be." I bend over and grab my knees. I'm going to be sick. This is not happening.

"Why are you so mad?" she asks in a whisper.

"Why am I so mad?" I come back up, with squared shoulders, as I walk into her again. Hands at my sides as my mouth touches her forehead. Enraged, I shout, "Because he forced you to…" I can't even say it. "Because, no one is allowed to touch you but me." I can't even think straight. The thought of what he did makes me crazy and knowing that it actually happened makes me want to cut somebody.

I take a step back, looking into her eyes. Getting lost in them as I'm lost in my thoughts. "He's dead to me, Penny. I can promise you that."

I have to get away from her before she thinks my anger is directed toward her. I've got no idea where I'm going, but I have to go somewhere.

CHAPTER 13
PENELOPE

BLAISE'S OUTBURST has me questioning everything I've ever thought about him. Is he really just trying to keep a distance between me and the students at Skull Creek High because he wants to be cruel? Or is it because he's jealous? I feel crazy for even thinking that and I hate that the possibility sends a swarm of butterflies fluttering through my stomach.

Blaise wanting me all for himself? It's absurd. Never once has he given me a reason to think that he feels anything for me other than unadulterated hate. From the first scar at fourteen years old when he pushed me down in my room, to the second one at sixteen when he lit my world on fire. And now, he's still cutting me and leaving marks that will last a lifetime, even if these ones aren't visible.

Maybe in another lifetime things could have been different. Our stars didn't align in this one. Even if I wanted to be his friend, or maybe more, it's not possible.

None of it matters. I keep saying that because it's true. I owe this night to myself and then I'm out of here the day after the funeral. Blaise will be going back to school after his time off for bereavement. His life will resume to normal, and so will mine.

I refuse to leave this town again as the girl that gets pushed around, even if I'm the only one who knows it. I will not be the girl that guys think they can slip a finger inside of and she'll never once tell them to stop. Or the girl who was told she couldn't go to a stupid party so she stayed home alone on her birthday. No. I'm going to that damn party and I plan on having the time of my life.

I was able to sneak Richard's truck out, leaving my car parked at the house. Blaise probably thinks I'm still in my room sulking. Richard's got a few vehicles in his pole barn and I figured it was safer to take one of his then drive my own car here. Especially since my tires were slashed a couple days ago and someone knows what I drive. I'm still not certain that it wasn't Blaise, but I can't take any chances.

It's pitch-black out and there's a nip in the air. I found one of my mom's old sweatshirts, from back when she wore casual outfits, and a black beanie from the garage. I won't look cute, that's for sure. I'll look like the walking dead in my all black attire and the mask. That's the point, though. To be inconspicuous.

Turning down the two-track, I'm sandwiched between a line of cars, moving at a slow pace over the uneven terrain. The bass from the car behind me is so loud that it rattles the dash.

The one and only time I came to one of these parties, it was intense. And I don't just mean the fallout of the night. It was packed with cars, people, kegs, and empty cans. There were fights breaking out, drunks vomiting, topless girls dancing, gawking guys who watched, and even a couple having sex right out in the open.

Pulling up behind a truck in the row of lined cars, I kill the engine. My entire body is consumed by fear as reality hits me. This is really happening. I'm going to this party alone. A loser. An unwanted guest.

The beauty of tonight? I don't have to be Penelope Briar.

I shoot Emery a quick text to let her know that I'm here.

Emery: Neon pink purge mask and Skull Creek High hoodie. Let's have some fun, girl! It's your birthday!

Someone lays on a horn in the distance and my body jolts. "Move, fucker," a guy shouts from a few cars back. There's someone standing in the way as the cars try to pile in. *He wasn't yelling at me.* I take a breath and open the door, closing it behind me.

People pass by and no one even gives me a second glance as I make my way up to the crowd surrounding a huge bonfire. The trees are all lit with neon string lights, just like last time.

As I near the fire, the heat of it hits me, causing sweat to break out underneath my clothes. Rubbing the sleeve of my sweatshirt where my scar lies, I remind myself, *I'm safe. It's just a fire. It's contained and it won't touch me.*

Scanning the party, I try to find Emery, but there are so many people that it feels damn near impossible. Someone nudges my shoulder, looks at my face and for a second, I freeze. Until I remember that tonight, I can be anyone I want to be.

As I'm walking closer to the fire, I hear a familiar laugh to my right. Looking in her direction, I spot her. Emery is standing between two men who she seems to be flirting with. One has his hand on her stomach and the other is saying something that has her swooning. She's wearing the mask she described and a black and white Skull Creek hoodie with a pair of jeans and her hair in a high ponytail. Even in a mask, she looks gorgeous.

As I walk closer, Emery looks at me. She doesn't know it's me—or maybe she does because she cocks her head to the side and tips her mask up. I give her a nod to acknowledge who I am.

Emery says something to the guys, then waves them goodbye and walks over to me. Looking left, then right, she takes me by the arm and pulls me to the side where there are less people. "I can't believe you actually came."

"You didn't tell anyone I was coming, did you?" I sound like a broken record, but I have to be sure.

"Pen," she says, "of course I didn't. You're my best friend, remember?"

Am I, though? I haven't even talked to her in two years. I've missed her, but it doesn't feel like we're best friends anymore. "Yeah. We are."

"You want a drink?" She gestures toward the keg, sitting next to the row of trees off to the side.

"Maybe just one."

"Good. Because you seem tense as hell."

My hands slide into the front pocket of my hoodie. "Doesn't it feel surreal, though? Being here?

"Not anymore. I've been to so many parties in this town that this one is no different. Aside from the fact that you have to guess who is who."

"Thank God for that."

There's a brief moment of silence between us and it actually hurts. There was never silence with us. "Em, I'm sorry for everything. I wasn't a good friend to you."

Emery chuckles, and I'm grateful that she's not angry. "You mean when you up and left me for no reason at all?"

"There were reasons I left. I just… I can't talk about them."

Placing both hands on my shoulders, Emery looks at me through the holes in our masks. "Pen. You can tell me anything."

"Can I? Because it seems like you and Lilith are pretty close now. You know how much that girl hates me."

"Lilith hates everyone. Besides, I was on the receiving end of their pranks, too."

I shouldn't be talking about this, but I can trust Emery.

"Remember the barn fire that happened two years ago on the night we came here?"

"Yeah. I heard a little bit about it. So what?"

Taking a step back, I pull up the sleeve of my shirt, exposing my scar. It's hideous. If I'd have gotten the medical attention I needed, it wouldn't look this bad. Showing Emery, showing anyone, just brings back so much pain inside of me. "I was inside the barn when it caught fire."

Emery lifts her mask, setting it on the top of her head. Her eyes wide as saucers. "You what?"

"Lilith, Chase, Blaise, and a couple others—they locked me inside and lit it on fire."

"No." She shakes her head. "They wouldn't do that."

"They did, Em. The next morning, I left." I don't tell her that the real reason I left is because I had sex with Blaise before finding out he was the one who set the fire. I didn't know until after the fact, and by then, it was too late.

"Ya know, you really shouldn't spread rumors unless you have facts. I honestly don't think they'd try and kill you. Sure, they play pranks and fuck with people, but they're not killers."

My heart hurts that she's taking their side over mine. "Why would I lie about this?"

"I don't think you're lying, but I also don't think you have all the facts."

She's defending them?

"Listen," she goes on," I'm gonna grab us a couple drinks, then let's go for a walk. It seems like we have a lot to catch up on."

She leaves my side and I'm standing here alone when I feel the presence of someone behind me.

"You look lost, little girl."

I turn around and I'm faced with a masked man. Solid black metallic finish on his face and his hood pulled up over his head. His voice isn't familiar, but something about him is.

"Not lost. Just enjoying the view of the fire."

"From all the way back here?" He takes me by the hand and starts walking. "It's warmer if you get closer."

I follow his lead, feeling strange about the situation—but in a good way. It's refreshing being somebody else in this town.

We stop at a few tipped over logs and sit down about five feet from the fire. I can feel the heat roll off it, but ironically, I feel safe. Maybe it's because of the guy beside me with his hand on my knee.

"Do you plan on disclosing your identity or you gonna make me guess?"

I bite the corner of my lip, though he can't see it. "I'll let you guess, but I don't think you'll get it."

"Ahh. I see you like games. All right, then. Do you go to Skull Creek High?"

I shake my head no.

"An outsider. I like it."

"Live local?"

"Wait. Don't I get a question?"

Black mask gives my knee a squeeze and chuckles. "Go for it."

"Do *you* go to Skull Creek High?"

"I do. Transferred last year from an even smaller town out in Arizona."

I breathe out a heavy sigh of relief. *He doesn't know me.* I'm not exactly interested in getting to know any guys here but having a friend at a party full of people who hate you isn't exactly a bad thing.

"Senior year?" I ask him.

He takes a sip of his beer then brings it back to his lap. His other hand still on my knee. "It's my turn, but yes. Final year before adulting begins."

"Not necessarily. You still have college."

"Only if I can afford it."

"There's something we have in common. I'd love to go away to a university. I've got the grades and all, but my scholarships will only cover two years at a community college."

"Hey, better than nothing." He tips his cup back and takes the rest of his drink down, then tosses the cup in the fire. "You wanna go for a walk? Get away from the noise?"

My mind instantly flashes to the last time I took a walk here. I was met by a mob of students who carried me away and tortured me.

"Maybe we could just walk over by the cars. I'm not a fan of the woods."

He laughs. "Scared of the big bad wolf."

"Something like that."

We both get to our feet and I'm surprised when he takes my hand in his. "So, you plan on telling—" His words trail off and I'm caught off guard as his hand slips from mine and his body goes stumbling forward until he's lying flat on the ground.

"Oh my God. Are you okay?" I drop down on my knees, but I'm shoved to the side by the guy who did this. He's tall, wearing a short sleeve t-shirt and a skull mask.

"Stop it!" I shout as the guy begins pounding into the mask on my new friend. His mask moves to the side and for a moment, I see his face before blood begins smothering it.

My hand claps over the mouth of my mask. Stomach twisting in knots so tight that I feel like I can't breathe. I take a few steps back as the guy just keeps punching, completely rearranging his face.

When a couple guys come over to try and break it up, I realize I have to get away from here and find Emery.

I'm walking backward, watching in hopes that someone breaks this up, but no one does. Spinning around, I walk briskly to the keg where Emery is standing.

I hope that poor guy is okay. He seemed nice, but someone must have really had it out for him.

Emery holds up a cup and I join her by the keg. "Did you see that?" I ask her, glancing over my shoulder to where the crowd is gathered around the guy lying there almost lifeless.

"No. But I heard it's Paxton Norwell, the new quarterback. Danny was just telling me that his friends are driving him to the hospital."

Holy shit! I wasn't expecting that. Not that he has to go to the hospital, that's a given. The guy was beaten pretty badly. But the quarterback was flirting with me?

"Come on," Emery gestures toward the trail, "let's drink, walk, and talk."

Hesitating, I stay back as she starts walking. "I don't know about that. Is there somewhere else we can walk?"

"It's just the woods. People are all over. You'll be fine." She passes me my drink and I just hold it in my hand. It almost seems impossible to drink through this mouth hole, even though everyone else is somehow making it work.

Against my better judgment, I walk beside her down the trail that started it all. This entire place is like a maze, but I've become familiar with it from living here. Sometimes I'd just go for walks on my own to clear my head. Other times, Emery would walk with me.

The farther we get, the more distance we put between us and the blaring music. There are a few stragglers out here. Some talking, some smoking pot, and some making out.

This is actually turning out to be an okay night, aside from the fight I just witnessed. I feel like Emery and I are on the road to recovering our friendship, and I'm surrounded by people and no one has called me out yet.

"Thanks for this, Em. I'm glad I decided to come."

"Yeah. Me, too. So, tell me why you really left Skull Creek."

I lift my mask on the top of my head and take a drink of my beer, a long drink. I'm not even sure I want to delve into this conversation right now. Being back on this trail, walking in the direction of the barn, is dreadful enough.

"Everything just became too much. I had to get away."

"You had to get away from everything? Or you had to get away from Blaise?"

I look over at Emery. "Why would you say that?"

"Oh, I dunno. Maybe because you had a crush on the guy."

"I did not," I spit out. "Blaise and I hate each other."

"It's me, Pen. You're not fooling anyone. I saw the way you looked at him."

Did she see the way he looked at me? Because we reciprocated unwanted glances.

CHAPTER 14
PENELOPE

BEFORE I KNOW IT, we're at the old farmhouse that I spent the night in. It sits toward the back of the property and the area where the barn was is directly in front of us. There's still some rubble on top of the dried-up space.

The crunching of leaves can be heard in the distance, which alarms every cell in my body. "I think someone's coming," I tell Emery.

There are no voices, though. It's actually freakishly quiet.

Holding my breath, I try to listen.

Nothing.

"Probably just squirrels."

She's right. My nerves are just getting the best of me.

"You wanna go inside?" She looks at me with this devilish smirk.

"The house? Hell no."

Picking up her pace, she hollers over her shoulder, "Come on. Live a little, scaredy-cat."

There are more leaves crunching behind me. I turn around to try and get a look, but it's pitch-black and I can't see anything. My entire body shivers, terror taking hold. Patting the front pocket of my hoodie, I make sure my phone is still there. We came out here with no defense if something bad should happen.

What if some serial killer comes out here and chops my body into tiny little pieces?

Pulling my phone out of my pocket, I turn on my flashlight. Emery is already at the front of the house and I begin full-on running to catch up to her. "Wait for me," I shout as she pulls open the front door and goes inside, leaving the door open behind her. "Darn it," I mumble, picking up my speed.

I reach the rickety, old porch. The boards creek beneath my feet, ready to give out with just a subtle jump. "Em," I whisper-yell, poking my head in the door.

She doesn't respond, so I step inside. Moving the flashlight on my phone all around as memories flood me all at once. "This isn't funny. We should get out of here."

Rumor has it, a farmer killed his wife here. The property was left to their son, but no one has lived in the house for years.

Last time I was here, I was in a state of brain fog and it didn't faze me. I also had Blaise's strong arms around me and felt untouchable. Right now, I'm scared. "Emery," I say again, taking a few more steps inside.

I'm struck silent when someone grabs me from behind, slapping a hand over my mouth. "You really should be more careful. Ya know that?"

Chase.

My body collapses in his arm when I lose my footing. With one hand over my mouth and the other wrapped around my waist, pushing my sweatshirt up, I'm pulled farther into the house.

"Put me down," I say, but my words are muffled.

"Not a chance, birthday girl. Always remember, we're two steps ahead of you, and one step ahead of Blaise.

What's that supposed to mean? That Blaise is always a

step ahead of me? Is he here? I try to look around, but I can't see anything. I also don't hear anyone else. Where is Emery?

Chase stops walking, giving me a chance to get back on my feet. Little good it does because he's still holding on to me as if his life depends on it.

He removes his hand from my mouth and places it around my waist with the other. "Did you really think we wouldn't find out you came tonight?

"I guess I just took you and your posse for idiots."

Chase laughs in a mocking tone. "Well, I'm glad you came because I still haven't had a chance to feel how tight your pussy is around my cock."

My stomach retracts when Chase slides his hand up my bra, cupping my breast in his hand. "Stop." My voice cracks. "I'll scream." It's a last-ditch effort, but we both know that no one will even care.

He doesn't stop. Instead, he begins pinching the bud of my nipple. "They're small, but I'm sure I could slide my cock between them and come all over your face."

"You're disgusting."

"And you're fucking stupid," says Lilith, coming out of nowhere without a mask on. "We need to hurry this shit up. I've got beer to drink and friends to hang out with. Unlike this sorry bitch who has no friends."

Swallowing hard, I push down the lump rising in my throat. My heart sinks into my stomach while dread washes over me. I should have known better than to come here. Let alone wander away from the party. "I'll tell everyone what you did. Everyone will know that you guys tried to kill me."

Chase laughs; this time, it's not sarcastic or ill-forced. He actually finds what I said funny. "She's fucking crazy. Maybe that's why no one likes her."

"I'm not crazy. I know it was you guys. I have—"

Lilith silences me by slapping her hand over my mouth. Pressing hard, her nails dig into the skin of my cheek. "How's that feel?" She digs harder, piercing the skin. "Do you remember the time you scratched my face? Still got a small scar on my chin from that shit."

I do remember. But she had it coming. Everything bad that happens to Lilith is warranted.

"Strip her down," Lilith demands of Chase.

He doesn't move as he holds me from behind.

"Now!" Lilith quips.

Chase lifts me up and begins carrying me into an open space in the house that I take to be the living room. "Please, Chase. I'll do anything."

Just like that night, I'm at his mercy.

"Anything?"

My eyes pinch shut as I nod. "Yes."

He keeps walking, holding me tight as we leave Lilith's sight. "I'm going to put you down. But I swear to God, if you run, I will catch you and what comes next will hurt." He sets me down on my feet and takes me by the arm as he positions me in front of the fireplace.

"How did you and Lilith know I was here?"

"You think this was your plan, but it was ours to begin with. Get you out here, have a little fun with ya."

"Blaise will find out. He'll kill you all."

That laugh again. "Oh, Blaise. Your almighty protector. I know you two hate each other, but you should actually thank him. Without him, you'd have probably been raped by the entire senior class."

Bile rises up my throat and I swallow it down. "Keep that in mind when you're stripping my clothes off because I'm telling him everything."

Chase's phone begins vibrating, and he uses his free hand to reach into his pocket.

This is my chance.

When his guard is down, I step in front of him, lift my knee and ram it straight to his balls.

"Ugh. You fucking whore!" he cries out in pain. His phone drops to the floor as he grabs his crotch.

Wasting no time, I haul ass and go to run out of the house, but I'm stopped by someone standing at the doorway. His or her arms are spread wide. It's too dark to see anything, but I recognize the mask. That's when it hits me. It's one of the masks I didn't recognize that night.

"Grab her!" Chase shouts as he wobbles back into the room with sore balls. It's hard to see anything, but I can feel Chase's venomous breaths hit my neck. "Fucking bitch." He grabs me by the hair and yanks me backward. I stumble and fall on my back, dropping my phone.

Shrieking, I try to get up, but it's no use. "Get off me," I scream, patting the floor to try and find my phone. The flashlight is still on, hitting the ceiling.

"Get her clothes off," Lilith tells him as she lingers over us.

Chase starts pulling my sweatshirt and even the fight I put up isn't enough. He tugs it over my head while Lilith tugs at my pants. I feel them slide down as tears fall from my face.

I just wanted to have fun tonight. I wanted to prove to myself that I'm not a pushover. I was wrong, though. I have no physical strength. My mind is weak. I'm useless. A waste of bones as Blaise once said.

Chase trails his tongue up my cheek, licking my tears. I turn my head and snarl in disgust. "Mmm, salty. Just like your personality."

"Fuck you!" I hiss, lying there like a stiff board, letting them do whatever it is they have planned.

Lilith shines her flashlight on me and orders Chase, "Get her up on the wall in the living room."

My tears slide as I shake my head no. "Please," I beg of him.

Where is Emery? I wanna scream at the top of my lungs, hoping she will hear me. Hoping anyone will hear me.

"Just fucking do it!" Lilith snaps.

I'm lying there in just a bra and underwear. Modesty be damned. I'm more vulnerable than I have ever been in my life and willing to do anything to save myself.

"You will all live to regret this," I choke in a pitted rage. "You will pay for tonight and for starting the fire at the barn."

"We didn't start the damn fire!" Chase hisses, slamming my wrist back down on the floor. "I don't know why you keep saying that. Yes, we locked you in the barn. But we never lit it on fire."

"Why did you do it?" I cry, unable to stop the tears that fall. "Why did you all make a mockery of me, day in and day out? What did I do to deserve it?"

"It was Blaise," Lilith begins. "Blaise started it all freshman year. He practically handed you over on a silver platter and told us to make your life miserable. So, we did. Then, he thought he could end it all when he told us to stop, but you were too much fun." Lilith smiles and it's unnerving. "You made it so fucking easy. You're our favorite toy, Penelope."

I already know this to be true. Blaise was always the mastermind. My heart aches. After everything, I wanted to believe he wasn't a terrible person. But, he is.

Lilith begins getting antsy, walking back and forth in front of where I lie. "Get her back in the living room. Get her against the wall and I'll take the damn pictures myself."

On the wall? What is she talking about?

Chase begins pulling me up while I kick my legs. "Quit fighting the inevitable."

"Emery!" I scream at the top of my lungs.

"Save your breath, sweetheart. No one's coming for you."

Like a slap in the face, it hits me. He's right. No one is going to save me. In this town, all I have is myself.

Chase tosses me over his shoulder and I pound my fists

into his back, squirming, fighting like hell. But it's not enough.

His hand smacks my ass hard and he laughs. "Keep trying. I like it when they fight back."

I growl, "I will never stop fighting!"

Chase drops me down to my feet and his arms instantly wrap around me as he pushes me against the wall. I look up and notice two metal clamps screwed into the wall. He grabs one hand and sets it in place, ready to close the clamp around it.

"Take the rest of her clothes off," Lilith says as she joins us. She's not alone, though. "Look who decided to join us," she says in a chipper tone, acknowledging the newcomer. It's hard to see, but it's definitely a guy with that build.

The other person wearing the mystery mask that night stands off to the side.

"Get your phone out," Lilith tells the person. "You're taking the pics." She's always barking orders like some damn queen on a throne.

"Let her go," I hear someone say. It's not a new voice, nor a stranger. His voice is laced with threat, though I can't see him.

"Blaise," I cry out, "please help me."

Chase freezes, looking at Blaise as he enters the room. He's wearing a mask. A skull mask. Blaise doesn't stop until he's directly in front of Chase. Cocking his fist, he unleashes it right on the side of Chase's head. Chase staggers to the side but comes back up with a twitch in his lips. Blaise does it again and again, until Chase falls to the floor. It's all too familiar to the fight I witnessed at the party only an hour ago.

In fact, it was the same mask. No. *Was it Blaise that attacked the quarterback?*

Oh my God. Could it be because he was talking to me?

"You're lucky I don't kill you right here and now," Blaise shouts between blows to Chase's face.

"Come on. We need to go," I hear the newcomer in the familiar mask say.

That voice.

It can't be.

"No," Lilith retorts. "Blaise does not call the shots here. I do." Lilith drops the light on the phone she's holding up. "We had a deal."

My head is spinning in a spiral of confusion. I have no idea what's going on as I stand here. My hands free, my legs able to move, but for some reason, they don't.

"Blaise," Lilith singsongs. "Are you backing out on me?"

Once Chase is incoherent on the floor, Blaise gets to his feet and stalks toward Lilith. "Fuck the deal."

Using this opportunity to get at least one answer to the dozens of questions storming through my head, I take steps toward the unknown person, though I'm pretty sure I know who it is since I heard her voice. She takes a few steps back and when a sliver of light from the moon casts through the window, I'm able to see her shirt. Reaching out, I grab her mask and pull it off.

"No."

"Pen, I can explain," Emery says with remorse. It won't work, though. I've been betrayed a lot in my life, but nothing cuts as deep as this does.

It's not even about tonight. I was gone for two years and left without a goodbye. Emery has every reason to be angry with me. I know she was there now. The proof is all over her face. This is about two years ago when my best friend put on that mask and stood outside of the barn while my enemies tortured me. This is about the fire and the unanswered cries for help as she stood by idly and allowed them to lock me inside.

"All this time. You were part of it." I can't think straight. I'm nauseous and on the verge of passing out.

"All of you." I spin around, looking from Blaise to Chase's lifeless body, to Lilith, and then to Emery. "You all hate me so much that you'd take pictures of me naked, to what? Show the entire student body? Students who already hate me because of you? You'd lock me in a barn and set it on fire…to kill me? Was that your plan?"

Emery drops to her knees in tears while Lilith just stands there with a smirk on her face. She's desensitized to all emotion, so I don't expect her to feel bad for what she did.

"Take your mask off," I say to the other guy who has not been identified.

When he doesn't, I pull it off myself, and he doesn't even fight me off.

Another punch to the gut. "Wade?"

Blaise comes toward me, putting a hand on my arm, but I swat it away. "No!" I snap at him. I try to say something to him, but the words get lodged in my throat.

I have to get out of here.

CHAPTER 15
BLAISE

"PENNY, WAIT," I holler as I chase after her. Bypassing my car, she heads for the trails.

"Leave me alone," she cries out as she begins to slow to a brisk walk.

I reach out to grab her, but she shifts to the right. I try again, but she shifts back. "Damn it! Would you stop and listen to me?"

"Give me your hand," I say to her, reaching out, offering to help.

"You expect me to hold the hand that's pushed me down for years. Not a chance."

"Just hear me out."

Her breaths are labored as she slows even more. As she goes to step over a log in her way, she trips. I catch her fall, but she drops weightlessly to the ground. "Why should I?" She sniffles as her cries ring out until she's full-blown sobbing. "Go back to your friends. Don't you have a *deal* with them?"

I crouch down beside her as she drops her face into her hands. "It's not what you think." I pull off my mask, followed by my sweatshirt. I wrap it around her shoulders as she sits here shivering.

Snarling, she looks over at me. "Everyone keeps saying that but I think I know enough."

Fuck. How did we get here? My fingers rake through my hair as I try to think of what I can say or do next to get out of this mess.

"You're right. I do have a deal with Lilith. I stay out of her way. You're wrong, though. They are not my friends. Not anymore."

"Stop talking." Penny pushes herself off the ground, but her body is too weak as her knees give out and she falls again, this time into my arms. She tries to push me away, but I hold tightly to her. "Nothing you say will ever make me forgive you. All these years...all these years you have tried to make my life hell. Congratulations. You did it."

"At first, I did. But did it ever cross your mind that I was never trying to hurt you? Maybe I was just trying to protect you."

"Protect me?" She cackles. "What a crock of shit."

"It's true. After the fire, everything changed."

"Oh. You mean after you tried to roast me? Gee, thanks for protecting me."

I can't tell her the truth. Even if she never believes it, I tried. Maybe I can't protect her from Lilith or Chase. But I can protect her from the truth.

Voices draw near so I give Penny a tug to try and pull her up. "Just leave me here. Let them have me. I don't even care anymore."

I look over my shoulder as they come closer. "I need you to wait here."

She doesn't say anything, but in the state of mind she's in and given that she has no strength, she won't get far.

I stand up, leaving her sitting there with my shirt wrapped around her.

Going back toward the farm, I'm met with Lilith and Emery. "Traitor!" Lilith says as she nudges past me.

"Not so fast." I snatch her arm and pull her body flush with mine. "You fucking touch her or say a damn word and I'll pin everything on you," I enunciate, "Everything."

"You wouldn't dare."

"Try me. She already thinks it was you. I can make it happen." I look at Emery. "And you, too. She remembers more than you bitches think. If you so much as look at her the wrong way, you're done for. Now, turn around and walk out of here and take a different trail. This one's in use."

Lilith snatches her arm back while Emery obeys my commands. It's apparent that Emery isn't cut out for Lilith's games. She has no idea what she got into by attaching herself to this noxious bitch.

"Fine," Lilith spews. "New deal. You keep my name out of your mouth and I'll do the same." She extends her hand, but I hold back.

"And Penny?"

She simpers with her hand still stretched out. "The little mouse can run back to where she belongs and I'll leave her alone."

"Get Chase out of the house. No cops. No ambulance."

"Make Wade do it."

"Wade won't be helping." She doesn't know it, but Wade was on my side the entire time. Penny doesn't know it either. She will, though.

"Ugh. Whatever. Let's just make this deal, so I can go get drunk. Tonight is turning out to be a real drag."

We shake hands and she goes on her way. A handshake that means nothing because that's what she gets when she makes a deal with the devil.

I go back to where I left Penny, hoping she's still there. When I don't see her, I begin to panic. She's going to walk up to that party half-naked. *Fuck!*

I start jogging down the trail but stop when I hear her.

"Over here," she says, pressed up against a tree.

Her expression is void. I'm not even sure if talking to her right now will do any good. I scoop her up in my arms, cradling her as I walk back to the farm where my car is.

When her eyes close, I'm relieved. She's gotta be exhausted from the events of the night.

This is exactly why I didn't want her to come back to this town. She should have stayed in Portland. This is why she has to hate me. It's why I can't love her like I want to.

CHAPTER 16
PENELOPE

MY EYES FLUTTER OPEN, and it takes me a minute to realize I'm not in my room. It's dark and the only light is coming from the open door of the bathroom. I'm wearing one of Blaise's t-shirts and a pair of his boxer shorts.

Wait a minute. I'm in Blaise's room.

I spring up and immediately see him. He's sitting in a desk chair beside the bed. His head is hung to one side, resting on his shoulder, arms hugging his bare chest and his feet are kicked up on the bed, snug against my leg.

Everything hits me at once. Part of me grasps at the possibility of it being a bad dream, but I know it's not. It all happened. Chase and Lilith stripping me out of my clothes, Emery being part of it, Blaise helping me.

Did he really help me, though? I'm hesitant to believe that was what he was doing.

Blaise begins to shift in his chair. He looks extremely uncomfortable and I almost feel bad that he's over there while I'm in this big, comfy bed.

His head lifts and he sees that I'm awake. "Hey," he says, smacking his lips together. "What time is it?"

My shoulders shrug. "No idea."

Slapping around at his nightstand, he picks up his phone. "Four a.m. Go back to sleep, Penny." He rests his head back on his shoulder and closes his eyes, but only for a moment.

When he realizes that I'm still sitting up, he looks at me again. "Get some sleep. We'll talk about it tomorrow."

"I need to know everything."

His shoulders drop and his feet hit the floor. "Seriously? At four in the fucking morning?"

All my questions hit me at once, but I start with the one that's heavy on my mind. "What was your deal with Lilith?"

Blaise leans forward, elbows pressed to his knees and face in his hands. He rubs aggressively, lets out a low rumble then stands up. "Move over."

"You want to get in the bed?"

"It is *my* bed."

Dragging my ass across the bed, I move as far to the opposite side as I can. Being this close to Blaise is dangerous, especially when he's not being a complete ass to me right now and wearing nothing but a pair of black boxer briefs.

Blaise sits down, props his hands behind his head and crosses his ankles. "Lilith has something on me. We made a deal that she'd keep her mouth shut if I stayed out of her way."

"Meaning?"

"Meaning she has something on me. Drop it."

I roll over on my side, facing him. "Fine. When did Emery become part of this?"

"No clue. I had no idea she was out there the night of the fire, so I guess then. Who the fuck knows? Emery would do just about anything for Lilith. *She w*ants to be Lilith."

It makes sense. Emery has always dreamt of being with the in-crowd. I feel like an idiot for not seeing it sooner. She threw me under the bus just to get a ride.

"You said you were protecting me. Why? I want the whole truth, Blaise."

Blaise slides down and turns on his side, now facing me. His eyes are soft right now. At this moment, I'm not fearful or on the verge of tears. I feel…content. I shouldn't. I should know better than to let my guard down in this town.

"I promised my dad I'd make sure you were taken care of."

"When? Why?"

"The day you left. That's when everything changed. It was no longer about making your life hell. It was all about keeping you safe. And you're not safe here."

Who is he to try and dictate my life this way? *I'm such a fool.* Here I was thinking for a moment that maybe he was protecting me because he cared. Even if he did fail miserably at his attempts to keep me safe.

"That's why you changed my tires?"

"No. I mean, yeah, but I also needed you to have a ride out of this town."

"Because you were protecting me due to a promise you made to your dad?" I'm trying hard to understand this. Was it all because of a promise? I hate that it hurts. So much for thinking he didn't want these people around me because he didn't *want* me to get hurt. Now, I know, he couldn't let me get hurt due to an obligation.

"I just don't know what to believe anymore. I feel like everyone in this town is lying to me."

"Hate to break it to you, Penny, but they are."

My voice softens. "Even you?"

Blaise scooches closer until his eyes are level with mine as we both lie on our own pillow. "Especially me."

I hate his honesty. I wish he'd just keep lying to me and tell me that he's the only one I can trust. I still wouldn't believe it, but it would make me hate myself less for the feelings that are overwhelming me.

"Because I couldn't stand the idea of anyone else hurting you and if you stayed in this town, it would happen."

"Newsflash, Blaise. I can get hurt anywhere. Ryan hurt me by cheating on me."

Blaise looks back at me with hooded eyes. "Fuck Ryan. He doesn't deserve you." Lifting the corner of the blanket, his body slides beneath it with mine.

He reaches over and begins trailing his fingers down my bare arms. "No one does."

Goosebumps break out on my arms and I shiver. Maybe it's the lack of sleep, or the emotional beating I've taken, but right now, it just feels nice to be touched.

There are still so many unanswered questions. Who really started the fire? Blaise hasn't denied it, but why would he start it then pull me out? Especially after he made a promise to protect me.

Nothing makes sense. But at this moment, I don't want to try and make sense of it all. All I can focus on is Blaise's hand grazing the skin of my stomach beneath my shirt as tingles rise up my thighs. His eyes look into mine like he's reading my thoughts on a piece of paper.

"I don't wanna hurt you anymore, Penny."

"Then don't," I tell him with a shake to my voice.

He slides closer and I stay cemented to my spot on the bed. I should move, but I don't. Run out of here and never allow myself to get this close to him again—but, I don't. Ignoring all the red flags and reasons to leave, I stay.

"Blaise." His name is a whisper rolling off my tongue.

Warm fingers line the hem of my panties while soft eyes bore into mine. He just lies there, watching me as his hand dips farther down. I take in a shallow breath, hoping he doesn't notice what he's doing to me.

With one finger, he parts my lips and slides it up to my clit. My body flinches when he begins rubbing circles. An overpowering feeling comes over me and it's almost too much; I want him to stop before I explode, but I also want him to keep going because it feels so good.

I pinch my eyes shut, hoping he's not watching me come undone at his touch. "Open your eyes," he tells me.

I do, but I question it. "Why?"

"Because I want to see them when I make you come."

His gruff voice alone sends me into a frenzy. Unintentionally, I lift one leg up, giving him better access. Is he judging me in his thoughts? Am I weak for giving into desire?

"Don't be shy. It's not like this is the first time I've touched your cunt."

I cringe at the word. "I'm not shy." It's not a lie. I'm not shy. I'm just highly inexperienced and fearful that I'll do something wrong. Like making a sound that is inadequate for the moment. What if I howl? Or bark? Oh God, is that possible?

Stop overthinking, Penelope!

Blaise slides closer, taking complete control as he pushes me onto my back. "What are you doing?" I ask him as he grabs the blanket on top of me and pulls it over his head. He disappears beneath it, his body leaving mine. My underwear slides down my legs and he takes them off.

One hand slides between my legs, spreading them apart. "Oh God," I roar when his tongue begins flicking at my sensitive nub.

When Blaise took my virginity, I don't think I got the full effect. It was painful and surreal. I was too focused on everything happening around us as firefighters extinguished the barn fire.

A few days ago when he fingered me, I felt it all. God, it was amazing. Like a high I've never experienced. It only lasted a few seconds, but I didn't want to come back down. Now, I want to climb that peak again. I want to soar from a mind-blowing orgasm, then I want to do it again because the pleasure is addictive.

Blaise slides a finger inside me and my back arches off the bed. He can't see me, which makes this all the more satisfying. No watchful eye as my mouth hangs open and my eyes glaze over.

Another finger joins and he begins pumping them inside of me while his tongue licks the length of my sex. I place a hand on his head through the blankets. "Blaise," I whimper, feeling like I'm losing control.

"Don't fight it, baby. Just feel it."

Just feel it.

Okay. I can do that. My heart rate excels and my head becomes cloudy. "Ugh," I moan. Rocking my hips to the motion of movements. He digs deeper inside of me, hitting a spot that sends my ass off the bed. I push down on his head, needing more of his mouth on my clit. When he starts sucking it between his teeth, every muscle of my vagina contracts. Every cell in my body is electrically charged. I see stars. "Blaise." I grab his head through the blanket, riding his face like I'm fucking him.

My body goes numb, chasing away the tingling sensation that took over.

"Mmm, Penny. You taste so damn good." He sucks and licks as I come down.

I smack my lips together, feeling dehydrated. Blaise pops his head out of the blanket and slides his body up on mine, then he kisses me. I can taste myself on his tongue. It's sweet. Like sugar water.

Blaise pulls open a drawer on his nightstand and grabs something. When I catch a glimpse of the condom, my eyes widen.

"Yes or no?" he asks.

Biting my bottom lip, I nod.

He takes off his boxers, tears the top of the wrapper off with his teeth and spits it to the side of the bed. Seconds later, he's sliding the rubber on.

His body is pressed so close to mine and I wish I could live in this moment forever. Everything feels right, even if it is so wrong. The painful truth that we will never be anything more than what we are hurts so bad. Tears prick the corners of my eyes. This moment is ours, but he is not mine. He never will be.

Would I want him to be? I think so.

"You ready?" he asks me, before lining the head of his cock at my entrance.

I nod again, and he slides in slowly. His face lingers over mine and the passion between us coils into something terrifyingly beautiful. Our eyes hold a stare as he pushes all of himself inside me.

Apprehension leaves me as my arms wrap around his neck and I pull his mouth to mine in a tantalizing kiss. His lips skate down to the crease of my neck as his cock glides in and out of me.

My breaths hitch when he picks up his pace, driving himself further and deeper. Blaise isn't small, by any means. Not that I have much to compare it to, but I've seen his dick. It's girthy and veiny, and it most definitely feels like it's spreading me open.

My head cocks to the side and he kisses his way up to my ear, grazing his teeth on my lobe.

He lets out a low rumble. "You're so damn tight." Lifting his head, he looks me in the eyes as he fucks me. "Who else has stuck their cock inside of you?"

"Only you," I speak on an exhale.

Pleased with my response, he rams harder. His mouth ghosting mine, he mutters, "Let's keep it that way."

His fists plant on either side of me. Blaise sucks in his bottom lip as he slides up and down my body. Our skin slaps with a wet smacking sound that only intensifies as he plunges into me at lightning speed. My head hits the headboard, so I stretch an arm back, holding it so I don't move further.

When a muffled groan escapes me, he slows momentarily. "You okay?"

I nod in response, so he resumes nailing his cock into me.

I'm more than okay. Aside from a trickle of guilt, knowing this is wrong, I want to do it over and over again until my insides can no longer take the pounding. And once I've healed, I want to do it again.

Blaise slips a hand between us, bracing himself on the mattress with the other. His thumb rubs vigorously at my clit, and the sensation rippling through me is mind-blowing. Warm lips land on mine again in a wet, sloppy kiss. Our bodies magnetically connect and my blood pumps rapidly through my body.

"Fuck, Penny." His voice is husky, eyes wide and full of lust. "I'm gonna come."

Holy shit. I think I am, too. My entire body shivers as my insides are zapped with electricity. It's…everything.

He thrusts again, deep and hard as we come at the same time. His body drops gently on mine as our chests heave together.

I never want to get up. It's crazy how one minute I can hate this guy and the next, I feel like I could potentially love him. It's not normal. I'm not normal. All of the rotten things he's done, and I hang on to these rare moments when Blaise breathes life into me. So far, he's the only person who ever has. Everyone else drains it—even him on a normal day.

After a few minutes, Blaise looks up at me. I'm thinking he'll say something cruel that will make me live to regret this, but to my surprise, he just lays his lips lightly on mine. "Go back to sleep for a bit. We've got a busy day."

CHAPTER 17
BLAISE

TODAY WE SAY goodbye to Richard Hale. A man of few words, but he didn't need them. His stance and the expressions he wore said them all. He was not a good man. I learned this when I was six and saw my mom's first black eye. As the years went on, new bruises appeared and new cries rang into my bedroom at night.

It was all confirmed when I thought Richard and Penny were sleeping together. The day I took her diary, I wanted to learn the truth. Lilith found it in the back of my car and she shared the secrets inside with the entire school. It was never supposed to happen.

But, then I knew. Penny didn't do anything wrong. It was all him.

His precious little angel, who we all thought he looked at as a loving daughter. Instead, he looked at her as an untouched girl in her transition to womanhood. He was turned on by the fact that she was a young virgin and he'd stand over her bed at night, watching her and jerking off to the sleeping beauty.

A lion ready to attack and take her innocence. I'd die before I let that happen. I got in his good graces. I was the obedient son. One who did what he asked while plotting for my own future. Take everything he owns. Penny and I were deserving of it. Not my bitch of a stepmother. We were the ones who endured years of disgrace. And one day, when I find my mom, I'll share it with her as well. And I will find her. One day.

Penny joins me in the kitchen, wearing a black, long-sleeved cotton dress that sits just below her knees and a pair of black flats. Her hair is all down. Her eyes are tear-soaked with bags beneath them. Her despair is obvious. And it should be after everything she's been through.

All the hell I've put her through, yet, she still looks at me like I'm her savior. I don't deserve it, but I certainly won't deny her. I could never deny her.

"Penny," I scream at the top of my lungs as I run up to the blazing barn. Fear ripples through me like a strong current, ready to throw me off the deep end.

Lilith runs toward me frantically. "We didn't do it. I swear. It was just a stupid prank. I don't know how —"

"Shut the fuck up." She better be okay. She has to be. "If anything happens to her, I swear to God I will burn every one of your fucking houses down."

Sirens sound in the distance and my entire body goes numb as I bust through the door of the barn. "Penny! Answer me!" My shirt gets snagged on a piece of wood, and I jerk back, ripping the fabric. Waving my hands in front of me, I make my way through the cloud of smoke.

Shit. I gasp when a large beam falls directly in front of me, missing me by mere inches.

"Penny," I try again.

She coughs. She's alive. "Blaise." I hear her choke through muffled cries and bouts of coughing. "Help me!"

Then I see her. Curled in a ball in the corner next to the hay bales. One catches fire and if I don't get her up now, she won't make it. "Get up!" I shout.

"I can't. My arm… My arm is cuffed to this beam." She wiggles, trying to free herself.

"Fuck!" I hurry over to her.

They're dead to me.

Every single one of them.

My eyes skim the barn, barely able to see anything through the cloud of smoke and debris falling, but I spot an axe hanging on the far side. "Stay here." Bad word choice. I don't have to see her eyes to know she just rolled them at me.

"Ahhhh," she cries out in immense pain, "My arm! Help!" The grisly sound of her desperation puts me in full-blown panic mode.

Jumping over fallen beams as the flames spread, I grab the axe and hurry back to her.

"God, Penny." I rip my shirt over my head and swat at her arm as the fire rides up the hay bales. I kick the bale that's engulfed beside us and wrap the shirt around her arm.

I raise the axe in the air. "Stay still," I tell her, before slamming it down on the chain attached to the beam. She pulls her arm back and gets up before another coughing fit begins and she crouches over. "I…I can't. My arm hurts so bad."

In a swift motion, I grab her and toss her over my shoulder. I don't stop as I run out of the barn, even then, I just keep going. Flashing lights draw near, but I run toward them. "No," Penny whimpers. "No ambulance. No cops. Get me out of here."

"But your arm."

"I'll be fine. Please. I don't want the added attention."

I turn back around to go to my car, but it's not there. "Fucking Lilith." She must've taken it and hauled ass out of here when she heard the sirens.

Penny pats my back. "Blaise. Look. Someone did this."

I spin around and my eyes land on a gas can sitting beside a tree. It's not your everyday red gas can; it's got a ring of silver duct tape wrapped around the bottom of it.

"Let the cops deal with it," I tell her, turning back around and moving as fast as I can while coughing up the smoke I inhaled. My

*chest hurts, my body feels like it's been beaten. I don't stop, though.
I head straight for the old farmhouse.*

She'll be safe here.

*Holding Penny in my arms, I turn to the porch of the farmhouse
and look out at the property. Lights flash all around. Firefighters
hurry to pull out their hoses as more sirens sound in the distance.
An orange glow lights up the night sky, while smoke hides the dark
clouds that were looming.*

"We need to hide," Penny coughs out the words.

*I nod, turn around and kick the front door open. It's pitch-black
inside, but there's a dim light casting through the windows from the
blazing fire.*

*Kicking my foot up behind me, I close the door. "How's your
arm?" I ask her. Looking down at her ash-smeared face.*

*"It actually doesn't hurt. I think my body is in too much shock
to feel that pain."*

*"Good." I set her down on her feet while bracing her by the
waist. "Think you can walk?"*

*She nods and takes a few steps over to the window. "What a
mess this night turned out to be."*

*"Yeah." I come up behind her, watching the firefighters battle the
flames.*

*Her arms fold over her chest as she stares out the window. "I
guess I just thought it would be nice to feel normal for a night. So
much for that. I'm too busy standing out to fit in."*

*Penny's never spoken like this before. Or maybe she has and I've
just never listened.*

*When she came into my life, I wanted to hate her. I wanted her
to know how much I had to hate her. I wanted Penny to feel the
wrath of my loathing, without it getting muffled by the bullying of
others. She was off-limits to everyone else, even though some—
namely Lilith—didn't care about that rule. Tonight is proof of
that.*

*This is all my fault. I've made her life hell, and for what? A few
high fives from the guys as I tortured my shy stepsister. Was it*

worth it? Not at this moment. Not when for the first time ever, I see her. I really see her.

A lost girl crying out in a world that's turned its back on her. A burnt arm that doesn't touch the pain she feels inside.

Suddenly, I feel a dire need to protect this girl, even if the one she needs the most protection from is me.

I draw in a breath of her smoke-infused hair, my lips touching the wispy strands. "Penny Pie," I say, turning her around to face me. Her downcast eyes lift, catching mine. Desolate, heavy, and alluring.

In one breath, I lean down, pressing my lips to hers. When she retreats, I place a hand on the back of her head, pulling her into a closed-mouth kiss. Our eyes bore into each other's and tears prick the corners of her eyes while something qualms in my chest. It's like nothing I've ever felt before.

"Blaise, I..." Her words trail off as her eyes close. My lips part slightly and I separate hers with the tip of my tongue. "I've never kissed a boy before," she finishes through a breath before she falls into the kiss. I know this to be true because I've had my eyes on her since she came to town. I've watched her every move, dictated how she lived, and made sure that everyone knew this girl was off-limits. No friends, except Emery. No boyfriends. I'd destroy any guy who so much as brushed against her shoulder. And no kisses—up until now—up until this moment.

What is she doing to me? What is this dreaded feeling in the pit of my stomach?

Our heads tilt, my heart racing. For a moment, I think I should end this now, but when she relaxes and slips her tongue in my mouth, I'm certain that nothing can stop this.

Penny places a hand on my shoulder and I grab her by the waist, leveling her body with mine. All my thoughts disappear into a cloud of misty fog. All I can focus on is the heat between us. This insatiable need to be closer to her than anyone else in the world. To mark her, claim her, and keep her forever.

So, I do.

In the heat of the moment, I lower Penny to the floor and I take what was always meant for me—her. Every part.

"You okay?" Penny asks me, snapping me out of the memory.

"Yeah. Just thinking."

"Well, it's good to see you two aren't making out this morning." Ana's voice hits me like nails on a chalkboard.

"Happy to see you're dressed as the dutiful wife for your husband's funeral. Speaking of, is the new boyfriend coming?"

Ignoring my snide remark, Ana turns her attention to Penny. "I really wish you'd consider staying longer. Forever, perhaps."

I toss Ana a glare, telling her to cut this shit out. Penny will not be staying here.

"Not a chance. I'll go to the funeral like I promised, but I'm leaving first thing in the morning." Penny exits the kitchen, leaving me alone with Ana.

"What did I tell you? She's not staying a minute longer than what we agreed on."

"And as soon as I have all of this," she waves her hands around the room, "she'll want to stay."

Clicking my tongue on the roof of my mouth, I glower. "Will hasn't been read yet, Ana. Might wanna quit planning your future."

Her eyes widen in surprise. "It doesn't have to be read. Richard told me it was all left to me and you don't get anything."

"Keep telling yourself that. I'm sure you'll find a new man to drain the life out of before taking all his money. Maybe next time you'll actually succeed."

"Regardless of what you think, I loved Richard very much."

I set my full cup of coffee down and glare at her with my

palms pressed to the center island. "He sure as hell didn't think so. Otherwise, he wouldn't have lied to you."

"What are you talking about?"

I suppose it's time to tell her the truth, and I'll love nothing more than to watch her drop to her knees in agony. "Bad news, Ana. Richard lied. This is all mine. But don't fret, you've got twenty grand coming to you. Enjoy that while it lasts." Not only did my dad and I discuss this a long time ago, I also got a call from the attorney last week, explaining the terms of his will.

She looks as if she's seen a ghost. "You're lying."

"Nope."

"He wouldn't do that. Unless, you twisted the truth. You manipulated and controlled him. And now, you're manipulating my daughter."

"Shut your mouth. Don't you dare talk to me about manipulation. You're the one who destroyed your relationship with your daughter years ago."

"I love Penelope."

"You love yourself," I spit out in a low growl. Stepping around the counter, I straighten the sleeves of her dress. "Now, go to the funeral. Put on a show for the town and then get the hell out of my house."

"What's he talking about, Mom?" Penny asks from the entryway.

"Penelope? How long have you been standing there?" Ana asks, crossing the kitchen and standing in front of her daughter. "Blaise and I are just having another one of our mother-son disagreements." She chuckles nervously. "You know how we are." Guiding her by the elbow, Ana tries to turn her to leave. "Let's go. We don't want to be late."

Penny tunes out her mom and comes farther into the kitchen, her eyes locked on mine. "What did you mean when you said this is your house? I thought Richard left it to my mom."

The will is set to be read tomorrow evening, but it's best Penny sees her mom crumble before she leaves.

I decide to give her the full story before Ana starts spewing her own fallacies. "He left it all to me. Your mom just assumed that it was all hers because my dad told her it was two years ago. A lot changed in two years. A lot of truths were revealed." I look at Ana, aware that she knows exactly what I'm talking about. "I guess you're not the only one who knows how to keep a secret."

Ana's posture dampens as if she was just called out for being poor in front of the entire town, though it's just Penny. "He's lying." She surveys me like I have all the answers. "You're lying!"

"It's not just mine, Penny. It's ours. I made a deal with my dad that I'd take care of you. I'd keep you safe while making sure you have everything you need."

"What about me?" Ana sulks, and I'm loving every minute of it.

"You get to pack your shit and get the hell out the minute Penny leaves."

"But, I'm your stepmother. Of course you'll help me."

Penny storms out of the room, leaving her mother in tears and me with a smile a mile wide.

"Quit your bitching. You still get your twenty grand and your secret. Take it and leave."

That's what was left to her. A measly twenty grand of *fuck off* money that she'll spend within twenty-four hours. It was a nice middle finger from my dad to his glorious wife.

Ana stomps out of the room. She's likely in denial, refusing to believe that my dad would basically cut her out of his will.

Penny might not accept any of the money that I'm going to offer her, but at least she knows the truth: her mom is a worthless bitch.

CHAPTER 18
PENELOPE

I'M DRIVING myself to the funeral. Riding with my mom is not an option, and I really think Blaise needs space that I'll gladly give him.

Once again, I let my guard down and opened up my heart —or spread my legs, rather—and immediately after, I remembered why I always feel a mountain of regret following our sexual escapades.

He could have just told me the truth. All this time he's known that he was the sole heir to his dad's estate. I was led to believe that it was all my mom's, and she thought the same. I'm not even angry about the fact that he gets everything. I'm just annoyed that he never told me. He made this absurd promise to Richard that he'd take care of me. How does he plan to do that? Cut me open some more then put a Band-Aid on my broken heart and hope all is well?

I wanna scream and rip my hair out at the same time.

Do the lies and secrets ever stop? When does it end?

As if finding out that two people I trusted betrayed me— Emery and Wade—wasn't enough, now I find out that I've been staying in Blaise's house, eating his food, and my mom is broke and homeless.

I should care that she doesn't have anything. But, I don't. I don't care at all. After years of being a gold-digger, she finally got what she deserves. Nothing.

Now that my head is clear, I'm ready to go into that funeral home, say goodbye to the man who would have been a pedophile if I'd allowed it, then flip the town off and leave for good. But not until I get the answer to my final question.

It's no surprise that the place is dead, no pun intended. Richard's life was all-business. He didn't have many friends, and I'm sure the ones he did have never liked him to begin with. To say he wasn't sociable is an understatement.

From what I can see, it's all my mom's friends gathered around her, hugging her while she weeps fake tears of grief. The level of phoniness makes me sick.

Be real. Be you. Own your mistakes. Try harder next time.

That's the way it should be.

Then again, I've lived my life with those standards and look at where it got me. Friends as phony as Mom's tears. A guy who can do something as little as bat an eye and I drop to my knees.

Zen music plays softly through the speakers while a slideshow of pictures show on a large screen in an open room in front of me. They're mostly of Blaise and Richard, but there are a few of my mom. One of me catches my eyes. It's the same picture that Blaise was holding last night. Is this what he was working on? Scanning pictures for the slideshow?

"Penelope, sweetie." One of Mom's friends from her book club wraps her arms around me. "I'm so sorry for your loss."

I'm not. "Thank you," I say before taking a step back. I'm not really a fan of affection from strangers, especially ones who behave like my mother.

Bypassing my mom, I walk into the room where Richard is. The smell of this place, alone, makes me nauseous. I've always tried to avoid funerals, but this one almost feels necessary. I never got a chance to tell Richard how I felt about him.

I left while he was in decent health and he died while I was gone.

I take a seat as others come in. The slideshow is stopped when the pastor enters. He stands at the podium beside Richard's casket and begins with his drawn-out sermon on life and death.

Fifteen minutes later, I feel like my armpits are protruding sweat as he wraps things up in a final prayer. Everyone is dismissed for a luncheon; one I'll be skipping.

Thankfully this was short, sweet, and to the point because the room is starting to feel suffocating. I need to say my piece and get out of here. Mom is already out of the room, probably sipping on champagne and gossiping about what everyone is wearing.

There are a couple people gathered around him, so I stay back while they view the embalmed corpse.

An elderly lady presses her lips together in a tight smile and is walked away by a middle-aged man. I'm not sure who they are, but I'm guessing it's his mom and a brother? Two people who were probably pushed out of his life because they didn't fit in with his lavish lifestyle. I wonder if that's how Blaise will be now that he has millions.

With only a couple other people in the room, I approach the open casket.

There lies Richard. A man of wealth, good looks, and a heart of stone.

His hands are folded neatly over his still chest. Eyes closed and mouth shut tight. I place both my hands on the side of the wooden box.

"Life isn't fair, Richard. You work your ass off to build an empire, neglect your son, marry a gold-digger, and you can't even take any of it with you. You didn't leave behind fond memories or a legacy. You left behind money. The root of all evil. From the first day I saw you, when you hugged me so tight in your arms and whispered, "You're the most beautiful girl I've ever seen," I knew I'd never be able to let my guard down. Then came your son. The devil incarnate. Between the two of you, I didn't stand a chance. One who hated me, another who favored me. You were a sick man. And I don't mean the cancer that ate away at your body. I'm talking about the depraved thoughts that lived in your head. The fantasies of having me to yourself, a child. I'm not sorry you're gone. I'm just sorry that your son has to work extra hard not to be you."

Blaise still has a chance to be a good person. He also shouldn't have to live his life standing by the promise he made to his dad. Chances are, he will die trying to live up to it. I'm not his responsibility.

I went to that party last night to prove to myself that I could. I left weak and emotionally unstable with less friends than I had going into it. I proved nothing to myself, aside from the fact that I'm still a pushover.

My head is strong and it knows what it wants. My heart is pure and I have good intentions. But when it comes to fighting back, I cower.

Maybe it's time to fight back. An eye for an eye. Not just for me, but for Blaise. He can have his life back without looking over my shoulder.

"This has been enlightening," I say to Richard. "Now, burn in hell." I blow him a kiss, feeling proud that I was able to get all that out, then I turn around and I'm face to face with Blaise.

His shoulders are drawn back as he stands there looking devilishly sexy in his black suit with his disheveled brown hair. "Everything you said is true."

"Eavesdropping on my conversation with a ghost? Nice one, Blaise." I go to step around him, but he moves in front of me.

"I take it you're leaving now?"

"I am. Isn't that what you want? Isn't that your way of *protecting me*?" I air quote the words.

I don't tell him my plan because I don't even know what it is yet. One way or another, though, I'm coming back as a force to be reckoned with.

"Yeah. But I also want you to accept some money once the estate is settled. Use it for a house, college, anything you need."

"My room," I say. "I want it back to the way it was."

He raises a brow. "Your room?"

"That's what I said, isn't it?"

"But you're leaving tomorrow. Why would you want your room back the way it was?"

My arms cross over my chest and for the first time in a while, I feel like I have some control over my life. "You never know when I might be back for a visit."

Wade comes walking into the room, pulling my attention away from Blaise. Just seeing him hurts. I really thought that he was one of the good ones.

"I have to go." I drop my head, avoiding eye contact with Wade.

"Wait, Penelope." Wade reaches out but doesn't touch me. "I never got a chance to explain why I was at the farmhouse."

My eyes roll. "Save it."

"I was helping Blaise," he spits out as I approach the doors to leave the room.

I turn around and look from him to Blaise. "It's true," Blaise tells me.

Wade continues, "Blaise called me and told me he needed help once he heard you were at the party. We knew it wouldn't end well."

A smile spreads across my face. He was just trying to help. Wade is one of the good guys. "Thank you," I say to him. I turn back around to leave but glance over my shoulder at Blaise and I see something in his eyes, something enlightening. My heart does a little pitter-patter as I smile back at him.

Goodbye, Blaise.

Weaving through the small crowd of people huddled around my mom where she talks about opening a local bakery, I laugh. The woman doesn't even know how to bake a frozen pizza.

An usher opens the door for me and I step outside, drawing in a deep breath of fresh air. I feel brand new. Like I've been reborn into someone with drive and fight inside her.

As I'm walking through the parking lot, feeling on top of the world—probably the only person in the world who leaves a funeral with a smile on her face—I see the enemy. Alongside her, my new enemy.

I reach into my purse and pull out my keys to my car. "You two have some nerve coming here."

"You're still in town? Wow, I thought you'd run back to Portland. Getting naked for us wasn't enough to get rid of you?" Lilith spews the idiotic remark.

"You know what, Lilith? Your time is coming and you better watch your fucking back."

I turn toward Emery who's just staring at me with uncertainty. Clenching my keys, I draw my arm back and plant my fist right on her nose. "That's for being such a bitch. Looks like someone won't be making the funeral, after all."

Blood streams down her face as she cups her nose in her hand. "How could you?"

I laugh, "How could I? How the fuck could *you*?"

Lilith steps in front of me with a snarky look on her face. "The only bitch I can see is the one standing in front of me."

"You're right. I am a bitch. You made me one. Better get your bestie to the hospital. I think it's broken."

Emery cries out when the blood drips onto her white dress. Who wears white to a funeral anyway? Stupid girl.

I shake my hand, working the cramp out of my knuckles as I walk to my car. Those two haven't seen the last of me. I'm going back to Portland, but not for long. When I return to Skull Creek, I'm coming back with a vengeance.

CHAPTER 19
PENELOPE

Two Months Later

IT'S BEEN TWO MONTHS. Two months since I gave Skull Creek a big fuck you and left that dumpster-fire town. Speaking of fire, I still don't know who set the plan in motion to try and roast me, a little over two years ago, but I'm not done attempting to figure it out.

That's the thing about shitty people in shitty places—you always want to push them down further than they already are. Even if they don't know they're at the bottom. I have every intention of showing them as I shove their faces in the dirt and dig my heel into the back of their skulls. They, being the girls who sought my demise—Lilith and Emery.

Let's not forget about Chase. He'll definitely get a nice taste of the earth as I drag him to his rock bottom as well. Then there's Blaise. The big fat question mark at the end of my last straw. Is he on my side, or is he playing another one of his sadistic games?

Regardless, I'm coming back with a wrecking ball, and they'll be none the wiser.

First, I have one stop to make on my way out of Portland.

I shift my brand-new car into park—one that Blaise bought me with dear old stepdaddy's money—and waste no time getting out as my feet take me hurriedly up the sidewalk. I don't even have to knock before the door swings open.

"Penelope? What are you doing here?" Ryan asks as he looks over his shoulder to see if Erica hears him talking to me. I know she's here. Her car is parked out front. "I thought you said—"

"Yeah. I said I didn't want to talk to you ever again." My shoulders rise, then fall as I speak. "But I changed my mind. There's actually one last thing I need to give you." I cock my fist and pummel my knuckles right on his nose. "Maybe next time you'll remember that before you fuck trash behind your girlfriend's back."

Ryan cups his nose, his eyes wide as saucers. "You bitch!"

Erica comes up behind him and I give her a hard stare.

"You can have his small dick, Erica. I didn't want it anyway."

I backpedal and turn away, shaking my hand, still displaying a smile that should have never faded. I put my trust in him for over a year and allowed him to steal my happiness.

Once I'm in my car, I wear a smile that cannot be erased. I do a burnout in front of Ryan's house, leaving skid marks for him to remember me by. Take that, fuckers!

These last two months since I've returned were spent rebuilding myself. I've focused on what makes me happy, instead of trying to please everyone else. I've dug deep and forced myself to feel things I never wanted to, but in the end, I found what I've been searching for my entire life—me.

Blaise has called...a lot. Well, he did, anyway. For weeks after I left, he'd call daily, sometimes multiple times a day. Never left any messages, though, and I never answered or returned the calls. Last month, ten grand showed up in my bank account. I let it sit for a while then another ten grand showed up two weeks later. It just kept coming. The old me would have been too proud to accept anything from anyone in that family. But, Blaise was right; I deserve some of the inheritance, too, so I'm keeping it.

A call comes through the speaker of my car, and I tap Accept when I see Dad's name flash on the screen.

"Hi, Dad."

"Hey, hun. Ya know, it's not too late to turn around."

I smile at the softness in his voice. Leaving isn't easy and I've gone back and forth on it since I left Skull Creek. It all came down to my reputation. I shouldn't care what they think, but after being the weak girl who ran for so long, I'm ready to go back and show my strength. "I know, Dad. This will be good, I promise, and I'll come for a visit in a couple months."

"If your mom gives you any grief about not staying with her, you just tell her to call me."

I laugh. "Duly noted, Dad." It's funny because he's the gentlest man in the world, so the thought of him giving that atrocious lady a piece of his mind is just too hard to imagine.

My dad doesn't know what happened during my short visit for Richard's funeral. In fact, he doesn't know much about my life in Skull Creek at all. He knows my relationship with my mom is rocky and I've made it clear I won't be staying with her in her new apartment in the city. She's also called countless times—I did speak to her once, just to tell her not to call me again and that when I was ready to talk, I'd call her. I don't hate my mom. I should, but I don't. Part of me hopes that one day we'll be in a good place again. That day isn't today, though.

"I'm about to get on the interstate. I'll call when I get there."

"All right. Drive safe and remember I'm only a few hours away. And, Penelope?"

"Yeah, Dad?"

"I may have put a few things in the trunk of your car for protection."

"Oh God, Dad. What did you put in there?"

"Let's just say it's an emergency kit: water, jumper cables, flares, pepper spray, and a taser."

I smile at his thoughtfulness but cringe at the thought of ever having to use the last two items. "Thanks, Dad. I love you."

"Love you, too, hun."

We end the call and I flip my blinker to turn left onto the busy interstate.

Skull Creek, here I come.

MY PALMS ARE SWEATING, and my heart is racing. I'm stuck three miles from my exit between a friggin' semi-truck and an RV with a sixty-year-old man who keeps winking at me through the rearview mirror. He's got a Great Dane in the passenger seat, who has a string of drool hanging from his mouth onto the dash.

I'm half-tempted to lay on the horn, but I know it won't do any good. Tomorrow is my first day of school, and I really wanted to get a good night's sleep, but it's already midnight. I could have started a day late, but I'm already coming into the school year behind. At least this way, I'm starting the first day of the second semester, so I won't actually be behind in the classes I'm taking.

I glance in the rearview mirror again, and sure enough, the long-bearded fella raises his eyebrows and winks again. Ugh, gross!

"Come on!" My palm hits the steering wheel hard and I straighten my back against the seat, trying to get a hold of my anxiety. It's not the traffic jam that's setting me off, it's just an added bonus to my impending panic attack. What's really got my nerves in a ball is the fact that I'll be walking the halls of Skull Creek High as a member of the senior class tomorrow morning. I've got no friends here. Not a single one. It's fine, though. I'm not coming here to make friends.

The brake lights go out on the car in front of me and I breathe a sigh of relief as we slowly start moving.

Seconds later, we're picking up speed and the closer I get to the hotel, the more I'm thinking I'd be okay just sitting in this traffic jam for the rest of the school year. Crazy how you want something so bad, then you get it, and you're not sure you want it anymore.

No. I do want this. More than anything.

I could've stayed in Portland and lived my life under the radar. Kept my friends that were actually really amazing, graduated high school and went off to college with another class of students who know nothing about my past. They see the scars, but they don't know where they came from.

Nope. Instead, I'm going back because I've earned the right to walk those halls with my head held high. Seeing the expressions on everyone's faces will be priceless.

CHAPTER 20
BLAISE

"DUDE, can you believe that shit with Lilith and Chase? Who would have fucking thought that he'd start banging her as soon as he recovered from the ass whooping you gave him." Wade rambles on as we make our way down the hall to the cafeteria for lunch.

"What I can't believe is that you're even surprised. Come on, man. It's Lilith and Chase." My shoulder nudges Paxton Norwell, the new kid whose ass I beat a couple months ago. He doesn't know it was me, but I certainly haven't forgotten him. In fact, I've made his life hell ever since.

"Watch it, fucker," he huffs a breath, but he keeps walking.

Restraint. Hold it together. He's still healing from his last ass beating.

I spin around, ready to pummel his ass again, but Wade grabs my arm. "He's not worth it, man."

"Like hell he ain't." I turn back around slowly. I'm not sure what it is about the guy that rubs me the wrong way, but I don't like him. Not even a little bit. He stepped into our school with this pretty boy facade, trying to get in everyone's good graces—and it worked, for a minute—but I see through the bullshit.

"One of these days, I'm gonna really lose my shit with that asshole." Not just him, but Chase, too. I've beat both their asses and they still have the nerve to look me in the eye when we pass in the halls. Chase spent a couple nights in the hospital recovering from his "accidental fall." Apparently, he had a serious concussion and some bleeding on the brain. Do I give a fuck? Nope.

"Asshole?" Wade laughs. "He's the epitome of perfection. Straight *A*'s, star athlete. In fact, I don't think I've ever seen him without a smile on his face, unless he's looking at you. Can't say you don't deserve it. You did break three of his ribs."

We walk into the cafeteria, and the crowd in the entryway parts. "He doesn't know that. No one does, so let's keep it that way. The last thing I need is an expulsion when I'm so close to getting out of this shithole."

I've got no regrets about what I did. He was cozying up to Penny, and I snapped. The way his hand rested on her leg sent fireballs shooting through my body. He was new and didn't know the rules, but he touched her, nonetheless.

Not that it matters. Penny is back in Portland where she belongs. She's safe there and I wish she would have never come back in the first place. Her visit was supposed to be an easy in and easy out. Instead, she got hurt more than she already was. Ever since she left, there has been a divide that was never there. In this school, there is my side, and there is theirs. They, being Lilith and Chase.

"Have you heard from her?" Wade asks, as if he was reading my mind.

We make our way to the front of the line by cutting at least twenty other students. No one dares to say a word. "Don't go there. I'm in a good mood today."

Wade grins, "Good mood, huh? I just had to stop you from tackling Paxton."

"Better than my worst days when you bring up shit from the past. I haven't heard from her and I don't want to. Now drop it."

It's a lie. Every morning I wake up thinking about her. Wondering if she's okay. Hoping that she's found some sort of peace outside of this town. I've been putting money in her account for a while now. She deserves that much. Hell, she deserves a lot more, but that's the least I can do. It's best that we cut all ties and never speak again. If we keep in touch, I'll want more, and there's no way she can ever come back. The students here are as ruthless as they come and they've always set their sights on her. As far as her and I go, I'm too fucked up, and she's utter perfection.

Shaking away the thoughts of the girl I need to forget, I snatch up my lunch tray. My feelings of contentment slowly fade and that dark cloud looms over me again. So much for a good day. All because he had to bring her up again.

With my tray in hand, I walk beside Wade to our table. Our crew mostly consists of guys from the football team, aside from Paxton. I've made sure he's deemed as contagious as Penny once was. Since the divide, Chase has tried to get him to join forces on their side, but Paxton wants nothing to do with those sociopaths, not that I blame him. Seems that he'd rather be a loner than step on that side of the tracks.

We've also got a couple cheerleaders and their friends that sit with us. One of which has her eyes set on me. Her name is Roxanne and she's not a bad-looking girl by any means, but she's not really my type. I'm not even sure if I have a type anymore.

"Hey, Blaise," she says, batting her lashes as she sucks on a spoonful of yogurt.

I tip my head to her with a half-smile. "What's up?"

This girl has been clingy as fuck lately. I shot her down

when she tried to suck my dick at a party one night and I'm pretty sure she looks at me as a challenge now. She needs to get off that shit because it's never happening.

I take a seat next to Ryder, a big, burly fullback. He's the comedian of the group. Always cracking jokes and trying to make everyone laugh.

"You don't wanna sit by me?" Roxanne asks as I set my tray down.

"Not really," I retort, knowing that it was cold and insensitive. Hints don't work with this girl so I have to lay it right out there.

Roxanne rolls her eyes and resumes sucking on her spoon like it's a full-time job.

Wade sits down next to me as I take a bite of my big-ass burger.

"What's the plan for Emery's party Friday night?" Ryder asks, breaking the tension at the table between me and Roxanne. "Do we go or make our own?"

Emery is still up Lilith's ass and I don't see her coming out anytime soon. She's having a big, back-to-school party this weekend, and while they're not our friends anymore, we will be going. "Oh, we'll be there with bells and whistles. I'd like to see that bitch try and kick us out." I speak with a mouthful of food. "I've got enough dirt on all three of those losers to make damn sure they never win this war they've waged."

Thing is, they've got shit on me, too. Well, Lilith, anyway. We've got a deal, though. She stays out of my way and I stay out of hers.

"We could all go together," Roxanne chimes in, warranting an unfocused glare from me.

"Dude," Wade gulps as his wide eyes look to my left. "No fucking way."

I follow his gaze to a table three rows over, and my heart drops deep into the pit of my stomach.

"Is that…" he continues rambling incomplete sentences. "It can't be."

My stare never falters as it hugs tight to the brunette bombshell. I'm frozen in place as I try to wrap my head around the fact that she's here. Penny, my Penny, is here at Skull Creek High. I'm pretty sure my heart has stopped beating altogether. I swallow hard, my face likely as white as the clouds hovering in the sky.

Wade nudges me. "What are you gonna do?"

My eyes skate beside her and that's when I see who she's sitting with—Paxton. In one breath, my chair slides back, tipping over and grabbing the attention of everyone in the cafeteria. All eyes are on me as I eat up the space between Penny and me with thunderous steps.

She looks at me with soft, wide eyes as I grab her by the forearm and jerk her out of her seat.

Paxton growls as I pull Penny up. "What the hell, man?"

"Shut your fucking mouth," I grind out as I get Penny to her feet.

She doesn't say a word as I lead her out of the cafeteria. Whispers can be heard all around us, but I pay no attention to them. Even Mrs. Jost stands by idly, showing no concern to my hold on Penny.

Once we're out the doors, I spin her around and press her shoulders to the brick wall, rustling a poster with details of the Valentine's Day Dance next month. "What the fuck are you doing here?"

She shouldn't be here. She was never supposed to come back.

"Surprise," she beams with little to no excitement.

"Is this some sort of joke, Penny? You're not a student here so dump your tray, say goodbye to your new friend, *Paxton*, and get the hell out of Skull Creek."

Her lips tug up into a snarky grin as she crosses her arms

over her chest silently. "I take it you're not happy to see me." She sniggers with a patronizing smile.

I haven't even had a second to collect my thoughts. She's standing right in front of me, but I still refuse to believe this is real.

"Happy to see you? No. I'm not. You're not supposed to be here."

"Why? Because it's *not safe*? Don't worry, Blaise, I can take care of myself."

"You've proven time and time again that you *cannot* take care of yourself. I've got too much shit on my plate to keep an eye on you, so whatever you have planned, it's over. Go home."

"I'm not leaving. For once, I'm actually excited to be back in this town."

I don't even hear anything she says as I skim her body from head to toe. She looks different. "Are you wearing makeup?" Since when does she care what she looks like? Penny never wore makeup. Her hair is curled, she's wearing… "What the fuck is this?" I tug down on her shirt that sits above her belly button, trying to hide her bare skin.

"It's called a shirt and I happen to like it. And yes, I am wearing makeup because it makes me feel pretty. Is that a problem?"

"Uh, yes. That is a problem. You looked fine the way you were, now go wash that shit off."

Penny blows out an airy laugh that catches me off guard. "No," she says point-blankly.

"Excuse me?"

"I said, no. I'm not washing it off. I'm not changing my clothes, and," she reaches into her back pocket and pulls out a student ID card, "I'm a student here, so if you don't mind, I'd like to finish my lunch. There's a nice guy in there who offered to let me sit with him since you and your posse have outcast him to the entire student body. I think we'll be good friends." She winks and tries to slide past me, but I cage her in by pressing my hands to either side of her head.

A raging fire ripples through me, on the verge of a full-blown explosion, but I hold it together. "Stay the hell away from him," I grit through a clenched jaw. "And what do you mean you're a student here? You can't be that stupid."

Her eyes widen and she cocks her head to the side. "Wow. So now I'm stupid? I have to say, I thought you'd be a little happier to see me."

I can't tell her that the moment I saw her in the cafeteria my heart stopped. I was mesmerized by her beauty and for a sliver of a second, I contemplated what life would be like with her here—as my girl—but that feeling quickly diminished when I remembered what her life would become. "You can't be here, Penny. It's not safe for you."

Flashing a cocky grin, her head tilts to the side. "I'm not going anywhere."

Who the hell is this girl? She certainly isn't my manageable stepsister.

It crosses my mind that she came back to see if there was anything left between us. It's not totally far-fetched. There's always been something there, even if we both fight it. Regardless, everything I did was to keep this girl safe and I'm not about to let it be for nothing. I can't let her see the effect she has on me.

"Look. If this is about us—"

"Blaise," she holds up a hand to stop me. "I know your ego is big and all, but I didn't come back for you, if that's what you're thinking."

Her truth hits hard, but it's best that way. It'll be easier to get her the hell out of here.

"All right." I nod slowly. "You seem pretty adamant about this, so tell me why. Why'd you come back?"

Penny's eyes soften and her gaze drops. Peering down at

the empty space between us, I see all of her—the quiet fifteen-year-old, then the sixteen-year-old who just wanted to fit in, and finally the scared girl who came back two months ago, hoping no one would remember, but everyone did.

"I can't let them win, Blaise." Her voice is somber, braided with a mixture of pain and fury.

There's a pang in my chest and I hate that emotion is stirring inside of me again. That is another reason why this girl needs to go back to Portland. She makes me feel and I fucking hate it.

"Them? Or me?" It's a valid question, considering I made her life hell just as much as Lilith, Emery, and Chase have.

She looks at me while her heart beats rapidly, I know, because I can see the thin fabric vibrating against her chest. "I haven't decided yet."

"They can't lose. Things have changed since you left, Penny."

"How so?"

"I don't have the power I used to." It sucks to say it. It kills me, but it's true. I was always the top gun at Skull Creek High and Chase stood right beside me. Students feared him because he's batshit crazy. They obeyed me because I had Chase at my side. I haven't lost all control, but I no longer have power over Chase and Lilith. I've got some shit that could ruin their reputations, but it's nothing against the damage they could do. It was enough to keep a level playing field, but now that Penny is back, all bets are off.

"Come on," she chuckles, "all hail Blaise Hale. You're the king of the school. Since when did you give up that title?"

"Didn't give it up. Chase and Lilith took it from me. They're together now, making them a force to be reckoned with."

"So stop them. But this time, don't use your power to hurt me. Let's work together to bring them down."

I don't mean to laugh, but it slips out with a heavy breath. "Work together? Me and you? Good one, sis."

"First of all," she holds up a finger. "Don't call me 'sis.'" She drops her hands and raises her shoulders with her eyebrows dancing on her forehead. "Second of all, why the hell not?"

"Um, how about because we're supposed to hate each other. Not to mention, I blinked two months ago and you were gone. Today, I turned my head and you were back."

"You knew I was leaving. At that time, I couldn't get outta this hellhole fast enough."

"So you get a new hairstyle, buy some new clothes and slap on some makeup and you *want* to be here? You certainly haven't grown any brain cells since you left."

Penny slips under my arm. "And I see you still enjoy the cruel jabs at my expense."

Her arms cross beneath her breasts, pushing her cleavage out of her U-neck shirt. I look around, making sure no horny high school boys are nearby before pushing her arm back down so her titties fall back into place. "Don't you know there's a school dress code here?"

"Why are you so concerned with the way I look? Aren't you the one who once called me," she air quotes, "'basic?'"

She's right, I did. Maybe I liked her that way. It kept all eyes off her, so I could have all the fantasies of what was beneath those clothes for myself.

"Still are," I lie right through my teeth. I can't let my guard down with this girl. If I'm nice, she really will stay. I need her to leave. There is no way I'm approving of this plan of hers and there's not a chance in hell that I'll join forces with her to try and take down Chase and Lilith. We will lose. *She* will lose.

"Well," she murmurs, "this has been a nice reunion, but I need to go eat before the bell rings. See ya around, Blaise."

"Not so fast." I grab her arm before she walks away. "Find a different table."

Her lips come together in a thin line as mischief dances in her eyes. "No." She snaps her arm away and trots off with sass in her steps, giving me the back of her hourglass frame.

"Fuck," I mutter, running my fingers through my hair.

This is bad. This is really fucking bad.

CHAPTER 21
PENELOPE

DEEP BREATH IN. Deep breath out.

He's changed. I'd hoped he was still the same asshole because it would make this all so much easier. I don't want to be in love with Blaise. In fact, life was so much easier when I hated him. I still feel it. That undeniable chemistry. The way our bodies swelter together. Hearts racing, pulses pounding. The throbbing in his throat was as visible as the beating of my chest. Yet, he'd rather me hate him than love him.

It wasn't that bad. Actually, it was torture. I didn't expect so many emotions to hit me at once. Seeing Blaise hurt more today than leaving him two months ago. How is it possible to miss someone when they're so close? If I could hold on to the guy inside of him, the one who comforted me the night of the fire, I would. I don't see him often, but when I do, I want to pocket him and keep him forever.

As I walk through the cafeteria doors, I pull open the notes in my phone and look at my list.

Retribution List
Find their weaknesses and expose them.
Lilith: GET ALL THE DIRT!

Emery: School records? Pretty sure she's cheating her way through classes.

Chase: Seek out other girls who may have been victims of his sexual assault.

Blaise?? Find out his part in the fire??

I'm looking at my phone when I crash head first into a steel chest. "Penelope. I thought that was you."

I look up and see Wade, with his lunch tray in his hand, wearing a smile. He looks the same but with longer hair. "Hey, Wade!"

"Visiting or here as a student? Because if you say student, I'm gonna need to prepare myself before I talk to Blaise again. He'll be pissed."

"Actually, Blaise and I just talked. He's not mad at all. In fact," I tug at Wade's arm, hoping to have a conversation with him before Blaise does. "I have a plan that could benefit us all. Come sit with me and I'll fill you in."

"Umm…" Wade runs his thumb over his chin as he glances behind me. I don't have to turn around to know that Blaise is standing there.

"Don't listen to her," Blaise says from behind me. His words hit my neck and send a rush of shivers down my spine.

Wade throws his hands up. "Sounds like a family issue that I want no part of." He dumps his lunch in the garbage beside us, sets his tray on top of the trash bin, and leaves the cafeteria.

I spin around and grumble. "You know, Wade is my friend, too. I know you've enacted this rule that no one is allowed to be nice to me in the past, but that changes now."

"You're right. You can have friends. Back in Portland." He grabs my shoulders and steers me through the doorway, back into the hall. "Do yourself a favor and go back."

I get away from his hold on me, the grin on my face never leaving as I cross the cafeteria, bypassing students who are paying little to no attention to me. It's actually a nice change from the usual insults and evil glances I endured in my prior years as a student here.

Paxton is still sitting in the same spot, so I take my empty seat beside him. Two months ago, at the party, Paxton and I talked. I didn't know who he was and he had no idea who I was. It was a nice conversation with a stranger who didn't know about my past in this town. I saw him sitting alone at lunch and invited myself to his table. Turns out, he's the male version of me, in the aspect that it is forbidden to befriend him.

Here I am, breaking the rules on my first day.

"Hey there. I was just finishing up and you've only taken one bite," Paxton says as he piles his trash on his tray.

"Yeah. I'm really sorry about that. You'll learn really fast that I'm not well-liked around here. I won't blame you if you turn your head and pretend I don't exist."

Paxton chuckles. "Listen. I've got no friends here, thanks to the assholes who run this school. Seems everyone is scared of them. If you're willing to reap the consequences, I'll take all the company I can get."

Picking up my apple, I roll it in my hand. "They don't scare me. Not anymore." I set my apple down and extend my hand to Paxton. "I'm Penelope Briar. Your new friend."

Paxton smiles and places his hand in mine. It's soft and warm, and I can tell it's never done a day's work, aside from handling a football. "Paxton Norwell. The new kid, outcast, and hater of all things Blaise Hale."

"I think we're going to get along just fine." I smirk as I shake his hand.

I pick my apple back up and take a bite into the fleshy skin. With a mouthful, I apologize again to Paxton. "I am sorry you had to witness that encounter with Blaise. He and I have a long history."

Paxton slides his chair back, tray in hand. "Don't ever

apologize for that douchebag. He's made my life hell and if it weren't for the fact that our hatred is so well-known and I'd be the first suspect, I'd probably kill him."

"Oh, you'd be surprised at how many suspects there would be. Me included."

Paxton laughs. "Well, I guess we better stick together then if we want to survive the rest of the school year."

"I like the way you think."

It's crazy how comfortable I feel with Paxton. He's devilishly good-looking with his blond hair, blue eyes, and muscular build. Normally I wouldn't approach a guy with his stature, but we have a lot in common. It's nice having someone on my side who can relate to being the reject all because someone gave you that title.

I untwist the top of my water, take a drink, and set it back down with the top still in my hand. "I'm actually really surprised that you've been outcast so easily. Quarterback of the football team and all."

"In a school ruled by the corrupt, it doesn't matter if you're rich or poor, smart or stupid, athletic or artistic. They don't give a shit."

There is so much truth to that statement it makes me sick. "Maybe it's time to change that." I take another drink then put the top back on my bottle.

"Now we're talking." He gestures to my tray. "You done with that?" I nod, and he grabs my tray and sets it on top of his.

I get to my feet and smile at his generosity. "Thank you."

"No problem." He angles his head toward the exit. "I better get to class. My fifth period teacher is a real stickler on tardiness. I'll see ya around?"

"Most definitely."

I watch as Paxton leaves. Once he's out the door, my gaze slides to the left where Blaise is standing against the back wall, his foot kicked up behind him and a toothpick pinched between his thumb and forefinger as he gnaws on it—watching me.

Warmth swarms my belly. My cheeks flush, and I hope I'm not wearing my lustfulness for the public eye to see.

We both just stand there, looking at one another, our cemented stare never faltering. The chatter of students rings in my ears, but I don't hear their words. All I hear is Blaise's heavy breaths from across the cafeteria, his eyes drinking me in like I'm his favorite beverage. My heart rattles against my rib cage, the air feeling thick and suffocating. I place a hand on the chair behind me when I begin to feel dizzy.

I should be over him. I was never under him—well, I was, but it can't happen again. I will not fall under Blaise's spell. He's a distraction, and I didn't come here for him. But, damn if I don't want to explore what's under those clothes, just to see if anything has changed. Or maybe just to see if his touch still ignites every cell in my body. I'd do just about anything to find out right now.

When he drops his foot from the wall and spits his toothpick onto the floor, the corner of his lip tugs up in a snarl. His eyes roll as he turns away.

My heart falls into my stomach. I might be ready to fight back, but I'm still stupid for thinking he'd ever look at me the way I look at him.

I GOT lucky and didn't have any of my three main enemies in my classes so far. That luck just ended and wouldn't ya know, two of the three are here in the last class of the day—Lilith and Emery. The good thing is, Paxton is here, too, so I take a seat next to him.

Since I've arrived, there have been whispers, snide remarks, and unwanted glances. Everyone seems to still follow Blaise's 'no talk, no touch' rule he put on me. He says he doesn't have the same pull in this school, but he definitely does. He just might not have as much as Chase and Lilith. I'm not surprised, though. Lilith has always been an equal to Blaise. Only difference is, Chase is now on her side, making them a pair of wrecking balls.

Lilith gets up from her seat at the middle table, Emery following suit. Her eyes lock on mine as she walks in my direction. I let out a low grumble as she drops her books on the table to the right of me. "Well, well, well. If it isn't the little bitch who spewed threats before she left town. Are you here to make good on them, or do you plan on rolling over and letting me stomp on you while you're down again?"

Paxton comes to my defense. "Get lost, Lilith."

I set a hand on his book, stopping him. I don't need, nor want, anyone fighting my battles. Not anymore. "I see you still have that cute little scar on your chin. Tell me, does it itch when I'm near?"

Lilith looks at me like air has just been pumped into her head. "Why would it itch?"

"Because I'm the reason for the damaged nerves under your skin."

"If you're insinuating that you get on my nerves, then you'd be correct." She looks around before leaning close and whispering, "What about you? Does that heinous thing on your arm itch when I'm near?"

If that wasn't a full-on admission of guilt, then I don't know what is. *I knew she was behind the fire!* Now, I just need to get proof, so I can expose her for attempted murder. I might not go to the police, but I'll certainly make it known to the entire school.

I sink back into my seat, without saying another word, and flip my notebook open while looking at the front of the classroom.

"Don't you know no one likes you?" she continues. "Why are you even here?"

Emery sits quietly beside her and doesn't even look in my direction. I can't even begin to process my thoughts on that girl. Part of me thinks I hate her even more than Lilith. At least Lilith was upfront about her distaste for me. She never pretended to be my friend. Emery, on the other hand, pulled the rug right out from under me. All the pain I've ever felt didn't touch the way she made me feel. The ultimate betrayal with no chance of forgiveness.

Mr. Grady goes to close the door, but it opens back up, almost hitting him in the face. When I see that it's Blaise, my eyes close momentarily, and I breathe a heavy sigh. *This will be interesting.*

It's not that I'm unhappy to see him. I know I'll be seeing him a lot. Especially since I'll be staying at his house. The hotel was a one-nighter. I wanted my grand entrance to be here at school. That way he knew it was no joke and that I was staying. It also took away the opportunity for him to tie me up and keep me from going.

My hands fold in my lap and I twiddle my thumbs as he comes closer and closer. There are four open seats, but he bypasses them all.

"You're in my seat," he scoffs, cold eyes digging into my soul.

He isn't talking to Paxton. He's talking to me.

I point to an open seat directly in front of me. "Go sit up there."

Lilith giggles then turns to Emery and begins whispering. Everyone in the class is watching us, and I'm trying really hard to hold it together.

"This is my seat. Has been since the start of the school year." He stabs a finger into the table where his name 'Blaise Hale' is carved into the plastic tabletop.

"But it's a new class." My eyebrows raise. "New semester."

"Yes, smartass. But, this is where I always sit in Mr. Grady's classes. So move."

My back straightens, and I grab my pencil, pressing it to the paper like I'm ready to begin taking notes. "I'm not getting up."

"Then I'll move you myself."

"You wouldn't dare," I challenge him, which was really stupid, because I know Blaise loves a challenge.

He laughs devilishly, before scooping up my books and dropping them on the table behind him.

I look past him and see that Mr. Grady has his head hung low, pretending he doesn't notice. Is he seriously going to let him get away with this? It seems money really does pay your way through anything. Heaving a breath, I press on, getting him to back down. "You hate Lilith and Paxton. Why would you even want to sit next to them, anyways?"

Blaise presses his palms to the table and leans forward, his breath riding down my neck. "Keep your friends close and your enemies closer. Now get up."

If I do as I'm told then I relinquish my claim that I'm not a doormat anymore. If I don't, he'll likely stand there all class or quite possibly, pick me up and place me in a new seat.

He's the one embarrassing himself, so bring it on.

I stare straight into his eyes, standing my ground. "You're in my way."

It's dog-eat-dog as we challenge one another. Someone will lose. Unfortunately, since Blaise is on a quest to get back the power Chase stole from him, backing down would only give his enemies more leverage. However, it also does the same for me. I'm not sure who I'm trying to prove myself to—me, him, or them. Regardless, I sit with my ass sweltering in a pool of sweat beneath my jeans. It literally feels like my entire body is on fire. All the attention laser-focused on me, the hushed sounds of students making bets on who will win.

Seconds become minutes before Blaise finally cracks. "Fine. Paxton, get up."

I breathe a sigh of relief that this is over, although I feel bad for Paxton. I know exactly how he feels as he stacks up his books, throws Blaise a sinister look, and heads for the second row in front of me.

Before he sits down, Paxton reaches for my books Blaise moved, but Blaise gives him a nudge and grabs them first.

"Listen, shithead," I hear Blaise say under his breath. "You stay away from my sister or you're dead."

Humiliation chews on my insides. Not only did he just threaten Paxton, he also referred to me as his sister. After all we've been through—all we've done—he still thinks of me as the kid of his dad's widow.

Everything has changed for me, but it's all still the same for him.

CHAPTER 22
BLAISE

SHE CAN FEEL me watching her. I know because she keeps biting her lip. She does that when she's nervous. It's either that or twirling her hair around her finger. When she's feeling timid but wants to hide it, she crosses her arms over her chest, hugging herself. I know all of Penny's quirks. She can pretend that she came back to town a changed girl, ready to take on the entire town, but I see through it. I know it's all a facade because there isn't a student in school who doesn't wear that same mask every day. They're all just skating by and trying to survive the torturous high school years.

Penny might think her visit for my dad's funeral was a waste of time, and maybe it was to her, but to me, it was a learning curve. I saw the truth. Believing fallacies for so long, it was eye-opening. I called Chase my friend. Would have taken a bullet for the son of a bitch. The thing is, I would have taken it because he would have pushed me into the line of fire.

"You're a real asshole, you know that?" Penny whispers, not even bothering to lift her head as she takes notes from Mr. Grady's lecture.

I shrug a shoulder. "Yeah. I know."

"Would it really hurt you to just be nice to him? He's a good guy."

Laughter erupts from my vocal chords, warranting a glare from Mr. Grady. My forearms rest on either side of my open book and I look at Penny. "You don't even know him."

"Not yet, but I will."

I glower, jaw grinding. She's testing me.

"No. No, you will not. You'll stay away from him or I'll put you right back on your short leash."

Her head shakes 'no' repeatedly. "Nope. Not this time." She turns toward me with a slew of confidence. "You have nothing I want and there isn't anything you can do to hurt me."

I raise a brow. "Is that so?"

"Mmhm."

"Well, *Penny Pie*," I lean closer, invading her personal space, "I happen to know a little secret about you."

She smirks, still holding that composure that irks me to the core. "My secrets have already been on blast. I've been to hell and back. Go ahead and give it your best shot."

Inching closer, my lips brush the lobe of her ear. I look past her and see Lilith watching with intent, so I keep my voice down. "How do you think everyone would react if they found out you fucked your brother and you liked it?"

Penny freezes. Silence consumes us as tension coils. I retreat back to my seat, lip curled in a grin. "That's what I thought."

Not a word is spoken between us the rest of class.

When the final bell rings, Penny is the first one out of her seat. Hopefully, I didn't just shatter her dreams of riding in on her high horse. Then again, let's hope I did, so she rides it right back out of town.

I don't wanna be the bad guy with her anymore, but I've got no choice if I want to keep the truth from her.

GETTING BACK INTO ROUTINE, I head to the weight room with Wade. I've got an immaculate bench press at home, but it's not the same as this place. Something about the gym here feels more like home than the house I live in. It's so quiet and lonely there.

Before my dad died, I lifted daily—mornings, after practice, any chance I got just to clear my head. It was the middle of football season when he passed, and I never made it back on the field to finish out my senior year as quarterback. Everyone thinks that's why I give Paxton such a hard time. Wade thinks it's why I kicked his ass. After that, he was off the field for the remainder of the season, too. There might be a few ill feelings about it, but it's the attention he gives Penny that irks me the most. I've never once seen the guy flirt with anyone but her. First, the Devil's Night Party, and now, she hasn't even been back in Skull Creek for twenty-four hours and he's already cozying up to her. Just thinking about it has me packing extra weight on the bar.

"Ready?" Wade asks, lifting the bar where he stands behind me.

My fingers wrap around the cold, metal bar and I lift up, bring it down, and up again, repeating the motions. "Yep."

"Norwell's getting a little too close to Penelope. We need to put a stop to that shit before she falls for his dumb ass."

Wade doesn't know about my past with Penny; no one does. He just assumes I'm this insanely protective brother who wants to hurt her and save her at the same time. It's not a false assumption. In fact, that's exactly what I want to do. Fuck if I don't want to hate her with every fiber of my being. I wish she was repulsive, so it'd be easier.

"Come on, man. Aren't we past all that bullshit? Let the girl make some friends this time around. She's not fifteen anymore. She can take care of herself."

I begin lifting faster, sweat dripping down the side of my face. "Have you forgotten what Chase and Lilith did to her at the Devil's Night Party? They stripped her down and assaulted her. Who's to say that this jackass, Paxton, isn't playing us, and he's really on their side?"

"That's highly unlikely. Paxton hates those guys as much as he hates you."

He's got a point.

"I still don't trust him. She can make some friends, but he won't be one of them."

"Something tells me you don't need to worry about that guy. I really don't think he has any interest in being more than her friend. But, is this really about Paxton, or is it about her?"

"Him!" I spit out in a huff, getting more and more agitated. "I don't like the guy. He had his hands all over her once, and it won't happen again." I continue lifting quicker than normal, causing Wade to hover his hands under the bar.

"I call bullshit. I think you keep everyone away from her because you want her for yourself."

The bar drops to my chest, and I screech, "Fuck!"

Wade leans over me and lifts as I push it up, locking it in place on the rack. I sit up immediately, grab the towel on the floor, and wipe the sweat from my forehead.

"Well?" Wade presses, "Am I right?"

I scowl at him, continuing to dab at the dampness on my hairline. "Why the hell would I want her when I could have any girl in this school?" I tip my head toward my bottle of water next to my gym bag. "Could you grab that?"

He picks up the bottle of water and hands it to me. I pull up the top and tip it back, taking a long swig.

"I see the way you look at her. I've seen it for a while."

Choking on my water, I'm caught off guard by his comment. "She's my fucking sister," I say through my coughing fit.

"Stepsister," he reminds me. "It makes perfect sense. You

hated her for years, tried to make her life hell and along the way, you fell for her. Just admit it."

Getting to my feet, I take a few steps away, still patting my forehead with the towel. I've never once admitted my feelings for her to anyone. It wasn't long ago that I was admitting it to myself. The truth is, I did fall for her. It was the night of the fire when everything changed. The moment I looked into her tear-soaked eyes as she was holding tight to her burning arm, something switched inside of me. All of a sudden, I knew I'd do anything to keep her safe from people like me. That's why she had to go. That's why she still has to go.

Turning around, I face my best friend and I give him one bit of my truth. "Maybe I did. It doesn't change anything, though. She can't stay in Skull Creek. They'll eat her alive."

"So you'll let her go again? Just like that, you'll let her walk out of your life forever?"

I nod. "If it means they can't touch her, then yes."

"Or we just stop Lilith and Chase, once and for all."

Now he sounds like Penny. The thing is, Wade doesn't know everything. He wasn't there the night of the fire. He has no idea that I'm not only protecting Penny from Lilith and Chase. I'm also protecting her from the truth. Because *that* would hurt more than any juvenile prank ever would.

I shake my head, disagreeing with him. "They can't be stopped. She needs to leave." I toss my towel down, ending this conversation.

He won't understand. No one will.

CHAPTER 23
PENELOPE

AFTER TYING up some loose ends on my schedule in the office, I'm finally leaving campus. School got out thirty minutes ago and the parking lot is pretty empty, but I do notice Blaise's car parked right in the front, with Wade's next to it.

I click the unlock button on my keypad, flashing the lights of my red Audi. It's certainly not the fanciest car in the lot—Blaise and Wade take that cake—but I never imagined I'd have a car this nice, so I'm still amazed that it's mine. It's not brand new and it's not one of the sporty-looking ones, but it's new to me. I once heard that if you give your car a name then it'll live longer. It's a bullshit myth, but I named her Cherry just to play it safe.

As I approach the driver's side door, alarms sound in my head. I don't even have to turn around to know someone is there. It's *who* it could be that has my hand frozen on the door handle.

"Ya know, you could probably get that brother of yours to buy you something a little nicer, considering your ho-ass mom can't afford anything these days."

Chase.

When I turn around, sure enough, it's him. My hand immediately raises to smack him, but he grabs me by the wrist before my palm makes contact. I could throw out the fact that his family doesn't have much either, but I'm not quite that evil. I will, though, if he continues to push my buttons.

"Whoa. Someone grew a pair. Try and smack me again. See what happens."

It was only a matter of time. I knew I wouldn't be able to skate through the final months of senior year without an encounter with my number two tormentor.

I turn around, holding my composure as I reach for the door handle with a shaky smirk on my lips. "Go away, Chase."

He slides up, pressing his ass to my door, holding it shut. He cocks his head to the side with a wicked smirk. "I've missed you, Penelope."

"The feeling is *not* mutual. Now move." I pull on the handle to no avail. He just presses his back end harder against my door, grinning like torturing me is his favorite pastime. "Now! Before your stank ass rubs off on the door of my new car."

He nudges closer to me and I move a few steps back. "Don't act like you've forgotten how good my cum tastes on your tongue."

"Ugh," my voice wavers, "you're disgusting."

With my keys clenched in my hand, my finger hovers over the panic button. I'm two seconds away from pressing it.

Chase looks down to where my key is digging into my palm with how hard I'm squeezing it. Before I can even react, he snatches them away from me.

He admires the keys while continuing to be the annoying asshole he is. "Word has it, you returned with a backbone. I'm not buying it. You still look like the same scared Penelope to me." He dangles my keys in the air with a cocky flash of his white teeth. "If I remember right, you like to barter. Tell me, what would you do for these keys?"

I jump up, trying to snatch them, but he raises them higher. "Stop being such a dick and just give them to me."

"I'll make it easy on ya. A quick handy in the back seat and you can be on your way."

"I'd rather drink my own vomit." I jump again, warranting another obnoxious smirk from Chase.

He's exactly as I remember him. Same clean, black haircut with shaved sides and a long top flipped to one side. Same crystal blue eyes that look like they are the gateway to hell. He holds the same air of too much confidence. And he certainly has the same stupid arrogance.

Chase shakes his junk with his free hand. "I got something you can drink."

My stomach churns and I'm getting really tired of this back and forth. My fists clench at my sides and when he opens his mouth to speak again, likely more degrading bull-shit, I raise my fist, cock it back, and lay it across his cheek, causing his head to snap to the side.

"Fucking bitch!" he spits as he reaches out and grabs me by the throat. His fingertips pierce the skin of my neck, thumb pressed firmly against my jugular.

"Let me go," I whimper through a strained breath.

"Let's get one thing straight, *Penny*," he enunciates the nickname Blaise dubbed me with. "You're nothing but a weak little girl. Always have been. Always will be. You can act tough, but when push comes to shove, you will fall down." He gives my head a shove, releasing his grip on me.

Gasping for air, I watch as he throws my keys across the parking lot.

The back of his hand grazes his cheek where I left an imprint of my knuckles. "Watch your back."

When he walks away, I draw in a deep breath, filling my lungs before crossing the parking lot for my keys. Thankfully, there's no snow right now.

I'm going to destroy that detestable boy and enjoy every second of his demise.

IT FELT like the day was going semi-decent until my run-in with Chase. Blaise wasn't quite the hardball I figured he would be. I expected him to be a little more boisterous about me coming back to town. Maybe a trip in the hall, a shove into my locker. At least, that's how it was in the past when I was a student here. Lilith gave me some shit, but I expect nothing less from her. It was Chase that really got my blood boiling. Just seeing him makes me feel sick. I instantly think of that night in the barn when he forced me to give him a blow job. There's no doubt that given the opportunity, he'd take advantage of me again.

He won't get the chance, though. Which is exactly why I just passed the Hale estate instead of getting settled in. Chase only lives ten minutes away from Blaise's house, so I decide to go check things out, just to see if there's anything I can use to my advantage.

I park across the street from the small, ranch-style house. Chase doesn't have the same luxuries as the group he runs around with does. There's a broken white fence wrapped around the yard, a dog chained up to a tree in the front, and a tipped over bag full of beer cans beside the open screen door.

I'm not sure how his family life is, but from the looks of it, it's broken. A few years ago, I would empathize with anyone who came from a broken home. Lord knows my family isn't put-together. After everything I've been through, empathy seems to escape me. These people destroyed any chance of me ever showing them compassion.

My phone beeps from the passenger seat and I pick it up to see that it's a text from my mom. Her calls and texts are totally random and it makes me wonder if she's drinking heavily, doing drugs, or quite possibly seeing a therapist. It's hard to say with her. I hope for the latter, but it seems so far-fetched that she'd ever admit she needed to work on her mental health.

Mom: Has Blaise been sending you money?

Why am I not surprised that her first message in over a week involves money?

I type back a quick response.

Me: I'm eighteen now. My finances are not your business.

Mom: According to your father, you bought a new car and phone. If he's sending you money, I should know. That money should have been mine, too.

I shake my head in disbelief at this lady. Obviously, the assumption that she's seeing a therapist is off the table.

Me: Why are you calling my dad?

Mom: You haven't returned my calls and I wanted to see how you were doing. He said you're in town. I'd like to see you. Just between us, though. Blaise doesn't need to know our business.

My heart begins racing frantically. Seeing her would be triggering and could set me back on all the progress I've made.

Me: I'm not ready. I'll reach out when I am.

I close out of the screen on my phone and drop it back in the seat, refusing to give her another second of my time.

When I look up, I notice that an old, rusted-out minivan has pulled into Chase's driveway. I straighten up in my seat and watch as an older lady—wearing a white shirt with a rip on the side, who I take to be his mom—tosses another can on top of the bag in front of the door. A tall, bearded guy, with a cigarette hanging from his lips, follows behind her and they walk inside.

I'm actually surprised. Chase is so well put-together. He always has on clean clothes. His truck is older, but it's nicer than any vehicle I had before the one I own now. I've never gotten the impression that money was tight for him.

Regardless, I still don't feel sorry for him. No matter what his life is like at home, it's no reason to treat people the way he does.

Unless, it's all he knows. There has to be more behind those walls than what I see from the outside.

I drive away from his house with every intention of revisiting. Chase has secrets, and I will find them out.

Once I have the dirt I need on these imbeciles, I can use it to my advantage to get the truth from them. Some would call it blackmail, though I'll call it a negotiation tool. When they fail to negotiate, I'll ruin them.

Three minutes later, I'm pulling up to the house that built me. It's the place that opened my eyes to a world of anguish. It drained me of hope, stole my innocence, and sucked the life right out of me. I actually feel like a fool returning, but I have to do this. It's time to face my demons head-on, so I can live a life without them.

Blaise's car is in its usual spot, so I park right beside him and go in the side door through the mudroom.

I'm not really sure if he's expecting me. He hasn't asked if I'll be staying at his house, but when I left, I did tell him to finish the remodel of my room in case I returned. It shouldn't be a total surprise when he sees me here.

Leaving my bags in the trunk of my car, I open the door and step inside. Just like last time, I'm hit with a tidal wave of memories. Music blasts through my ears, and I'm not sure where it's coming from, but it's loud as hell. I close the door behind me and creep down the hall. I'm not really sure why

I'm trying to be so quiet, especially with the heavy metal music blaring, but I am, nonetheless.

I come to a complete halt when I see Blaise standing in the kitchen over the stove, humming along to the tune of a song I don't even know. The smell of grilled cheese fills my senses. *Is he cooking?*

He looks so vulnerable right now and part of me wants to just turn around and leave. I could come back when he's doing something a little less…human. Maybe when he's sleeping.

When his eyes snap to mine, it's too late. "What the hell?" he speaks hastily. "What are you doing here?"

I stuff my hands in the back pocket of my jeans and shrug my shoulders. "Surprise, again."

Smoke begins smoldering from the pan, so Blaise kills the flame before redirecting his attention back to me. "Are you staying here?"

A frown tips on my lips. "Are you inviting me?" I am regardless of what he says, but I don't tell him that. It's best to ease into it.

"Well, you're sure as hell not staying with your mom. I know that. The only other option is for you to do what I said and leave town. I'd heed my advice and go if I were you."

"Told ya. I'm not going back to Portland."

Blaise digs the spatula under his sandwich on the pan and scoops it up, then drops it on a paper plate. "It's your funeral. Don't say I didn't warn you."

I walk farther into the kitchen and pull out a barstool. "I can't believe you're cooking. Aren't you like a multi-billion-aire now?"

The music stops when Blaise clicks a button on the remote. "Henry is out for the day. A guy needs to eat. Why do you act so surprised?"

"I've just never seen you do anything for yourself, that's all."

Blaise drops the plate down in front of me and I look at him with a sweep of confusion. "What's this?"

His brows raise. "It's a grilled cheese sandwich."

"I know that. Why did you put it in front of me?"

"It's a long drive back to Portland. You should eat before you go."

I'm fighting off the warm feelings swarming in my stomach. My head shakes as I look down, biting back a smile. "You're never going to stop trying to get rid of me, are you?"

He goes back over to the stove and relights the burner, then slops up another piece of bread with butter and drops it in the hot pan.

Watching Blaise cook is just too weird. I look down at my sandwich and it's the perfect amount of golden and brown.

"For what it's worth, I'm not *trying* to get rid of you." Blaise turns around with the spatula in hand. "I *am* getting rid of you. So eat your food and be on your way. You've already missed your first day of your second semester at Hallstone High. Wouldn't want you falling too far behind."

I pick up my sandwich and take a big bite. Ooey gooey cheese drips from my lip and I lick it up. It's actually pretty good. "Are the renovations on my room done?" I ask, completely ignoring his comments at me leaving.

Blaise clicks his tongue with a snarky look on his face. "It's done. But don't get too comfortable."

"Good. It's late and I'm tired. Busy day at school and all."

The pan starts simmering and he turns around to flip the sandwich. "One night. You leave tomorrow."

I bite my bottom lip with a smile. "Thanks, *bro.*" It's a sarcastic title that I rarely use, but it seemed fitting.

"Don't thank me."

Blaise finishes up and sits down across from me to eat. An awkward silence surrounds us and all I can hear is the sound of him chewing.

"Ya know," I say with a mouthful of food, "I'm getting what I came here for, with or without your help."

Blaise lifts his eyes from his plate. "And what exactly is it that you came here for, Penny?"

"Answers and revenge. You all made my life hell. I'm not sure I'll ever fully recover from the shit you and your crew put me through."

"This revenge you speak of, am I on that list?"

How does he know there's a list?

He continues, "Metaphorically speaking."

"That depends." My fingers run around my lips, wiping away the breadcrumbs. "I guess. I don't really have enough information to decide what you deserve."

It's no secret that Blaise was awful to me. The years I spent here were nothing short of harrowing. He should be at the top of my list. I should hate him for everything he did to me. But, I don't.

Leaning forward, he locks his elbows on the island counter. "Well, if I am, I say bring it on, baby. I like feisty Penny."

I drop the crust of my sandwich on my plate and push it toward him as I stand up. "You've never met the girl I've become. I might just make you eat your words."

"Where are you going?" he asks as I walk away.

"Getting my bags. I need a shower and some sleep."

It was a long drive in and I only got about three hours of sleep last night. A hot shower, warm pajamas, and a solid eight hours of sleep sound like the perfect way to end this day.

Just as I go to open the door to the mudroom, Blaise reaches out from behind me and grabs the handle. "I'll get 'em."

I turn around and look at him, just to make sure it is in fact Blaise. My eyebrows hit my forehead. "Come again."

"I said I'll get your bags. Go upstairs. I'll be there in a minute."

"Okay. Thanks, I guess." I duck under his arm and slither out from beneath him as he squeezes the handle. Blaise walks out, closing the door behind him, leaving me confused about his intentions.

CHAPTER 24
BLAISE

A GUST of wind blows as tiny pellets of ice smack against my cheek, slapping me out of this fucking trance I'm in. At least, that's how it feels. If I could go back to the years when I couldn't stand the girl, I'd do it in a heartbeat. It was so much easier being mean to her and enjoying it. Something tells me that I'm fighting a losing battle when it comes to talking her into leaving; she seems hellbent on staying, no matter what I threaten her with or whatever nasty words I say. Hell, she might not even care if the entire town knew we fucked.

Right now, I just might say screw the naysayers and go fuck her again. Sure would relieve some of this pent-up stress my dick is holding.

I pop her trunk and grab not one, not two, but three huge-ass bags, shaking my head the entire way back to the house.

Yep. She's not planning on going anywhere, anytime soon.

Kicking the door open, I drop them at my feet and just stand there, staring at her luggage.

"We should go." I slouch down to where Penny lies on the cold floor curled in an old blanket I found. Her eyes are wide open as she stares straight ahead at the wall.

The sun has risen and I peeked out the window to make sure the fire was out and the coast was clear.

"Blaise," she says, pushing herself into a sitting position, while holding tight to the towel wrapped around her arm. "Why would anyone do this to me?" Tears slide down her cheek and I sweep them away with my thumb as they continue to fall.

"I wish I knew because I'd make them all pay." I grab her good hand and pull her up until she's on her feet. "You okay?"

She nods, although I know she's not. She's physically hurt and emotionally wounded. I'm not sure she'll ever be okay again.

"My dad's driver is on his way. We better get you to the doctor to have your arm looked at."

"No," she yelps, "I don't want anyone to know. I just...I don't want the added attention."

"But, Penny—"

"I said no, Blaise."

There's no doubt that she'll have a nasty scar, whether it's looked at or not. I'm pretty sure she'll need some skin grafting at the very least. "Okay," I finally say, leaving the decision up to her.

Penny has always tried to make decisions for herself, but no one let her. She's wanted to leave this town ever since she arrived, so she could go live a normal life with her dad. She would have done anything to get away from me. Now, I'm starting to think she was right to try and flee my clutches. If she stays in Skull Creek, she might never leave alive.

"Thanks for grabbing them," Penny interrupts my stroll down memory lane. She reaches down and grabs one of the bags and I grab the other two. "The room looks great. I'm actually very impressed. I might never wanna leave." There's a sarcastic kick to her statement, but I know she's doing it to get a rise out of me.

I follow behind her up the stairs to her room. It was her room, then it wasn't, and somehow, it is again. My dad wanted it renovated for her because he had this sick obsession with his stepdaughter. He thought that giving her fancy things would bring her back, probably so he could corrupt her and claim her body.

"Pen," I say as we walk down the hall, a bag in each hand at my sides. "I know you want answers, but do yourself a favor and stop searching for them."

She turns around and presses her back to the door, pushing it open. "I'll never stop until I know who and why."

Fuck it. Maybe I should just tell her and get it over with. Let her do with the information what she will. It sure would make this nagging fucking headache go away that I've lived with for over two years.

"I ran into Chase today," she says out of nowhere.

I drop the bags at my feet with a thud. "And?"

She sits down on the end of the bed and folds her hands in her lap. "He hasn't changed. Tried getting me in the back of my car."

"He what?" I spit out, eating the space between us. "Tell me you didn't—"

"God, no." Her lip curls up in disgust and a rush of relief washes over me. "I'd rather have sex with you then…" She shakes her head, changing her train of thought. "Anyways, he insulted me, threw my keys, and spit out a few threats. Nothing I can't handle."

"Why the hell didn't you call me?"

She laughs, like it's the dumbest question I've ever asked. "Call you? Why would I do that? You're not on my side, remember?"

Aren't I, though? It sure does feel like I'm on her side. If I wasn't, I'd welcome her in this town and let her stay, only to watch her life crumble at her feet.

"Look," I say, sitting down beside her, "you're right, I'm not on your side, per se, but I told you before, everything I said and did was to protect you. Not just from me, but from them. That's why you need to go back to Portland. Not because I don't want you here." My entire body flushes with heat as the words leave my mouth. I've never been this honest with her, or anyone for that matter.

Her body turns to face me as she tucks one leg under the other. "You're serious?" Her voice is solemn and laced with wonder. "You really think you're protecting me?"

"I'm trying. You're making it really fucking hard, though."

Her eyes beam into mine and I can feel the sparks ignite in my body from just her look alone. "But, why?"

Answering that question feels damn near impossible. So I go with the first thing that comes to my mind. "We're family."

Probably wasn't the best response. The way she's looking at me tells me it was the worst answer I could give her.

Penny gets to her feet and paces in front of me, her arms draped at her sides. "Family?"

"Okay. Bad wording. I know you hate it when I refer to us as family."

"Well, Blaise," she drawls, "can you blame me? Look at what we did. It feels so gross."

My brows raise and I bite my bottom lip. "It definitely felt a certain way, but gross wasn't on my list."

She stops walking and stands in front of me. Her hair is piled in a bun on top of her head and her eyes are swollen from lack of sleep. "It's not funny."

"I wasn't laughing. In fact," I stand up, aligning our bodies, "I don't find anything funny about the way it felt to be with you. Not once, but twice."

Right before Penny left Skull Creek in the fall, things were different. At least they felt that way to me. We connected on an entirely different level. Feelings surfaced that I'd been shoving down for so long.

"Don't remind me," she huffs, giving me the impression that she's either denying it or she outgrew those feelings already.

It makes sense that she'd be standoffish. I'm not exactly pleasant company.

I bring my hands to her arms and run my fingers up and down the sleeves of her sweatshirt. "If it weren't for all the obstacles in our way, do you think you'd wanna be reminded?"

Soft ocean eyes beam into mine. Her mouth opens to speak, but the words don't come out.

"Answer me," I demand. "If our parents never married and the past didn't exist, what would you want from me?"

"I...I don't even know. It doesn't matter. The past does exist. The pain you inflicted on me is as real as the scar on my arm. I'm still not sure you didn't have something to do with it. You've never denied nor claimed responsibility."

She's right, I haven't. Maybe it's because part of me does feel responsible.

I take a step closer. Warmth radiates between our flush bodies. "That's not what I asked."

"Pranks and acts of hatred aside? I think I could easily fall for you." Penny purses her trembling lips. I can tell that admission was taxing for her.

If only I could tell her I feel the same. The possibility of sweeping her away to somewhere where the past doesn't exist, crosses my mind. We could run away together and start over somewhere else, anywhere else. I've got the money to make it happen.

I'm supposed to be pushing her away, so she'll leave town, but right now, I want to keep her forever.

Leaning closer, I ghost her lips with mine. "Give up your search for answers, Penny. Leave the past where it belongs." My mouth then crushes hers, sweeping my tongue between her clenched lips and prying them apart. Her hands slap my shoulders, fingers digging through the fabric of my t-shirt.

"Blaise," she hums, attempting to push me back while I pull her closer. "The past does exist. We can't."

My fingers pinch her chin, guiding her mouth closer. "Right now, nothing else exists."

She continues to shake her head while trying to break the kiss, so I drop my hold on her. "What the hell, Penny?" I huff, unsure why she's being so resistant. Penny never resists me. Unless... "Are you back with that nitwit, Ryan?"

"God, no. This has nothing to do with Ryan. It's just...wrong."

"Come on," I grab her by the waist and tilt my head, ready to go in for another kiss, "no one needs to know."

She blows out a heavy breath. "That's the problem, Blaise. No one needs to know because no one can know. Because this is wrong."

I throw my hands up in defeat. "What's so wrong about it, Penny? Huh? We're not blood-related. Our parents were married, but one of them is dead now. It's not like we grew up together. Tell me what the fucking problem is."

After a beat of silence, while she chews on her bottom lip, she finally speaks, "All right. We can do this if you tell me the truth about the fire."

"Jesus Christ. Are you ever going to get over that shit?" My voice rises. I've got no control over it. She's infuriating. I'm so sick of this conversation. "It was over two years ago. Move the fuck on."

"Move on?" she shouts. "How am I supposed to do that when I have to look at this every day?" She pulls up the sleeve of her sweatshirt, exposing the eaten flesh on her arm. "Someone tried to kill me, Blaise. There was a gas can. The same kind of gas can I saw in your garage the next morning. Tell me that's not a coincidence?"

"It's a fucking gas can," I shout back, running my fingers through my hair and turning away from her. "Ninety-nine percent of the population has them. So what if it looked like the one you saw at the barn."

Penny wafts sarcastically. "You really do think I'm stupid, don't you?"

Her head shakes repeatedly as she stands there, watching me and waiting for a response. Only this time, I don't give her one.

I'm too fired up and I'll likely regret anything I say.

"Get some sleep, Penny," I say, before walking out of the room and slamming the door shut behind me.

My back presses to the closed door, and I release the pent-up air in my lungs. "Fuck!" I mutter under my breath.

No matter how hard I've fought to keep this secret from her, she wants it revealed. I just hope she's ready for what's waiting for her on the other side of the truth.

"Last chance to go get that burn looked at," I say as Dad's driver comes to a stop in the garage.

I'm happy to see my car is sitting out front. Lilith better hope she didn't scuff it up at all.

"I told you, I'm fine." Her voice is a whisper that only I can hear. With her chin to her chest, she remains still, even though the car has stopped.

My fingers graze her chin, turning her head toward me. "Everything is going to be okay. Do you trust me?"

When she doesn't respond, I press my lips to hers, tasting the saltiness of her dried tears. "We'll find out who did this and we'll make them pay. Okay?"

She nods under my touch, and I kiss her once more, before opening the door to get out. "Let's get inside, so you can get cleaned up."

Once we're out, I pull Penny's hand to go inside, but she resists.

"What's that?" she asks, looking past my shoulder.

I follow her gaze to the counter in the garage that holds a tool-box, a couple spray cans of paint, and…two gas cans. I look back at her quickly. "What? The gas cans?"

"Those aren't just any gas cans, Blaise. They're the exact same as the one we saw by the tree at the barn."

"So," I laugh, "gas cans are a common household thing. Come on, let's get inside."

Her hand jerks out of mine and she takes a step back, bumping into the back passenger door of the car. Tears well in her eyes and I'm not sure what she's so worked up over. "Not everyone puts a silver ring of duct tape on their gas cans." She looks pale, like she's seen a ghost, as she pulls open the driver's door.

"Marlon," she says the driver's name, "whose gas cans are those?" Pointing to the cans on the counter, her eyes never leave mine.

Marlon pokes his head out the door and looks at them. "Those ones are used by the Hales in emergencies. Why do you ask?"

She presses further. "Did you put the duct tape on them?"

"No," he chuckles, "Carl, the other driver, did that. He claims those ones are his. Mine are over there." he points to three others with no tape on them. "Apparently, he doesn't like people using his stuff. Kinda weird, if you ask me."

Penny nods while looking at me with a burning glare. "Yeah. Yeah, that is weird."

"I actually found one sitting outside the garage this morning. It was completely empty. You kids know anything about that?"

Penny's eyes widen and she breaks the stare she's held on me this entire time. "Wait. What did you just say?"

"That's enough, Marlon," I interrupt and grab Penny by the hand. I've got no idea what she's insinuating here, but Marlon isn't helping matters. "Come on." I pull her to the mudroom door, give the handle a turn and escort her inside.

"Let me go," she snaps, jerking away aggressively.

"Tell me you don't think—"

"What? That you were behind this?" Her shoulders rise as tears fall. "I dunno, Blaise. Were you?"

I laugh because it's actually funny. Once I realize she's serious, I hold my composure. "You're serious? I risked my life to go inside *that barn. I carried you out. Why the hell would I do that if I started the fire?"*

Penny brushes her shoulder against mine as she walks past me. Stopping at the door to go inside from the mudroom, she turns around, gripping the handle behind her. "Just because you didn't start the fire, doesn't mean you didn't put the plan in motion. Lilith brought your car back. Who's to say she didn't bring your gas can back, too?" The handle turns and she pushes the door open, then slams it behind her.

Oh, hell no, she doesn't.

"Penny," I holler, tearing the door open and chasing after her as she walks steadfast toward the stairs. "I didn't do it."

"Save it." Her voice trails down the steps. Seconds later, I hear her bedroom door slam shut.

Someone started that fire, but it sure as hell wasn't me.

CHAPTER 25
PENELOPE

AFTER A SEARCH ON SOCIAL MEDIA, I was able to get Paxton's cell phone number. I shot him a text last night and asked him if he'd meet me in the library before school. He responded with a 'k.' I'm hopeful that he'll help me out because he has just as much hate for this group as I do.

So, here I am. Twiddling my fingers while I sit at an empty table in the library. When I hear the shuffle of feet, my head shoots up.

"Hey! You came!" I beam, a tad too eagerly.

Paxton flings his backpack over his shoulder and drops it on the table with a thud. "Told you I would. What's up?"

"Remember how we said we have to stick together to survive this semester?"

With narrowed eyes, he takes a seat across from me. "Yeah," he drags out the word.

"What if I told you I think we can live instead of survive?"

Paxton looks left, then right, making sure no one is around. "I'd ask what your plan is?"

I fill him in on all things Lilith, Chase, and Emery. I go as far as telling him about Emery's betrayal, and even the fire.

"They actually lit the barn on fire with you inside?" His eyes are wide as if he can't believe what I'm telling him.

Pulling up the sleeve of my shirt, I show him the proof. "I have the scars to prove it."

"And you think your own stepbrother would really do that to you?"

"That's the thing. I'm not sure if Blaise did have anything to do with it."

"All right. Tell me what I need to do. My reputation can't get much worse, might as well give it a shot."

I lean closer, my arms stretched out across the table. "How good are you with computers?" I ask in a whisper.

"Computers and technology are two of my favorite pastimes. I'm actually planning to go to school for computer engineering."

This partnership just keeps getting better and better.

"I need you to get me Emery's school records and keep an eye on Chase. Something weird is going on with him at home."

Paxton massages his temples. "Damn, Penelope. That's some serious trouble if I get caught."

"Please," I beg. "You're my only hope. I've got no friends. No family. No one." I sound pathetic, but I'm desperate at this point.

After a few seconds of thinking, he finally says, "I'll see what I can do."

Paxton and I make a plan to discuss more in the student courtyard at lunch. For the first time in a while, I feel hopeful. I feel like everything might actually fall into place.

I'M WALKING at a leisurely pace to my locker to put my books away for lunch. I'm on high alert because I know that you can never be too careful in these halls. You just never know when someone might pop out of nowhere and attack.

"Eww," Lilith grumbles snidely as I pass her and Emery.

Normally I'd keep walking, maybe hang my head low and pretend I didn't hear it, but not this time.

"Eww is right. Your friend smells rancid." I keep walking, a smile growing on my face as I try to hide it.

"What did you say?" Lilith's voice rings in my ears and the next thing I know, I'm flying forward and stumbling over my feet.

Somehow I manage to catch my fall, and when I look up, I see why. Paxton places an arm around my waist, but I spin around to face Lilith and Emery.

"You bitch!" I screech, charging at her and taking her straight down to the floor. My thoughts escape me as hands fly in every direction. I'm not sure if they're mine or hers. My scalp feels like it's been set on fire, but I ignore it completely. Just as I get a hold of her wrists and pin them over her head, spit flies in my face.

"Get off me, you crazy-ass psycho." Lilith squirms beneath me, trying to get me off of her, but I don't budge.

My hair still feels like it's being ripped from the follicles and when I glance up I see Emery with a fistful trying to pull me off Lilith. "Stop it, Penelope," Emery yells.

"Traitor," I scoff, releasing my hold on Lilith and reverting my attention to Emery. She looks frail and void of emotion. I shove her back and she lands on her ass, sliding a few inches across the dirty hall floor. "Is her friendship worth it to you? Do you have everything you want now? Popularity and what, a bright future ahead of you?" I laugh in a mocking tone because she's absolutely ridiculous.

Emery goes to stand, but I knock her down again. "You're going to live to regret ever taking this girl's side. Mark my words." I can feel someone pulling me back by the shoulders, but I keep spewing all the hateful words I've wanted to say for so long. "Three years from now when you're tending bars and eight months pregnant, I hope you remember how good you had it before you stabbed me in the back."

"Is that a threat?" Emery hisses with stone-cold eyes. "What could you possibly do to hurt me?"

I chuckle deviously, giving her no response. I don't know what I plan to do to hurt them, but I will find a way.

"Come on. They're not worth it," the voice from behind me says. I glance over my shoulder and see that it's Paxton. All this time, I thought maybe it was Blaise. Instead, Blaise is standing at his locker with the door open while he watches everything unfold.

Paxton pulls me away while Emery helps Lilith up. My heart hurts. It's a pain I've felt time and time again over the last couple months.

Choking down the lump in my throat, I follow Paxton's lead. "They'll get what's coming to them."

We approach Blaise as we walk down the hall and I'm still fired up when I slam his locker door shut. "Do you see why I can't let it go?" I shout loud enough for everyone to hear.

He just looks at me like I'm washed-up garbage.

Why do these people hate me so much?

As soon as we're away from the crowd, I stop, crouching down with my head between my knees. "I can't do this. This fake bullshit. Maybe I was stupid for coming back."

"You're brave for coming back. A lot braver than I would have been." Paxton kneels beside me and places a calming hand on my back. "I'm going to help you, Penelope. I promise."

I look up and see the delicacy in his eyes. I've only known Paxton for a short time, but so far, he's the kindest person I've met in this town. It would be so easy for him to just turn his back on me, knowing the repercussions of being my friend, but he doesn't.

"Thank you," I say to him, in all seriousness.

Paxton helps me up and we head out to a picnic table in the courtyard for lunch. It's pretty cold out, and there are light snowflakes falling, but I prefer it out here, away from the crowd of miscreants.

"So," Paxton begins as he unpacks his lunch—we opted on grabbing brown bag lunches from the cafeteria to avoid the line. "I did a little digging and it shouldn't be too hard to tap into the school records. As far as Chase goes, I just need his address and I'll…"

Paxton's words trail off and I follow his gaze behind me. "Just fucking great," Paxton growls.

I turn around momentarily before returning to my sandwich. "What do you want, Blaise?" There's a glimmer of possessiveness in his eyes that tells me this won't be a pleasant encounter.

"Aren't you two just the cutest little outcast couple?" There's a sarcastic bite to his words, but I think he's just jealous.

Paxton blushes and takes a bite of a granola bar. "We're friends. Nothing more. Nothing less."

I chime in with my two cents. "Even if we were more than friends, it's not your business."

"Actually, it is. You're staying in my house and I'd prefer if you don't socialize with the likes of this loser."

My eyes roll as I spin around on the bench. "And what makes him a loser, Blaise? Being my friend?"

"No. That actually makes him a disobedient fool. What makes him a loser is the fact that no one likes him."

"Yeah. Thanks to you."

"Truth be told, it's thanks to you." Blaise grabs me by the arm and pulls. "Would you excuse us, Paxton? I need a word with my sister."

Against my better judgment, I don't fight back. Might as well hear him out so he can be on his way.

"Why would it be my fault that no one likes him?" I ask, jerking my arm until it's out of his hold.

"His downfall began at the Devil's Night Party last year when he was feeling you up. So, it's your fault he had to be shunned."

That's right! Before I was lured to the farmhouse, Blaise beat Paxton up. It slipped my mind, but now it makes total sense. "You beat him up because he was touching me?" Blaise is exaggerating on that heavily. Paxton put an innocent hand on my knee, that's all.

He raises a lazy shoulder. "Rules are rules."

"He was new. He didn't even know about your stupid rule. I thought you just didn't like him. Why would you care if he touched me?"

Blaise's cheeks flush lobster red, but he doesn't respond. "Just go eat somewhere else and stay away from him."

"No!" I spit out before heading back to the table. I glance over my shoulder and see that Blaise is still standing there. "Just ignore him. He'll go away eventually," I tell Paxton.

"Eh, I'm not so sure about that. What sort of fucked-up family life do you have?"

My head turns, and I see out of the corner of my eye that Blaise is still there. "You don't wanna know, believe me."

Paxton takes a drink of his Coke and sets it back down with a cheeky grin. "Ya know. If you wanna get under his skin, I know a way."

"I dunno. I think I've already got myself in enough trouble with Blaise. The outcome of my antics when it comes to him is never good."

"Oh, come on. It'll be funny. Besides, I can take care of myself. I'm not exactly skin and bones. Just follow my lead."

Nervousness washes over me in anticipation of what Paxton's about to do.

Paxton begins leaning across the table and I know exactly

what's coming next. I have no time to stop him as his lips meet mine in a soft kiss. It's completely causal. Closed-mouth, no fireworks display, no instant chemistry.

Before I can even close my eyes, Paxton is being pulled away. I jump up from my seat and hurry to the other side of the table, throwing myself between them.

"Touch her again and you're dead," Blaise howls.

My arms stretch out between them and I glare at Blaise. "Would you stop it? It was perfectly innocent."

"You kissed him!" he snaps back.

I drop the hand that was extended toward Paxton and shove both of my palms into Blaise's chest. "So what?"

There's anger behind his eyes, but more than that, there's despair. "Why the hell would you do that?"

Suddenly, this little prank doesn't seem so little. I actually feel bad, like I betrayed Blaise in some way.

"It was nothing," I say softly.

"It didn't look like nothing!"

I glance behind me and see Paxton packing up his lunch.

"Blaise, I can promise you I have no interest in Paxton and he is not interested in me. He's just helping me since you won't."

"Why are you so fucking naive? Of course he is. You're drop dead gorgeous and smart as hell."

Butterflies flutter through my stomach. "You think I'm gorgeous?"

Blaise raises his shoulders tensely, almost like he just realized what he said. "Grab your food. You're eating with me."

"At your table?" I shake my head. "No thanks."

Paxton is walking away and I should go grab him and apologize, or thank him, rather. I'm not really sure. The plan was to piss Blaise off and it worked, but I feel bad that he finished his lunch and I haven't even eaten anything again.

Blaise pivots around and tosses my sandwich in the

brown bag. "Yes, at my table." He starts walking off, and I follow behind him.

"Wait. I can't sit with you."

"Why the hell not?" he huffs, taking long strides toward the open cafeteria doors.

"Because people will wonder why. You've never been nice to me."

"Fuck everyone else."

I finally catch up to him when we're approaching the table full of students, who never even looked in my direction all the years I went here.

All eyes shoot to Blaise, then to me. "Guys, you remember Penelope?"

They nod and welcome me with a "hey, hi, hello," while Blaise pulls out a chair for me to sit down.

I'm a ball of nerves when I'm finally settled in my chair and I hate the attention laser-focused on me. Blaise takes it upon himself to pull my half-eaten sandwich back out of the bag and hands it to me. It's actually pretty embarrassing how much he's catering to me.

I look over at him and notice that he's not paying any attention to the gawking of the people around us—he's just watching me.

One bite has my mouth parched. It feels like I haven't had water in days. My dry lips smack together as I chew, then I swallow hard, feeling the ball of bread slide down. Should I say something? Ask about the weather?

"So, are you two like an item?" a girl sitting beside Blaise asks. I've seen her before, but I don't know her name.

Everyone laughs, so I join in like it's comical.

"She's his fucking sister, you idiot," Wade barks at her.

"Stepsister," I blurt out. The girl looks at me as I correct Wade. "Our parents were married. We're not *actually* brother and sister."

Blaise tosses an arm over my shoulder and gathers me

under him like he's this big, protective brother. "Close enough."

Bile rises up my throat, forcing out my bite of sandwich.

"I'm Roxanne, by the way." The girl leans across the table, bumping food trays and milk cartons as she goes. "You two, like, live together?" the girl asks as I shake her hand back. Her poking and prodding has me wondering if she's got a thing for Blaise.

"Sure do," Blaise says.

I shake my head and squirm out from under his arm. "Just until I graduate, then I'm going to Arvine University. Blaise's dad, my delightful stepfather, is paying my tuition."

Blaise looks at me with wandering eyes. "Really?"

"Yup." I know he's surprised that I'm actually accepting the money. For a while, I wanted nothing to do with it, but now, I look at it as a way to make my future brighter.

"Interesting." Roxanne taps a finger to her chin. "And Arvine, huh?"

"It's my dream school."

"Isn't that nice. It'll be like a little high school reunion," Roxanne says with a sarcastic knock to her statement.

"How so?" I take another bite of my sandwich, awaiting her response.

"Oh, you don't know? Half of the people at this table are going to Arvine, including Blaise."

This time I choke and cough and hack. It's actually pretty gross.

"Are you okay?" Roxanne asks.

I break through my coughing fit and finally swallow down the bite, chasing it with my water. "Yeah. I'm fine."

"Thank God. We wouldn't want Blaise's *sister* dying at our table." Roxanne chuckles annoyingly.

Once I've got my reflexes under control, I look at Blaise. "I didn't know you were going to Arvine. I thought you planned to leave Washington."

Blaise shrugs his shoulders. "Changed my mind."

This is a weird turn of events that has me wondering if I should change my plans. Spending four years at a school with Blaise sounds like temptation on a silver platter.

When the lunch bell rings, everyone scatters without even a goodbye. I take my time packing up my trash and Blaise stays sitting.

"That wasn't so bad, was it?" he says, stretching his arms out on either side of him and resting them on the back of the chairs to his left and right.

"I wish you'd stop telling everyone we're family."

"Maybe I will if you stop digging into the past."

"This again, really?" I walk toward the garbage can, and Blaise jumps up to follow.

"Yes, this again. How exactly is the new kid helping you?"

Once I've dropped my trash, we leave the cafeteria, walking side by side down the hall. "He's helping me dig up dirt on Lilith, Chase, and Emery. When I have it, I'll use it to get answers."

Blaise drops his head back and sighs heavily with his hands snug in the front pockets of his jeans.

"Let it go, Penny." He drags out the words. "You're gonna regret this."

I stop walking and turn to face him. "For the last time, I'm not letting it go. And to be honest, it really bothers me that you are taking their side."

"I hate those fuckers as much as you do. How am I taking their side?"

We start walking again and I lay it out there for him. "If you were on my side, then you'd help me. I know we've never been friends, but I thought we made some sort of progress last time I was here. I guess I was wrong."

My pace quickens and Blaise grabs my shoulder. "Wait."

I take a deep breath and look at him. He glances around at

the students hustling to get to class and licks his lips. "Follow Lilith after basketball practice. You'll get what you need."

His hand drops from my shoulder and he walks away.

Repeating the words over and over in my head, I'm shocked that Blaise actually gave me something useful.

Follow Lilith after basketball practice. You'll get what you need. It's a start.

CHAPTER 26
PENELOPE

I'M SWEATING SO bad I'm almost positive the girls in the locker room will be able to sniff me out. They just had two hours of basketball practice and I probably still smell worse than they do.

Practice cut out twenty minutes ago and I can still hear them chattering from where I'm hiding in the janitor's closet.

It's starting to feel suffocating. I take a deep breath of the heavy air as I look at the time on my phone.

Five-fifty.

For the love of God, go home and shower.

Voices come closer and I hold my breath, trying not to make a sound.

"See ya at class tomorrow," one of the girls says.

"Bye, Lil," another says.

"Good practice, ladies," comes from the coach.

I listen intently to the footsteps as they slowly subdue.

"About time," I hear Lilith say. "I thought they'd never leave."

Yeah. You and me both. Wait. Who is she talking to?

Lilith begins giggling and I can see the shuffle of feet in

the light through the crack under the door. "That tickles. Oh my God, stop." She giggles some more.

Who the hell is she with?

My heart begins racing in anticipation of finding out.

"Let's go to my office before one of the janitors sees us."

No way! Lilith and Coach Anderson? This is insane. A smile draws on my face. This is really fricken good. I have to get out of here and get proof. With this sort of leverage on Lilith, she's sure to crack and admit the truth about the night of the fire.

My hands press to the cold, hard floor, and I push myself up. Stretching my arms, I work out the kinks in my spine from stuffing myself in a corner for over an hour. Desperation at its finest.

With my ear pressed to the door, I listen.

Nothing.

I grip the handle and turn it slowly. "What?" I gasp, trying again.

Oh, no!

I shake the handle, trying to open the door, but it's no use, it's locked.

"You have got to be kidding me." Did I really just lock myself in the janitor's closet when I had Lilith's secret within reach?

I immediately unlock the screen on my phone. I could call Paxton, but that just feels weird. I only met the guy yesterday. Well, technically we met at the Devil's Night Party, but...oh my God, stop thinking so much.

Without a second thought, I hit Blaise's name on my contact list.

It rings and I tap my foot on the floor, hoping like hell he answers.

"Hello," he says on the other end of the call.

"Uh, thank God. Blaise, I've got myself into a little pickle."

I bite hard at the corner of my lip, feeling my tooth puncture the skin.

"And how does one get into a pickle? I can see how a pickle would get into you. It actually sounds kinda kinky. We should try it."

"Would you stop talking? Listen, I did what you said and was ready to follow Lilith after practice. In fact, I heard her and Coach Anderson but… I sort of got myself locked in the janitor's closet."

Blaise busts out laughing, and it's so obnoxious that I have to pull my ear away from the phone.

"It's not funny. I'm seriously stuck here."

His laughter continues to erupt, infuriating me further. "Blaise," I bark, "I'm in the one next to the girls' locker room. Come get me out of here."

"I could come get you, but you'd owe me one."

"Fine!" I stammer, "Just hurry."

Being indebted to Blaise is risky. At this point, though, I'll gladly do whatever he wants if it means leaving this closet unscathed. It suddenly feels like the walls are closing in, ready to swallow me whole.

So much for getting proof of Lilith and Coach Anderson's illicit affair. It doesn't matter, though. Now I know, so I can catch them next time. Once I do, the ball will be in my court.

Twenty long minutes later, I hear footsteps drudging down the hall. I shoot up from my sitting position and go to the door.

"Penny," Blaise whispers.

"Yes. I'm here." I start twisting the handle again, knowing full well that it's not going to open.

"Would you stop that? I can't get the pick in there if you're wiggling it."

I take a step back, knees knocking in anticipation. *Please let him get it unlocked.*

Seconds later, the door opens and light floods the closet.

Throwing myself into Blaise's arms, I breathe out a sigh of relief, then realize what I just did. Dusting off his arms from my touch, I retreat. "Sorry. I just got a little excited."

Blaise looks down at me. "What are you sorry for?"

I give him a sideways glance, wondering if he's fucking with me. But the look on his face says he's serious. "Throwing myself at you."

"You don't have to apologize—" His words end when he shoves me into the closet. "Shh. Someone's coming."

Unintentionally, I hold tight to his arm. "Do you think it's them?"

"Shh!"

The steps come closer, and Lilith's annoying laugh carries into the closet. My eyes shoot wide open. "It is them."

"I said, shhh!"

My entire body is shaking, my arms hugging tightly to Blaise's strong bicep.

"Gimme your phone," Blaise whispers.

I hand it to him and he unlocks the screen with my passcode. "Hey! How did you know that?"

He doesn't respond, just cracks the door a bit more and opens the camera on my phone.

One shot, two shots, and then a video. I can see on the screen that Lilith and Coach Anderson are kissing, likely a kiss goodbye after a quickie in his office. I still can't believe she's sleeping with him. He's married with two young kids.

Blaise backsteps and slowly closes the door. "Got her."

Once again, I throw myself in his arms then immediately back off. This time, though, Blaise doesn't let me loosen my hold on him. He pulls my body flush with his, one hand on my waist. "Seems you owe me one, Penny Pie. I'd like to collect right now."

My neck cranes as I try to look at him in the darkness. There's only a small sliver of light shining into the room, and

I can't see his face to know if he's being serious. "Right now, right now?"

"Mmhmm. Right now." He pushes my head down, but I resist.

"I'm not doing that here!"

His hand slides up my sweatshirt, fingers grazing the skin along my rib cage. "I could leave and close the door behind me, locking you in here. A deal is a deal."

"You wouldn't!"

"You're right, I wouldn't. But I still wanna collect."

"Someone could catch us. Could you imagine how everyone would react?"

"School's out. Everyone's gone home. Live a little," he says, pressing his lips to my neck and planting kisses down to my collarbone.

My head tilts instinctively and goosebumps cascade down my body. I'm at his mercy when he pops the button of my jeans.

This is really happening.

I take in a shaky breath when he slides his hand down my pants and beneath my underwear.

"Relax, baby."

The way he says baby makes my insides quiver, causing me to lift my leg, propping it on a box for better access.

Blaise wraps a warm arm around me, beneath my shirt, and pulls me close, continuing to iron out my neck with his lips. His skin against mine is everything.

Two fingers rake up my slit and begin rubbing feverish circles around my clit. My body jolts at the rush of adrenaline coursing through me.

This boy has been many things: my tormentor, my enemy, my saving grace, and now a man with magical fingers. He has a name in these halls for being high-handed. Being here with him, right now, makes me feel like I hold just as much power.

A moan escapes me when his pace quickens. "Oh God,

Blaise," I whimper, biting on the collar of his hoodie while his teeth graze the skin of my collarbone.

His fingers dip inside me, sliding in and out in a slow and rhythmic motion. My body fills with an insatiable heat. Burning from the inside out as I grind against his hand.

My arm descends and I stuff my hand down his joggers, getting a nice grip on his cock. So hard and hungry, just for me. I did this to him.

Blaise curls his fingers inside of me causing my eyes to roll in the back of my head.

With his cock in my hand, I slide my fingers up and down with the little space I'm given. His above average length makes it hard with his pants still on.

Sounds I didn't even know I could make escape me as he begins drumming against my G-spot. It doesn't even matter that we're at school in a closet, I'd gladly let him do whatever he wants to me if it feels this good.

Blaise growls a raspy sound in my ear. "Tell me you like it."

"I fucking love it." My own admission has my heart beating rapidly.

"You've got a dirty mouth now, Penny. You never used to talk like that. Maybe I need to shove my cock in it and wash it out with my cum."

God, his words are so degrading, but they only arouse me further.

"Is that what you want? Do you wanna suck my cock?"

I wanna tell him no. He needs to keep doing what he's doing because I'm almost there.

"Yes," I cry out when he moves faster, digging deeper.

Blaise lifts his head and looks at me. He bites hard on his lip with a lust-filled expression. It's a vulnerable moment, him watching me as I'm on the brink of explosion.

I rest my head on his shoulder, but he shakes it off. "Look at me. I wanna see your face when you come on my hand."

Doing as I'm told, I lift my head. Our gazes hold as my entire body fills up with a dire need of release. Tingles shoot through me from head to toe. With a held breath, I clench my walls around his fingers and howl in immense pleasure.

"That's right, baby. Keep going."

He doesn't stop. Just keeps finger-fucking me and before I know it, I'm soaring again. Soaking my jeans and filling his hand with my release.

I try to steady my heavy breaths when he pulls his hand out of my pants, and the next thing I know, I'm on my knees. His cock springs free from his joggers, and he slides them down to his ankles.

Without instruction, I immediately take the shallow end of his cock in my mouth. My tongue swirls around his head, licking up a salty bead of precum.

Stroking and sucking, I do the best I can with the little experience I have. The last time—the only time—I did this, it was forced. My mouth pools with saliva and I attempt to push the thoughts away.

Blaise rolls his hips, fingers wrapped around the ponytail on my head. He tugs, forcing my head to drop back with my mouth still on him. I look up and see him peering down at me with watchful eyes.

"Damn. You're a fucking pro. Have you done this before?"

I swallow hard and watch as he does the same, then I break our stare.

"Shit, Penny. I forgot."

Shaking my head, I keep sucking, hoping he doesn't turn this into a big deal. I'm not surprised he remembers. What Chase did only elevated his hatred for him. It was the final knife in his back that ended their friendship.

Blaise pulls back, his cock leaving my mouth, but I keep my hand on him and slide it up and down his length, using my saliva as lube. "What are you doing?" I ask, licking the wetness from my lips.

"You can stop."

"Blaise," I drag out his name. "Don't make this a thing. It's fine."

I've accepted what happened and I rarely even think about it. The only reason I did now is because it's the first time I've done this since the incident.

"A deal is a deal. Now quit trying to be nice." My lip curls into a smile. "We both know you're not."

Blaise exhales a laugh. "You're right, I'm not. Now bend over."

He pulls me up until I'm on my feet, wraps an arm around my stomach and bends me over. My hands find the shelf on the back wall, and I use the bottom one as a base.

The second my jeans come down, I'm practically fiending like an addict to have him inside me. The idea of getting caught is terrifying, but exciting at the same time. It's a rush I've never felt before. Blaise wastes no time shoving his cock inside of me. There is nothing gentle about the way he fills me up, pulls himself out, and does it again, and again.

My nails dig into the wooden shelf, splinters burrowing beneath my fingernails. It's been so long and the way he stretches me open is both painful and pleasurable.

Blaise grunts as he pounds into me, his balls slapping against my pussy. Two hands pinch my shoulders tightly, using them as cushioning for his drive.

"Fuck, Penny. You're so warm. Let me stay forever."

My heart skips a beat then falls right back into a pounding rhythm. Blaise and I both moan in unison as we reach the height of our climax. He thrusts a couple more times, grunting and pulling my hair harder before coming to a dead stop.

We both remain still as we steady our heart rates. "Wow," I say through a heady breath.

Blaise drops his hold on my ponytail and slides out of me, evidence of our orgasms spilling down my leg.

Normally regret would consume me at this point, but I'm not even sorry I allowed this to happen. In fact, I'm feeling pretty satisfied as I wipe myself up with some paper towels I found on a shelf. Fortunately, I started taking birth control when I returned to Portland. Not because I planned on sleeping with anyone, but I like to err on the side of caution.

Once all articles of clothing are back in place, Blaise and I just stand there looking at each other. I'm waiting for him to say something, though I think he's waiting for the same.

"Thanks for your help today," I finally say, trying hard to hide the smile that is pulling at my lips.

He winks, warmth blanketing my body. "Thanks for the closet quickie."

I swat playfully at his arm then push the closet door open. "Let's get out of here."

We're walking down the hall to leave and I'm totally shocked at how much Blaise has changed since the last time I arrived in Skull Creek. I'm not sure who to thank for that, but I decide to ask the burning question in my mind. "Can I ask you something?"

"Shoot."

"Don't get mad, 'kay?"

Blaise gives me a sideway glance. "Not a good way to start this conversation, Pen. What's on your mind?"

I pull my keys out of the side pocket of my bag and fidget with the lucky penny keychain my dad gave me last summer. "Did you ever find your mom?" Bringing up this topic of conversation never ends well, but I'm hopeful he won't lash out at me this time.

His eyes stay straight ahead as we walk, and I watch him out of the corner of my eye. His content expression shifts to something blank and unreadable. "No."

"Have you tried?"

We keep walking, but he still hasn't answered by the time we approach his car, so I follow him to the driver's side door. He grabs the handle, stops, and looks at me. "No. I haven't tried." The door opens, and he climbs inside. Before he closes it, he says, "See ya at home, Penny."

Blaise takes off, burning rubber as he exits the parking lot. I walk at an amble pace, keys dangling at my side, thinking about what I can do to help him.

If anyone had asked me a year ago if I'd ever do anything to help Blaise, I'd laugh. It's just that he's all alone and it has to be sad sometimes. I sure as hell was when I lived in this house. Not to mention, his dad died, he has no siblings—aside from me, which doesn't even count—his mom is gone, and all his friends, except Wade, are douchebags.

By the time I reach my car, I have a plan. I really don't want to do it, but I think I need to go see my mom.

CHAPTER 27
BLAISE

IT'S past dark and she's still not here. *Where the hell could she be?* It's not like she has any friends in this town. Then it hits me. I bet she's with that fuckboy, Paxton.

I try to call her again, but just like every other time, it goes straight to fucking voicemail.

"Dammit!" I slam my phone down on the kitchen counter.

"Should I put dinner away?" Henry asks, peering at the lasagna I asked him to make.

I know Penny likes it. Wanted to do something special for her after her long day, but apparently, my kindness, though rare, goes unnoticed once again.

"Yeah. Put it away. She can warm it up later if she's hungry." I snatch my phone off the counter aggressively and walk with heavy steps to the basement door.

Just as I open it, the door to the mudroom flies open and in walks Penny.

Slamming the basement door shut, I close the space between us. "Where the hell have you been?"

Penny examines me with a raised eyebrow. "I was out. Why?"

"No shit you were out. Where?" I'm trying hard to push down my frustration, but she's staying in my house and doesn't even have the decency to answer my calls. She could have been dead in a ditch for all I know.

She slides an arm out of her jacket, then the other, and folds it over her arm with shifty eyes. "I went to see my mom."

Her feet move past me and I follow behind her. "Your mom?"

Penny takes a look at the spread of food on the counter. "This looks good. I'm starving."

I grab her jacket from her hands and toss it on the kitchen table. "Quit changing the subject. What made you decide to go see your mom?"

Spinning on her heels, she faces me with agitation. "Do I need a reason? She's my mom."

Henry begins setting dinnerware at the table for me and Penny, completely ignoring us, though, I'm sure he's listening.

"She might be your mom, but she's also a royal bitch that you can't stand. So yeah, there has to be a reason."

"Thank you, Henry," Penny says, taking her seat. "I love lasagna."

"You're welcome, Ms. Briar. But you should thank Mr. Hale. It was his idea."

Henry walks out of the room, leaving us alone.

Penny looks at me with a lecherous stare. "Did you do this for me?" There's a glint of a smile on her lips.

"It's nothing. Now tell me about your mom."

"You remembered?"

"It's a meal. Not a fucking trip to the Eiffel Tower." Why is she beating around my questions and acting so shifty?

Or am I the one acting strange? Fuck. I dunno.

"It's sweet," she says, rubbing her hands over the sleeve of my arms. "Now drop the hardass charade and come eat with me."

I glower at her a moment longer before my shoulders fall and I take her hand, leading her over to the table.

Penny scoops us both a piece of lasagna and we each grab some of the garlic bread.

After I take a bite, I continue to pry, "Was your mom happy to see you?"

She chuckles. "Is that woman ever happy to see anyone?"

"Right. Dumb question. Well, did you get what you went there for?"

Her fork stabs into the lasagna and she lowers her eyebrows. "No."

Part of me is pleased with that answer. I don't know what she expected, but I hope it wasn't a relationship with that wretched bitch. Then again, I might have to come to terms with that possibility at some point in the future.

I don't even know why I'm thinking like this. It's not like Penny is a permanent fixture in my life. *Is she?*

We continue to eat while that thought lingers like a dark cloud. I'm not sure what will happen next. Penny said she's going to Arvine U, which was my plan, too. For fuck's sake, I'm going to end up burning the entire school down if I have to watch her get hit on by college guys left and right. Maybe us attending the same four-year university is a bad idea. *Unless we go together.*

Sure as hell would be nice to have her at my beck and call for a blowie or a quick fuck. Might also keep the lonely nights at bay. I'm starting to enjoy her company.

What the hell am I thinking?

"What are you thinking about?" Penny asks, snapping me out of my trance.

"Are you really accepting tuition money from me and going to Arvine U?"

She blows out a laugh. "That's what you've been thinking about?"

"Well, are you?"

She forks her lasagna and takes another bite with her elbows pressed to the table. Our parents would have a field day with that one if they were around. "I thought about it. I've got the grades, I just never had the money, until now. What about you?"

I'm still surprised that she's accepting anything from me that came from my dad. "Yeah. I mean, that's been my plan since freshman year. But you knew that, didn't you?"

Penny pins a hard glare on me. "Are you insinuating that I'm following you there?"

Slumping my shoulders, I lean back in the chair. "I don't care if you are. I'm actually flattered that you love my cock enough to follow it to college. That's four years of hardcore sex. Are you ready for that?"

"That's all you think about, isn't it?" She shakes her head with a grin on her face. "For your information, I'm not following you. They have a great communications program that I'd like to enroll in. What about you? What are you thinking of majoring in?"

"Business. Maybe. I'd like to start something of my own that I can pass down to future generations."

"I like that." She smiles.

"All right then. It's settled. We're going to school together."

"Together?" Her teeth bite into a chunk of garlic bread.

"Okay. We're going to the same school. How's that?"

She shrugs her shoulders with a smirk on her lips.

Looks like Penny and I get four more years together.

The rest of dinner, I watch her when she doesn't realize I am, and my heart jumps every time our eyes catch.

Fuck. I'm falling hard for this girl. And it's only a matter of time before I have to watch her heart break in two, especially now that she's going after Lilith with proof of Coach Anderson's affair. I might just have to tell her the truth about the fire before it's revealed by someone else.

CHAPTER 28
PENELOPE

LYING to Blaise today wasn't part of my plan. I didn't think he'd drill me about going to my mom's house. Didn't think he'd really care. I mean, why would he? I know he hates her, but she's still my mom.

The truth is, I did get what I went there for. It cost me every dime Blaise put in my savings account, but it was worth it in the end. I got information on where his mom might be and there's no price tag on reuniting Blaise with his mom.

My phone begins buzzing in the front pocket of my hoodie, so I walk away from the kitchen table where Blaise and I were studying. It's so weird doing normal, everyday things with him, like eating dinner, doing homework.

It's Paxton.

"Hey," I whisper.

"You got a minute to meet up?"

I walk out of the kitchen quietly and steal a look at Blaise, who has his nose stuffed in a history book.

"Yeah. Where at?"

"Could you just come to my house? I'll text ya the address."

"All right. I'll wait for it."

I end the call and take one last glance at Blaise to make sure he doesn't notice. If he sees me leaving, he'll ask a million questions I don't have answers for. My guess is that Paxton got the school records I asked him to get.

With soft steps, I go upstairs and get my keys off my dresser, then sneak back down and out the front door.

It's freezing out, and I wish I'd grabbed a jacket, but I can't risk going back inside.

A text comes through from Paxton with his address and I'm surprised at the location. He lives on the same street as Chase. In fact, he's only a couple houses down from him.

Maybe it wasn't the school records he got, maybe he got some intel on Chase for me.

My entire body shivers as I climb in the driver's seat and close the door. I start the engine and immediately crank up the heat. "Easy on Me" by Adele plays through the speakers, and I sing along as I make the short drive.

I'm following my GPS to make sure I get the right house, and sure enough, he's practically Chase's neighbor. Only two hundred yards separate their two houses. Paxton's is a little more welcoming with a manicured lawn and all the shingles in place. It's small, though. It has me wondering if he's an only child.

Before I even open my car door, Paxton is walking down the paved driveway. He's wearing a pair of black sweatpants, a cut-off t-shirt, and white socks, with no shoes.

Instead of coming to the driver's side window, he goes to the passenger door and gets in. "Hey, sorry. I'm watching my little sister and can't leave the house."

There goes my assumption that he's an only child. "Aww, you have a little sister?"

"Two of them. Natalie is eight, she's the one I'm watching. Cadence is fifteen and mostly stays in her room."

'That's awesome. I always wanted a little sister."

"They're not all they're cracked up to be. So, is Blaise your only sibling?"

"Ugh," I grumble. "I hate when people call him that. Yes and no." My head wafts back and forth. "Our parents married when I was fourteen. I only lived with them for a couple years before I moved in with my dad. His dad passed away a couple months ago, and at this point, I don't think of him as a brother."

Paxton laughs. "Probably better that way. No brother should look at his sister the way Blaise looks at you."

"Whaaaat? Blaise doesn't look at me a certain way."

Paxton shifts in his seat so that his body is facing me. "Girl, he most *definitely* does. You've only been here for a couple days and I can already tell he's got it bad for you."

I'm not sure why that comes as a surprise to me. After all, I did just have sex with him a few hours ago. Not to mention, he's been oddly sweet and attentive. Even had dinner made just for me.

"What about you?" I ask, changing the subject. "Do you have an interest in any of the students of the almighty Skull Creek High?"

He sweeps the air with his hand. "Nah. None of the people here are my type."

"Well, what's your type? Maybe I can help."

Paxton laughs. "Probably not the type you're thinking of."

I want to ask him, but I'm worried my assumption is way off, like it usually is. "You like… I mean—"

"Guys?" he interrupts, "Yes. Am I that obvious?"

"I didn't want to ask and be wrong. It's crazy, I barely know you, but I feel like we've been friends forever."

"It's not crazy. I actually don't make friends easily. At my old school, I was sort of a hothead. Wasn't always the nicest guy to be around. Once I came out, I just felt like a new person. I was no longer on constant defense."

"Well, I'm glad you came and sat by me at the party last semester. If it weren't for that night, I'd probably be too afraid to approach you. I don't make friends easily, either."

Paxton looks taken aback. "Wait a minute. What party?"

My head slants as I look at him to see if he's serious. "The Devil's Night Party? The night before Halloween? You came and sat next to me by the fire and we were talking when the fight broke loose."

Paxton's expression goes blank. He turns his head, staring out the windshield, then he looks back at me. "That was you? Shit," he runs his fingers through his hair, "I had no idea. I mean, it was a good conversation, but I actually came and sat down that night to try and make someone jealous." He laughs. "I had no idea it was you."

"Really?" I'm actually taken aback. I would think he'd recognize my voice. Not that it's important at all. "Who were you trying to make jealous?"

"It was stupid. Just some junior that I had a little thing for. He's in a relationship now and it doesn't even matter. I can't believe I didn't know it was you this entire time. That was right before I got my ass handed to me."

"Yeah," I sigh. "Blaise should have never done that. I didn't even know it was him until later that night.

Paxton clamps his fingers into a vise grip and looks like he's seen a ghost.

"What's wrong?"

"It was Blaise? Penelope, I've been trying to figure out who jumped me ever since that night. I didn't know it was him." He drops back in the seat. "I should have fucking known. It makes sense, though. He did it because I was talking to you. Because he has some sick obsession." Anger takes hold of Paxton as he slams his fist into the dash. I jump back, startled at his outburst. "Screw that rich bastard. I'm gonna kill him."

"Paxton. Let it go, please. Blaise has changed."

"Like hell he has," he shouts. "He is still the same guy he was then and he wouldn't hesitate to break the bones of any guy who so much as looks at you."

My heart splinters in two at the thought of Paxton hurting Blaise, even if he did hurt him first… "What…what are you gonna do?"

"I don't know. But I'm doing something. I gotta go." He reaches for the door handle, but I grab his arm to stop him.

"Wait. Did you call me here because you got some information?" I feel selfish for even asking, but I need to know what he found out.

"I'll text you the video. Tell your *brother* he better watch his fucking back."

Paxton gets out and slams the door shut behind him. I sink back into the seat and wish I'd kept my damn mouth shut.

Two minutes later, my phone beeps, and I pick it up from the center dash.

It's a text from Paxton.

Paxton: I'm not mad at you. I'm mad at him. Sorry I lashed out. Hope this video helps with your retribution.

I wait anxiously as the video loads.

"Come on. Come on."

It starts playing and I turn up the volume on my phone, the sound coming through the speakers of my car.

It's a video of Chase. He's standing in his front yard with an older man I don't recognize. It's not the same guy I took to be his dad. He looks left, then right, and hands the guy a bag of some sort. Their voices are too far away, so I can't hear anything but Paxton's breathing.

"Looks like Chase is making a drug deal," Paxton's voice comes through the speaker. "I'd say cocaine by the looks of it."

Holy shit!

The guy hands Chase a wad of cash, then shakes his hand and walks toward a shiny black car.

"Do your thing, girl," Paxton says before the video cuts out.

I got you, you son of a bitch.

CHAPTER 29
PENELOPE

BLAISE never even noticed I left last night. In fact, he was still at the table studying when I got back. I was mentally exhausted from the knowledge I learned, and the knowledge I shared, so I took a quick shower and went to bed.

Regret consumed me when I woke up this morning. I wish I'd never told Paxton that it was Blaise who attacked him. I seriously had no idea he didn't know.

Stupid. So fucking stupid.

Regardless, I need to rectify things. Paxton seems to be a good person and he's been kind to me, so I'd like to try and fix this.

"Blaise," I say, poking my head in the basement door. I don't know why he still stays down here when he has this entire house. It's always been his comfort zone, so I guess it does make sense that he'd avoid the change.

I push the door open farther and go down the stairs. "Hey," I say, catching him off guard.

His eyes lift from his phone. "Good morning." His tone is placid and he seems distracted. "I'm glad you came down. I need to talk to you about something. It has to do with—"

"Actually, I need to talk to you, too." I have to get this out before school. I'm so worried about what Paxton might do and what Blaise will do to him in return. It could be bad. It could be really bad.

Blaise sticks his phone in the front pocket of his black jeans. He's all dressed for school with a solid white t-shirt that hugs tightly to his muscular frame, and a pair of black boots. "Okay. You go first."

"Remember at the Devil's Night Party when you attacked Paxton?"

His eyes snap to me. "Wait. How did you know that?"

"I saw you, Blaise. You attacked him right in front of me. It was your mask."

"You didn't see shit."

"I know what I saw, dammit." I can feel myself growing angry with his failure of admission. "You beat him up because he was talking to me, then you ostracized him."

Blaise sweeps his hand through the air, blowing out a heavy breath. "All right. Fuck!" He raises his voice a few octaves. "He had his slimy hand on your leg. Something snapped inside of me and I lost control."

"And you couldn't just admit that you lost control? Instead, you had to continue to make his first and only year at this school hell?"

"He stole my fucking spot on the team."

This conversation is going nowhere.

"Then you stole it back and gave it to someone else. For what? Power?"

"What's done is done. So you know it was me. What are you gonna do, rat me out?"

I walk closer, hoping this conversation smooths out a bit and doesn't escalate into a screaming match. "I had no idea he didn't know it was you and I may have slipped to Paxton."

Blaise shrugs his shoulders as if I just told him there was a chance of rain today. "So what? I don't care if he knows. I just never made it a point to relay the information."

"Whew. Okay, good. I'm glad for that. The thing is, he's really pissed, and I'm worried he's going to retaliate."

He laughs and laughs and laughs.

"Blaise," I snap. "This isn't funny."

He walks toward me and puts an arm around my neck. "Come on, Pen. We need to get to school."

"What if he jumps you or starts a fight? I don't want you to fight back and hurt him. He's been a good friend to me."

"Yeah," Blaise glares at me condescendingly, "a friend who wants to bone you."

My head shakes. He's so insistent that Paxton has a thing for me. It's not my place to share Paxton's business, although he did say he's out. Either way, I'm not going there. "Even if Paxton was interested in me, I'm not interested in him. So just drop it and please fix things with him. For me." I'm asking a lot, but with this new side Blaise has given me, I'm hopeful he'll consider it.

We're walking upstairs, me in the front, when Blaise smacks my ass.

"Hey," I screech.

"Ride with me to school, and I'll think about it."

"Don't you think people are going to get the wrong idea if we keep spending all this time together? You already invited me to sit with you at lunch, with a table full of people who have all been under the assumption that you hate my guts."

"You really think I give a shit what anyone says about me?"

Honestly, no, I don't think Blaise cares what anyone thinks of him. The thing is, I care. I've had the title of a nobody ever since I stepped foot in this town years ago. I'm a joke to everyone. A continuous prank. The one who stands out because she can't fit in. I came back ready to prove to them I'm more than meets the eye and if rumors spread that Blaise and I have something going on, it will push me down further than I've ever been.

"Wait a minute." Blaise stops walking, stepping right up to me as I pull on my coat in the living room. "You care, don't you?"

"You're technically my stepbrother. Everyone knows that our parents got married."

"Who gives a flying fuck? Screw them, Penny. In ten years, will the opinions of these people really even matter?"

My head tilts to the side as I look at him. He really has changed. Or maybe this Blaise has been in there all along, and I just failed to notice.

I was never trying to hurt you. Maybe I was just trying to protect you.

Those were his words. I know that my first few years in this house Blaise hated me. It was clear as day with how awful he was to me. At the end of my stay, though, I think I grew on him the same way he's grown on me.

"Okay. Humor me. You're saying that you wouldn't care if the entire town knew what we did?"

He smirks, meeting my stare. "What did we do, Penny?"

My eyes close, head shaking with a smile. "You know what we did."

His hands find mine, and my eyes open. "Say it."

"We…had sex. A couple times." It feels so weird saying it out loud.

Blaise grazes his thumb over my knuckles and my heart skips a beat.

"No, I wouldn't care."

And now my heart has doubled in size. There's no hiding my giddiness as I squeeze his hand back. "Okay. Maybe someday we'll stop pretending that there's nothing between us and show the world we're unbreakable."

"Someday?"

"Yeah." I nod. "When I said I didn't come back for you, I

meant it. I came back in search of myself. But I think I found her in you." Being this vulnerable is scary. I'm putting my heart in the palm of his hands and I really hope it doesn't come back to bite me in the ass. Oddly enough, I don't think it will this time. "But I still have to get my answers, so I can fully heal. You understand that, right?"

"About that, Penny." His fingers sweep through his hair. "We're gonna be late for school, but we need to talk soon. There's something I need to tell you."

"Oh?" My eyebrows pull together. "Sounds serious. What is it?"

"Later." He reaches down and grabs my backpack off the floor. "We gotta go."

I don't hassle for more because I need to talk to him, too, and I need more than a couple minutes. He needs to know that I think I found his mom.

MY STOMACH IS in knots as Blaise and I walk side by side through the halls. We're thrown a few awkward glances. People stop with their chatter and stare, wondering why he's hanging out with the girl that he swore off to the entire student body. It's been a couple years, but they haven't forgotten.

Blaise looks over at me and it's like he senses my nervousness. His hand reaches for mine, but I choke and pull away quickly. I'm not sure why I do it. It's petrifying being under the scrutiny of a hundred teenagers who would love nothing more than to voice their opinions in a hostile manner.

Blaise shakes his head and picks up his pace.

"Blaise, wait," I say in a whisper-yell. He keeps going until he's at his locker. It pulls right open and he huffs as he grabs his books off the shelf. "I'm sorry. I'm just not ready—"

"Save it, Penny." He slams his locker shut and narrows his eyes until he's walked past me.

"You don't understand," I shout as he walks away, leaving me standing there with everyone watching.

I feel like I've been kicked in the gut. As soon as I pulled away, I knew he was going to make it something it's not. This isn't about him. I don't care if people know that I've fallen for him.

I'm watching him walk away when Paxton comes out of nowhere and sidles up right behind Blaise. I gasp when I see him cock his fist back. "Blaise," I scream through the hall. But it's too late. Paxton punches the back of Blaise's head, causing him to stumble forward until he trips and falls to the floor. Paxton straddles Blaise's lower half, holding him down. "No!" I begin running down the hall toward him. "Paxton, stop!" I shout as he continues to pummel his fists at Blaise's face repeatedly.

"Stop!" I try again, grabbing Paxton from behind and pulling him backward. He gives his arm a jerk, shaking me off, and resumes laying punches on Blaise.

I see blood. Lots of blood.

My heart drops so far into my stomach. I clap my hands over my mouth as I watch everything unfold.

This isn't happening. This can't be happening.

What feels like minutes—but is more like seconds—later, Paxton is being apprehended by a couple male teachers.

"Blaise," I cry out as I hurry to his side. He looks me right in the eye, blood streaming down his face. I'm not sure where it's coming from. I look around, thinking someone will come help, but no one does. "Someone help him!" Why isn't anyone helping? "It's okay, Blaise." My head rests on his chest and I hold him until one of the staff comes to his side with a first aid kit.

"Holy shit," Wade says from behind me, though I can't see him. I'm too focused on Blaise. "What the hell happened?"

"Miss," one of the teachers says. I'm not sure who she is and I assume she doesn't know me. "We're going to need you to back up, so the ambulance can get to him."

My mind goes foggy, and I can't think straight.

"Miss, we need you to move."

This is all my fault. I told Paxton it was Blaise who attacked him and now he paid him back in full.

"Ma'am!" The lady shouts. "Move, please."

Someone grabs me from behind, pulling me back. I look up and see it's Wade. "Wade, he's going to be okay, right?"

Wade nods, likely telling me what I want to hear.

Two EMTs come walking hurriedly down the hall. "Penny," Blaise grumbles.

Pushing my way to his side again, I lay a hand on his chest. "I'm here."

An EMT tries to steer me away, but I put up a fight, tears falling recklessly down my face. "Let me go. I need to be with him."

As he's rolled away, I hear him one last time. "I lied."

CHAPTER 30
PENELOPE

I LEFT school and went straight to the hospital. Blaise is conscious and he's going to be okay. He has a concussion, needed a few stitches in his head, and has some bruises, but nothing that won't heal. They're keeping him overnight to make sure there's no internal bleeding, but he should be able to come home tomorrow.

I'm so angry at Paxton. He could have handled this in so many different ways and he went with the worst one possible. Not only did he just put a huge target on his back, he likely lost me as a friend.

He's been texting me nonstop, but I've ignored them all. Now that I'm somewhat calmed down, I decide to read them.

Paxton: I'm sorry, Penelope, but he deserved it.

Paxton: Don't be mad at me for doing exactly what he did.

Paxton: I'm sorry. Text me back.

Paxton: Okay. I fucked up. I should have just talked to him, but my anger got the best of me. The guy ruined my chance at getting seen by a recruiter for Arvine University at the game the following week. I don't have the money he does. I needed that ride, Penelope.

Paxton: That doesn't matter. Look, just text me or call, so we can talk. You're the first person to befriend me at this school and I don't want to lose you.

Paxton: You really like this guy, don't you?

I swipe out of the screen and flip my phone over on my lap, looking back at Blaise and watching him sleep.

My heart twinges at the sight of him. He looks so peaceful. This is the first time in my life I've ever seen Blaise in this state. Not because he's injured. Because he's helpless. He's real. Raw. Bold. Beautiful. He's a human with a beating heart who has endured so much loss.

His eyes begin to flutter, and I spring up and go to his side, taking his hand in mine.

"Penny," he says through a cracked voice.

"Yeah. I'm here."

He tries to sit up, but I place a hand on his chest. "Don't get up. You need rest."

His dry lips smack together. "What the hell happened?"

"You got hurt, but you're going to be okay."

"Hurt? How?"

My hand squeezes around his. "There was a fight at school."

He nods as if the memories are coming back to him. "Paxton?"

"Yeah."

His eyes close again. "Gonna kill that little bitch." His mouth falls open as he drifts back to sleep.

I let go of his hand and pick my phone off the bed.

The best friendships usually begin as enemies. After all, that's how me and Blaise got where we are. Maybe there's hope for a friendship between Paxton and Blaise one day.

Me: All right. We can talk.

Paxton texts back immediately.

Paxton: I'm in the waiting room.

Oh, shit. He's here. I haven't left Blaise's room since I

arrived. It never crossed my mind that there could be people out there waiting to see how he's doing.

Blaise is on some pretty heavy meds and sleeping peacefully, so I leave him to go into the waiting room. As soon as I'm visible, Wade and Paxton both jump up.

"How's he doing?" Wade asks, rushing to my side.

I glower at Paxton, hands on my hips. "He's asleep, but he'll be fine. The worst is some stitches on the side of his head. He's gonna be pissed that they had to shave a line of his hair."

"Oh, shit." Wade chuckles. "You're screwed, Pax. He's never forgiving you now."

"Pax?" I say in question, looking at Wade. "Since when are you two friends?"

Wade's eyes skate from me to Paxton. "We're not. I mean, this is the first time we've talked. "

"Mmhmm." I smirk, looking between them. I sense something is going on here. "I find it odd that you're being so kind to the guy who just beat up your best friend."

WADE'S SHOULDERS rise and fall. "Can't say Blaise didn't deserve it. I mean, he kicked Paxton's ass first."

IT'S TRUE, but still, two wrongs don't make a right.

Paxton stands idly by with his hands in his jacket pockets.

"You wanna talk now?" I ask him.

He nods toward the empty chairs and we sit down.

"Look," he begins, "I didn't plan that. I swear I didn't. But he was walking down the hall with a cocky-ass look on his face and I reacted."

Wade takes a seat on the other side of me. "I'm not defending Paxton by any means, but Blaise did do the same shit to him. He's a firm believer in an eye for an eye. He'll get over it."

"I'm just glad he's okay. That's really all that matters to me."

"Guess he won't be crashing Emery's party with me tomorrow night." Wade laughs like it was a joke, but it actually piques my interest.

"Emery's having a party?"

"Uh, yeah. Not that you'd wanna go."

This is perfect. Just the news I needed to put a Band-Aid on this shitty day. "Actually, I'm considering it now."

Wade draws back. "Blaise isn't gonna like this. I really think you should reconsider."

"I need to handle something. Shouldn't take long. Would you mind staying with Blaise while I make an appearance?"

Wade drops his face into his hands, rubbing his temples aggressively. "You're asking for trouble by going to that party."

"Please," I beg of him. "I have to do this. It's important to me."

His head lifts and he looks at me. "I can't lie to him."

I nod, knowing that asking him to lie would be wrong. "You're right. It was stupid to ask."

"However," he chimes in. "I do plan on going to hang out with him a bit when he gets home. If you need to run some errands or whatever, I'll stay with him. Just bring Paxton with you. I don't like the idea of you *running errands* alone."

Is this his nonchalant way of giving me his approval? Sure does sound like it.

I'm not too keen on the idea of forgiving Paxton this quickly, but Wade is right, I shouldn't do this alone.

LOOKS like I'm going to a party tomorrow night.

CHAPTER 31
PENELOPE

AFTER SITTING at the hospital all night, Blaise was finally released to come home. He's under strict orders to take it easy, so I've got him set up in the basement with everything he should need.

I haven't told him I'm going to the party. Just said I had to run some errands, and Wade was coming to hang with him for the night.

He's still pretty doped up but that isn't stopping him from trying to cop a feel.

Blaise wraps his arms around me and pulls me down on the couch with him. "You need to rest," I say, once again.

"No. The only medicine I need is this." He cups my crotch, curling his fingers into the fabric of my leggings. I'm half-tempted to let him have his way with me, because I'm pretty turned on by this playful side I'm seeing.

"Didn't mean to interrupt," Wade says, coming out of nowhere.

I jump up, my cheeks flushed. *We're caught.*

"He already knows."

My eyes shoot wide open. "What?"

A dozen questions run through my head. How does he know? What does he know? What is there to know?

Wade knocks Blaise's feet off the couch and drops down. "It's all good. I don't judge, and personally, I don't think there is anything to judge. It's not like you're actually brother and sister."

My face drops into my hands. Humiliation is still working its way through me. I screech when Blaise slaps a hand to my ass. "See. We're good."

I spin around to look at him, unable to hide the smile on my face. He pulls me down and presses his lips to mine. "Is this real?" I mutter into the thin space between us. It feels like a dream.

"As real as my erection, that'll be waiting for you when you get back."

I kiss him once more before I stand up and look at Wade. "Don't let him have any more of his prescription pain meds until I get back."

It's the drugs talking. There's no way things are going to be this *easy* with us.

I'M WAITING on Paxton so we can head to the party when he finally emerges from his front door.

"Hey." Paxton slides in the passenger seat of my car. "It's fucking cold out there."

"Yeah. It's brutal. Good thing Emery's party is inside."

"Hey," he grabs my attention. "You still mad at me?"

I'm not really sure how to answer that. "I'm not mad, but I'm not happy with the way you handled things. It is what it is, though. We can't erase our past mistakes; we can only learn from them."

I shift into drive and head to Emery's house with my nerves

at an all-time high. Paxton and I talked a little more last night and he agreed to go with me today. I'm still pretty upset with him, but the more I think about it, his anger is valid. I'm not saying it's excusable, but I'm hopeful we can all move on from this.

Paxton looks tense as he buckles his seatbelt. "You're sure you know what you're doing?"

"Definitely. I've been to Emery's house at least a hundred times. It's been awhile, but they have a theater room with a huge-ass projector screen. The plan is to just play it there."

Wade put together a little video for tonight's entertainment. I'm giving Lilith one shot to come clean, and if she doesn't, I'm blasting her dirty secret for the entire party to see. I never got anything on Emery, which sucks, because she's the one who hurt me the most, but there's always next time. I'm sure after tonight she and Lilith will continue to try and make my life hell, so there's no doubt there will be another chance to return the favor.

We pull up to Emery's house just as my phone buzzes in the pocket of my hoodie. I pull it out and my jaw immediately drops open when I see the text.

"Oh my God," I say out loud, unknowingly.

Unknown: Hi. I received a call from you about my son, Blaise. You mentioned the passing of his father, can you confirm this is true? I can't have this conversation until I'm certain.

"Who is it?" Paxton asks.

I hold up a finger, halting him.

I immediately text Blaise's mom back.

Me: I can promise you that Richard Hale is dead. He can't hurt anyone anymore.

Unknown: I hope he's rotting in hell. How is Blaise?

Me: Great. Well, not so great. I actually think he'd love to see you.

Unknown: Can I call you in the morning? I'd love to make a plan to meet up with him.

Me: Absolutely.

I'm in shock as I close out of the screen on my phone. I'm sure Paxton picks up on my surprise because he's all up in my face.

"Who was that?" he asks, trying to read my expression.

"Blaise's mom." I blink repeatedly. "I can't believe I found her after all these years."

All it took was money for my mom to tell me the truth. My mom met Richard when she was working as a nurse at the cancer clinic. My guess is, she sought him out because he had money and, well, he was terminally ill. She'll never admit it, though. They started having an affair and Blaise's mom found out. Apparently, Richard was physically abusive toward his at-the-time wife and when she threatened to take Blaise and run away, so he'd never see him again, Richard threatened Blaise's life, and her freedom. She was sent away with enough money to survive with the promise that Richard would kill Blaise and pin it on her if she ever came back. Sick bastard. I surely hope he is rotting in hell.

My mom gave me the last known address of Blaise's mom. When Richard passed away, she took everything of substance from his office. I did a search and got a phone number. She had moved since then, but the new owners were able to give me her new address. A little digging and I found the number to her workplace and left a voice message on her private line.

I'm still in shock. Blaise is going to be so happy to reunite with his mom. Five years ago, she disappeared without so much as a goodbye. I know he's tried to find her with no luck.

"Are we ready to do this?" Paxton asks.

I nod. "I think so."

Paxton swings open his door while I take an audible breath and do the same. It's unreal seeing this many people at Emery's house. She always wanted this attention, and now she has it. Too bad she had to become Lilith's clone to do so.

There are cars parked up and down the long driveway,

some even on the lawn. Her dad's gonna be pissed about that. He was always a stickler about his yard. I swear there was a landscaper here every day that I visited.

"We need to stick together, okay?" I tell Paxton. I'm trying not to show my worry, but any party I've ever attended with this crowd has ended badly. They can gain the upper hand in a matter of seconds, and this time, I might not make it out alive.

"Don't worry. I've got you." Paxton takes my hand, and I immediately feel a sense of relief. People might get the wrong idea here, but I remember what Blaise said yesterday. *In ten years, none of these people will even matter.*

The closer we get to the house, the louder the voices and music become. From what I see, everyone is having a good time. There are no fights, no guys jumping off roofs. It's still early, though.

"Hey," Paxton says, tugging my hand. He tips his head in the direction of a couple people talking. "Is that Chase?"

My neck stretches out as I try to get a better look, but it's too dark to tell. "It could be. But who is he talking to?"

Paxton pulls me to the left and we veer off the driveway. "This way."

Leaves crunch beneath our feet, and for the first time ever, I wish we had some snow to hide the sound. It's certainly cold enough as I shiver beneath my winter coat.

We creep along a row of trees until we're within range to hear the conversation being had. It's definitely Chase talking.

"We agreed on two-fifty. I want it all or no deal."

Shit. Is he making another drug deal?

"We also agreed on fifty pills and this looks like half."

My hand claps over my mouth, masking the gasp. "That's Emery," I whisper.

"Every damn time I bring you the goods, you pull this shit. Just take the pills, feed your addiction, and give me the fucking money."

Addiction?

I pull my phone out of the pocket of my coat and swipe open to the camera to begin recording.

Emery snatches something from Chase's hand, likely a bottle of pills. "Or," she pipes up, "you can take the hundred dollars I'm giving you, let me keep these, and I'll keep your secret that you have to sell drugs to keep up with your show of being one of us."

"Being one of you?" Chase bites back. "Says the girl who pops pills daily. Listen, little girl, we made you and we can break you."

"Fuck off," Emery slams a wad of cash into Chase's chest. "Take it or leave it. My guess is, you'll take it, so you can eat another damn day."

I'm speechless. I never would have guessed this was going on behind closed doors. Chase selling drugs to get by. Emery being one of his clients to feed an addiction.

I end the video and we hang back until Chase is out of sight.

"Well, that's a turn of events." Paxton ducks under a branch and heads for the open driveway.

Yeah. It most definitely was.

As we walk toward the crowd, I organize the videos on my phone, just in case I need to use them. I'm hopeful Lilith will comply and it won't come to that.

"There she is," I say, spotting Lilith. Chase joins her side and throws an arm over her shoulder then whispers something in her ear. I wonder if she knows he's been dealing drugs. Lilith has a lot of money and if she cared for Chase at all, I would think she'd find a way to help him. Then again, this is Lilith we're talking about.

"I'll wait here and I won't take my eyes off you. You can do this."

My heart is pounding in my chest, palms sweating, head dizzy. *I can do this.*

At an amble pace, I eat up the space between Lilith and me. When I'm about ten feet away, her attention snaps to me and my entire body burns from her venomous glare.

"You've got to be kidding me," Lilith singsongs, pulling away from Chase and walking steadfast toward me. "You have some nerve showing your face here. Haven't you learned your lesson about showing up where you're not wanted?"

I swallow hard, putting on a mask of badassery. "It seems I haven't. I actually came to see you, Lilith."

"Me?" She laughs. "I hate you, Penelope. Why the hell would you want to see me?"

I lean into her personal space, hoping the tremble of my body isn't visible. "Because I've got something that could destroy you."

Lilith cackles again. "Destroy me? Impossible."

"Oh, it's possible, and it's real. So unless you want the entire school to know your secret, you better give me what I want."

Lilith shoves her hands in my chest, walking me backward, so we're away from nosey ears. "What the hell are you talking about?"

"Who started the fire, Lilith? Tell me now or I'll go inside Emery's house and play the video showing what you've been doing in your spare time."

She steps up to me, nose to nose. "You're bluffing."

"Try me." I take a step forward, bumping her chest with mine, eyes glaring.

We hold this stance for far too long, but I refuse to back down. Finally, Lilith takes a step back. "You're gonna regret this."

My tongue clicks on the roof of my mouth as I smirk. "Maybe I will. Maybe I won't."

Lilith opens her mouth to speak, but the words get away

from her. I follow her gaze behind me and see Emery standing there.

Her eyes are glassed over, expression blank. More than likely, she's high again. "You're not wanted here, Penelope. Go home."

I shake my head. "No, I'm not leaving until I get what I came here for."

"Go home, bitch!" Chase shouts.

Everyone begins chanting in unison, "Loser, loser, loser."

My thoughts escape me. All I can focus on is the words they keep repeating. "Stop!" I shout.

"Loser. Loser. Loser."

Everyone is looking at me. *Everyone.* I can't breathe. I can't think.

"Move," I tell Lilith, who's blocking my path now. My entire body itches at the unwanted stares coming from my classmates.

"MAKE ME, BITCH." *She goes to shove me. I glower, trying to go around her, but she steps back in front of me. "What's the matter, birthday girl? Mad that your own family doesn't even acknowledge the day you were born?"*

THAT DAY I felt like a loser. Everyone laughed and gossiped while encouraging Lilith to break me piece by piece. I was the butt of their jokes. Made a mockery of on my own birthday. Deep down, I believed the words Lilith said.

"Loser. Loser. Loser," the crowd continues.

The thing is, I don't care. Not anymore. Fuck them all. Every single person standing here hoping to play a part in my demise has their own skeletons that will fall out one day. Can't say I wouldn't love to watch it unfold.

Someone grabs me from behind and pulls me back as the

chanting continues. "Come on. Let's just go," Paxton says with two hands on my shoulders.

I walk backward, my eyes deadlocked on Lilith. She's laughing at my expense and having the time of her life. I just glower back at her, hoping she can see in my eyes that her day of reckoning is upon her.

Once we're far enough away and I'm sure I won't get jumped from behind, I turn around and keep walking with Paxton at my side.

Wait. He's leading me to the car!

"No!" I spit out, stopping my movements. "This isn't how my story ends. I came here for something, and I'm not leaving until I get it."

"We should just try another time. They've really got it out for you tonight."

I shake my head, heading back toward the party, as Paxton follows my lead. "No. This ends tonight."

We walk around to the backside of the house and go through the door of the walkout basement. I know this house like the back of my hand. I can hear the stampede of party-goers moving around upstairs, music blasting, people laughing.

"The theater room is upstairs." I just need to sneak in there and connect to the Bluetooth.

"You're sure about this?"

"Paxton," I say, tears welling in my eyes, "I've never been surer about anything. It's time they atone for their sins."

Paxton nods in agreement. "Give me your phone. I'll connect it. You just hang back and try not to be seen."

My lips press together as I fight back the tears. Tears of anger, sadness, and also appreciation for Paxton.

We creep up the stairs and open the door at the top. Once we're in the crowd, I keep my head down, trying to blend in, pressing my back to the far wall. There are people gathered outside the theater room. I can see the door is open and it's also full of people. My eyes snap to the projector.

Paxton gives me a knowing look. Wasting no time, he goes straight to it.

"Lookie here," a guy I don't recognize says. "It's Skull Creek's biggest loser."

My arms cross over my chest and I look away, hoping this drunk idiot will leave me alone.

"Loser. Loser. Loser," he begins, although he can't be heard over the loud chatter.

"Do I know you?"

"No, but I know you." It's apparent he's had too much to drink, the way his body sways back and forth. "Pretty sure you were told to leave."

He must've been outside during my altercation with Lilith. "Get lost."

Instead of doing what I asked, he slides his body up to mine. "How about we get lost together. I've never had a loser suck on my dick before."

"Ugh," I grumble in disgust, shoving him away from me. He staggers, losing his balance and falls into a group of girls. Their drinks spill down the front of their shirts and they make a big fuss, grabbing the attention of everyone in the room.

I should have known this wouldn't go smoothly.

Paxton looks at me and gestures toward the screen. "Now?" he shouts over the crowd.

I nod. "Yes. Play it."

The video of Lilith and Coach Anderson begins playing, but there's no sound. No one even notices. Paxton adjusts the volume on my phone, and we can finally hear them over the surround sound. Everyone stops what they're doing and all eyes shoot to the projector.

People gasp, hoot, holler, and eventually, more people start coming into the room. Phones are pulled out, recording the video.

It wraps up, but Paxton put it on loop, so it'll play three times, making sure it isn't missed. Next up is Chase and his deal in his front yard.

"What the hell is this? Stop that!" Lilith screeches as she comes barreling into the room. She heads straight for Paxton, shoving him out of the way.

No. We haven't got to Chase and Emery.

I push through the crowd, making a beeline for Lilith. Once I reach her, I shove her until she stumbles back a few steps. "I gave you the chance to tell me the truth and you declined my offer. Now everyone can know what a little whore you are."

Lilith raises her hand, slapping me hard across the face. The pain isn't even noticeable as I push her again, knocking her on her ass.

"You want the truth?" she howls. "Fine." She gets herself up and knocks my phone out of Paxton's hand, then messes with hers for a minute.

"What are you doing?" I ask her, unsure if this is good or bad.

Lilith smirks as she interrupts the video with one of her own.

It's the barn engulfed in flames. Firefighters are blasting it with hoses, trying to put it out. I'm trying to process what I'm looking at, but the memories of that night flood me all at once.

"Shut it off!" I hear Blaise's voice coming from behind me. I don't even turn around. I'm too captivated by the glowing embers on the screen. Watching board by board fall and crumble into the mosh pit of flames. Blaise steps in front of me. "Let's go." He walks his body into mine, trying to get me to move, but I don't. I pay no attention to the swelling and bruises on his face. His weak demeanor and his presence. All I can focus on is the video.

Blaise and Lilith quarrel as he tries to stop the video, but it's too late.

My heart drops. I feel like I've been smacked in the face with a two-by-four.

Clear as day, I watch my mom sneaking behind a tree. She reaches down and grabs the gas can, then disappears into the woods.

Blaise and Lilith both freeze, watching me. Waiting for me to break down. "Why…why was she there, Blaise?"

Frozen in place, I just stand there, watching the video replay in my head.

"Penny. Let's go." Blaise pulls me away. My feet move, but I'm not sure where I'm going as he leads me out of the room. My body is in a state of shock.

"Did she start the fire, Blaise? Did my mom try to kill me?"

"I told you to let it go, Pen. Dammit, you should have just let it go."

My own mother. The woman who brought me into this world and is supposed to love me unconditionally.

It looks like I got what I came here for. Now, I'm not sure I want it anymore.

CHAPTER 32
BLAISE

"PENNY," I shout once more before I hear her bedroom door slam shut.

I can't believe she thinks I started the fire. I ran in to save her without even giving it a second thought. I was ready to burn for her.

I'm heading to the basement when my phone rings in my pocket. I pull it out and see that it's a call from Lilith. Before she can even speak, I tear into her. "So help me God, if you bitches had anything to do with that fire last night, you'll never show your face in this town again."

"Blaise," she says, "we didn't do it."

I feel the strain of the chorded veins in my neck bulging out. "Quit lying to me, you stupid bitch!"

"I'm not lying. We didn't do it, but I know who did. I stood back while the others went to the party. I saw you carry Penny out of the fire."

Shit. She saw us? She better not have fucking watched us through the windows. Wouldn't put it past this masochist.

"Why the hell didn't you leave? You could have been seen." Not that I care, but it's a dumb call on her part.

"Curiosity, I guess. Anyways," she continues, "Once you were inside that old house, I saw Penelope's mom. Blaise, I think she did it, and I have proof."

"Wait? What do you mean you have proof? Why the hell would Ana be out there?"

"Well, it looks to me like she wanted to kill her daughter."

My body goes numb as I look around to make sure Penny can't hear any of this, then I walk over to the kitchen table and sit down.

"That's insane. She wouldn't try and kill her own daughter. Send me the video."

There's a long silence that has my blood boiling. "Send me the damn video, Lilith."

"I sent it."

I put her on hold while I watch, and sure as shit, there's Ana. She's snatching up the gas can and running off.

"You can't tell Penny. You hear me? She can never know. It'll kill her."

Another beat of silence.

"It wouldn't break my heart one bit to hurt that girl. But, I've got a deal for you."

"You would, you evil cunt!"

"I'll keep this secret, but you stay the hell out of my way. I do what I want, when I want. If you get in my way, she's toast."

Penny rolls onto her side, facing me on my bed, tearing me out of my thoughts.

"Blaise. Tell me now. Please."

After the fallout from last night, I got Penny out of there and brought her home. She cried for hours, asking for answers, but I promised her I'd tell her everything today. And I will.

It was my plan to tell her yesterday, but dumbass Paxton had to go and jump me in the hall. He's still on my shitlist.

I slide down so that I'm looking right at her with my head pressed to the pillow. "Okay. I'll tell you everything."

Ana comes walking into the kitchen, clicking her heels against the hardwood floor. She looks primped and primed, nothing like a woman who just lit a barn on fire the night before.

"Blaise!" Ana huffs, her face pale, like she's seen a ghost. "What are you doing here?"

I stretch my arms on the back of the chairs on either side of me, a shit-eating grin on my face. "Good morning, Ana. Did you sleep well?"

She shuffles a bit with her purse, then drops it on the counter. "I umm, I didn't expect to see you. Yes, I slept well. Thank you."

I've already talked to my dad. He knows what Ana did. His fixation with Penny has him on board to make this woman's life a living hell. We're gonna strip her of everything she loves and enjoy every second doing it.

"It takes a real piece of work to sleep well after trying to kill their only child. Doesn't it, Ana?"

Ana stops fidgeting with her phone and looks at me, astonishment written all over her face. "What are you talking about? Who would ever do such a thing?"

"Oh, I dunno. You." I push the chair back and get to my feet, closing the space between us. I get a firm grip on Ana's chin, getting right in her face, so she hears me loud and clear. "I know what you did last night and I've got proof. You tried to kill Penelope. If it weren't for me running in that barn to save her, she'd have much more than a third-degree burn on her arm."

I can see the bob in her neck from her rapid pulse. She trembles beneath me, stuttering over her words. "That's…that's insane. I'd never—"

"It's on video. You did, and if you know what's good for you, you'll listen loud and clear."

"Blaise," she interrupts me, "I'd never hurt Penelope. I love her."

"Then why'd you start the fire with her inside?"

"I…I didn't know she was in there. I wasn't trying to hurt her." She jerks away and I let her, only so she can finish what she has to say. Spinning on her heels, dropping her face in her hands, she *begins sobbing. "Your car was there. You're always at that barn. I thought it was you inside."*

My jaw drops open. Me? "You tried to kill me?"

It almost makes me feel a little better, knowing she wasn't trying to kill her own daughter, but it's still psychotic as hell. Sort of funny, too. She actually thought she could get rid of me. It's no doubt that it was for my place in Dad's will.

Her head shoots up from her hands and she palms her hips. "That's not what I meant."

She goes to walk away, but I grab her by the wrist. "This is what you're going to do. Listen to me very clearly. You'll let Penny leave and go live with her dad where it's safe. I don't trust the kids in this town, and I certainly don't trust you. If you don't, she'll know everything. She'll know you're the one who almost took her life."

"It doesn't change anything. I hate her, Blaise. Even if she wasn't trying to kill me, she still attempted to murder you, and hurt me in the process. It hurts. It hurts so damn bad."

"Trust me. I get it. I prefer you stay far away from that lady. All she cares about is money and she doesn't care who she hurts in her quest to get it."

"I'm sorry I doubted you, Blaise. All this time I thought you wanted to hurt me, but you really were just trying to protect my feelings and keep me safe. I wish you'd told me sooner, but I understand why you didn't."

Our mouths connect and it's everything. It doesn't matter where we came from, who our parents are/were, or what happened in the past. Everything we went through brought us here today. "I love you, Penny."

Her eyes light up, glimmering in the streak of sunlight cast on her face. "I love you, too."

We lie in bed, talking for another hour about the past, the present, the future.

"I gave her all my money," Penny says out of nowhere with a downcast gaze.

Bracing myself on my elbow, I look down at her. "Why would you do that?"

"There's something I have to tell you. You can't be mad, though."

I drop back on the pillow, mentally preparing myself for what she's about to say. So much has happened over the last twenty-four hours that I'm not sure anything could surprise me. "All right. Let's hear it."

"I found your mom."

My head shoots up and I look at her. "You what?"

Penny meets my stare and sits up. "My mom knew where she was this whole time. I found her."

Words escape me as I try to think of something to say. *She found my mom?*

I feel excited, nervous, scared, unsure. So many emotions hit me at once. Memories of my childhood replaying in my head. My mom was so kind and attentive. Her heart was huge and she always had a smile on her face.

Penny goes on to tell me everything my mom told her. About the abuse and the threats. How she was forced away. Then, she gives me her number. I have so much to think about before I make the call, but one day, I hope I have the courage to do it. Until then, I've got the one person I want right by my side.

I tug the blanket up and put a hand on Penny's waist, pulling her body flush with mine.

Her eyes widen when my rock-hard cock grinds against her and she bites her lip, knowing that drives me wild. "You're still healing. I think we should wait."

"I'm fine. I promise. Besides," I slide my hand down her shorts, cupping her pussy. "This is the best medicine."

Penny maneuvers her hips, getting closer, and I know she wants it just as bad as I do.

Two fingers slide inside her swollen pussy. "Tell me this is mine," I say in an authoritative tone.

She doesn't answer, so I pull my fingers out. Her eyes widen and she glowers at me. "Don't stop."

"Tell me then."

Leaning forward, she speaks into my mouth. "It's yours." She grabs my cock through my boxer shorts and I twitch in delight. "And this is mine."

"Damn straight it is." I shove the blankets off us and roll over on top of her, parting her legs with my knee. Our mouths cement together as I finger-fuck her, grating my hungry cock against her leg.

Penny bucks her hips up, wanting more, so I slide another finger in, filling her up. It's a satisfying feeling, knowing that I staked a claim on this girl two years ago and her pussy hasn't been touched by another dick. I know damn well that dick-wad, Ryan, never stuck his dick inside her. She is mine in every sense of the word. Her heart, her soul, her body.

Penny closes her eyes, dropping her head back. Her legs spread wider, arousal soaking my fingers as I slide them in and out of her tight sex.

She moans in pleasure and I pick up my pace, bending my fingers and pumping them deep inside of her.

I watch her expression as she tenses up, holds her breath, and releases into my hand.

In a matter of seconds, I rid us both of our clothing.

My body cloaks hers, feeling her puckered nipples against my chest. Craning my neck, I take one into my mouth, sucking hard as I line my cock with her entrance. "God, you're so fucking beautiful," I mutter into her mouth as I slide inside of her.

Sweltering from the inside out, I go deeper, giving her my full length. So tight, warm, wet, and mine.

I sweep a hand under her head and lift, bringing our mouths together.

She pants a heavy breath into my mouth, nails digging into my back. "Blaise."

The way my name rolls off her tongue throws me into a frenzy. I pick up my pace, fucking her hard and fast. Feeling her insides envelop my cock.

Two hands find my shoulders. Pushing down, driving me deeper inside of the gateway to heaven. God, this girl is so perfect. I want to make a home inside her pussy and stay here for an eternity.

"Fuck, Blaise. I'm coming again."

I thrust again, unable to hold it. Electricity ripping through me. Every cell in my body is overcharged and ready to combust. "Fuck," I groan into the nape of her neck. I thrust once, twice, and release, spilling my cum inside her.

Dropping down, I refrain from putting my full weight on her. Her arms wrap around my back as I nuzzle my head between her titties.

A few minutes pass while we catch our breath and steady our heart rates.

"Can we stay in bed all day?" Penny asks through a shaky breath.

"We *are* staying in bed all day."

When we do finally get out of bed, we'll come back here at night and every night after that, as long as she'll stay. Because I never wanna let this girl go again.

CHAPTER 33
PENELOPE

MY HAND SWINGS back and as my palm meets the side of her face, I howl, "How dare you!"

Mom cups her cheek with both hands, eyes as wide as saucers. "Penelope Briar. What in the world has gotten into you?"

As if she doesn't know.

"What's gotten into me," I laugh. "What's gotten into me? Oh, I don't know. How about the fact that you lit a fucking barn on fire with me inside it. Do you see this?" I hold out my arm, showing the evidence of her destruction. "You did this to me."

"Honey, I..." she stumbles over her words, trying to find the easiest way out of this. "It was...it was an accident."

"An accident," I laugh again, though it's mocking and loaded with sarcasm. "You accidentally bump into someone. You accidentally spill a glass of milk." My voice raises and I show no restraint. "You don't accidentally set your daughter on fire!"

There are tears in her eyes but they do nothing to console me. I've known this woman my entire life. When she cries, it's because of her own woes. Those tears have nothing to do with the way her actions affected me.

Her face drops into her hands and she begins sobbing uncontrollably. "I'm so sorry," she says through bouts of sniffles. "I didn't know you were inside."

I grab her hands, pulling them away from her face so she's able to look me in the eye when I speak. "That may be true. You thought Blaise was inside, though, didn't you? You tried to kill him so you could be the sole heir to Richard's estate?"

Her only response is more of a blubbery mess as black mascara slides down her cheeks.

"How'd that work out for you, *Mom*?" I smile, loving every minute of her downfall. "Probably didn't expect Blaise to run to his daddy and tell him everything, did you?"

That grabs her attention.

She stops crying, sweeping away the tears while smearing her makeup even more. "Blaise told Richard?"

I nod. "He sure did. The day after the fire, he told his dad everything. You were never getting his money. This entire time you thought you had it in the bag. Boy, were you wrong."

It's humorous how quickly her expression changes from remorseful to downright angry.

"That son of a bitch!" she grumbles, eyes narrowed at the floor. "He played me. For two entire years, he played me."

"Karma's a bitch, ain't she?" I snatch my purse off the counter in her small apartment kitchen. "If you ever need anything, *don't* come to me."

"Penelope! Wait!" she hollers as I slam the apartment door closed behind me. She tears it back open but I'm already halfway down the stairs. "Please, don't leave me. I'm all alone now."

When I reach the bottom, I turn and look at her, a brief moment of sympathy weighing heavy on my chest. "Get some help, Mom. Once you've thawed your heart out, maybe

I'll be willing to do some counseling with you to repair what you broke."

With that, I leave, knowing that the door is closed on my relationship with my mom. I'm hopeful one day in the future she'll reflect on her life and decide to amend her mistakes. Maybe then I'll crack the door back open, but I'll never fully trust her enough to let her back in.

☠

I'M on pins and needles waiting for Blaise to finish his call with his mom. He's pacing the back deck with ankle-high snow boots on, a pair of gym shorts and a cut-off shirt. He's gotta be freezing his ass off out there. We got dumped on with a foot of snow last night and, of course, it's the day we both return to school after taking a few days off so we could recuperate.

Blaise ends the call and the smile on his face tells me it went well. I don't even hesitate to tear the sliding door open. "Well?"

"Let me in first. It's fucking cold out here." He shivers and walks through the door, tracking snow on the floor.

I close it behind him and turn around. Blaise wraps his arms around me, kisses my forehead, and looks at me. "She's coming to visit next week."

"Yay!" I beam with excitement. "Do you think she'll end up staying for good?"

"I don't know. We'll have to see. I'm gonna offer her the house. She deserves it and we're leaving in five months for dorm life anyways."

This is the best news.

I'm so happy that Blaise has the chance to rebuild his relationship with his mom.

Mixed feelings swirl inside of me. Relief and happiness for him; anguish and disappointment for myself. There is no chance of that happening on my part. The woman I once called 'Mom' is gone. I've got all the family I need. I have a loving dad in Portland, and I have Blaise.

She did this to herself, to us. It's her loss, really.

I drop my arms and take a step back. "All right. Let's get to school and see what's in store for us today."

Blaise grabs me by the waist, refusing to let me go. Planting kisses down my neck, he says, "What if I try to hold your hand in the hall?"

I chuckle, remembering how mad he got when I pulled away last time. "I dunno. I guess you'll have to try and see what happens."

☠

WE ENTER the school and I keep my head held high. Students stare, they whisper, they laugh. We ignore it all. Blaise reaches over and grabs my hand and I tangle my fingers around his. We share a smile then return our focus on the hall as we walk. Crowds part in our path, stopping to see if this is a joke. But it's not. Blaise and I *are* together.

For the first time since the fire, I'm wearing a short-sleeved shirt. My scar is on full display for everyone to see. It's crazy, but I'm not even embarrassed by it anymore. It's my scar—my battle wound. Proof that I can overcome anything thrown my way.

Everyone knows that my mom started that fire. They know I was inside and could have died at her hands. I'm not even sure if my mom realizes the extent of her destruction. I'm not sure she even cares.

Lilith's video went viral, and Coach Anderson was terminated from his position. She claims she was coerced into a sexual relationship with him and got off scot-free. Instead of ruining her, we actually built her up. She's been deemed a legend for sleeping with the coach. By the girls, anyway. To the guys, she's a whore who spread her legs for a forty-year old, married man. We all have a silent understanding that she'll stay out of our way and we'll stay out of hers.

Passing by Chase, he hangs his head low, avoiding eye contact. Emery and Chase's videos never played, but it never had to. A few days ago Emery's parents found her stash and she didn't hesitate to rat Chase out as her dealer. It's no surprise she was as shitty of a friend to them as she was to me.

Emery is currently in rehab and Chase is out on bail and facing charges for possession and distribution of narcotics. It's highly unlikely that he'll be attending school this fall. Can't say I'm sorry he got caught. Karma really is a bitch.

"Hey, Paxton." I wave as we pass by him and Wade. Blaise has agreed to give Paxton the benefit of the doubt. He kicked his ass and Paxton returned the favor. The score is settled so we're leaving it at that.

We reach Blaise's locker. My hand drops from his and he wraps an arm around me, tugging me close. In front of watchful eyes, Blaise presses his mouth to mine, kissing me with so much passion that my knees go weak.

"They're all watching," I whisper into his lips.

"Let 'em watch."

So I do. I fall into the kiss, knowing that together, we're unstoppable. Blaise has his title back as the king of the school, and I'm the queen at his side.

EPILOGUE

PENELOPE

"DAMN. THIS IS NICE," Blaise says, scoping out my dorm room. "In fact, I think it's better than mine."

I place a canvas painting of an angel and a devil holding hands on a nail on my wall then step off the bed. "It's a pretty small room, but it works." My back is still facing Blaise as I admire the wall hanging.

Closing the space between us, Blaise wraps his arms around my waist from behind. His chin rests on my shoulder and he takes in an audible breath. "I missed you last night," he hums into my hair.

I pivot around, arms wrapping around his neck. "It was one night." I lick my lips when I see him watching mine. "We agreed that the dorms and separate rooms would be a good thing."

"I got so used to having you in my bed every night. Not to mention all these horny college boys that walk the halls in search of a lay."

With unwavering eyes, I grin. "It's a dorm of girls and I have a very, very," I emphasize, "badass roommate."

I'm not lying. Leah has the brawn of a man and doesn't hold back when it comes to voicing her opinion.

"I just worry. You're easily the hottest girl on campus, and I know how guys are."

His declaration has me blushing. I'm far from the hottest girl on campus, but I'll take the compliment, knowing that he truly believes I am.

"I'll be fine. I promise." I kiss his parted lips. He wastes no time, sliding his tongue in my mouth.

I know Blaise worries. It's what he does. He's so scared that there will be a replay of the events that took place in high school. I've assured him many times, this is a different crowd and not everyone is as cruel as Lilith, as deplorable as Chase, or as deceptive as Emery. Not to mention, as erratic as him.

Everything slips away. Every worry he's bestowed on me. All the strangers surrounding us outside that door. None of it matters as I fall into this kiss. Our hearts beat in sync, his thumping against my chest and mine against his. Sometimes I wonder how I got so lucky, then I remember that luck had nothing to do with it. I fought hard for these feelings—for this love. I'm so consumed by Blaise that it's both terrifying and exciting. What makes it even better, I trust him now and I know he feels exactly the same way.

"Stay with me tonight," Blaise breathes in my mouth.

I laugh into our kiss, gulping the air he just exhaled. "It's only our second night here. I prefer not to break the rules so soon."

"That's the thing about rules." His hand skates up my shirt, leaving a trail of goosebumps in the path of his fingers. "They're made to be broken."

The door to my room flies open and Blaise and I both backstep away from each other. I pull my shirt back down in place and wipe the back of my hand across my mouth.

Leah throws her hands up in surrender. "Whoa. Sorry, roomie. Didn't mean to interrupt."

I laugh at her liveliness. "No worries. Blaise and I were

just leaving. I'm going to Blaise's for a couple hours, but I *will* be back later."

"Maybe." Blaise steers me to the door. "She *might* be back later."

"Might wanna knock before you come in. Haven't had my own space since I was in my mama's womb. Haven't been laid in three years. You just never know what might be going on in my bed, if you know what I mean."

"Um, okay." I grimace. "I'll try to remember that."

Blaise gives me a concerned look, likely worried about the sanity of my new roommate.

"Come on," I say, pushing him out the door and closing it behind us. Before he can speak, I hold up a hand. "Don't. She's a sweet girl."

He zips his fingers across his lips. "Wasn't gonna say a thing."

We both laugh as we walk down the hall. It feels so nice not to stand out. We're just an average couple in a big school, full of people who don't know us and don't care what we do. It's a nice change of pace from Skull Creek.

Our last couple months there weren't all that bad, but every time we turned a corner, someone would stare and whisper. *Aren't they brother and sister? That's so disgusting. Their parents are married? I hear she's a whore and she's slept with his dad, too.*

Eventually, I learned to ignore it, until I didn't care at all.

It's a quick drive to the guys' dorms on the opposite side of campus. One of the perks about Arvine is the freshmen can have cars, whereas some schools don't allow that. Naturally, Wade and Blaise are in a dorm together, and Paxton, who has become a pretty good friend to all of us, is three doors down from them with Ryder.

"How are the guys settling in?" I ask Blaise as he shifts into drive and pulls out of the parking lot.

"I'd say pretty good, considering Wade and Paxton stayed

up until three in the morning playing video games and laughing their asses off at absolutely nothing."

I bite back a smile, which Blaise catches when he glances at me. "What's that look for?"

"What look?"

"That giddy-ass grin on your face."

"Nothing. I'm not grinning."

He reaches over and tickles my upper thigh. "What are you hiding?"

It's not my place to say anything, and there's a good chance I'm totally off base, but I don't tell him I think there's something going on between Wade and Paxton. Actually, I know there is. Paxton told me he had a crush on Wade. Wade's never came out and said that he likes guys, but I've had a feeling ever since he drove me home from Poppy's last fall. He talked about how he'd love to go somewhere where he can just be himself and doesn't have to pretend. After that, I picked up on things, such as the way he looks at Paxton.

"Don't make me pull this car over and fuck it out of you."

"In that case, my lips are sealed."

Blaise slams on the brakes, throwing my body forward. Thankfully, I put on my seatbelt.

"Are you challenging me?"

I laugh at him as he undoes his seatbelt and leans over the center console. "We're in the middle of the road. Get back over there and drive." I shove him, but he only comes closer, stealing a kiss before he retreats and drops back in his seat.

"I'll get it out of you one way or another."

His hand rests on my thigh the rest of the short drive. Once we get to the dorms, he parks and we make our way up to his room. People are still moving in, so there are guys carrying furniture, bags, dressers, and even huge-ass televisions.

Blaise pushes his door open and to our surprise, it's

empty. His eyebrows waggle as he grins. "Looks like we've got the place to ourselves for a bit."

"Lucky us."

Blaise kicks the door shut and tackles me from behind, lifting me up and carrying me over to the bed. In one swift motion, I'm on my back with his chest pressed to mine. Our eyes burn into each other and I swear I could live in this moment.

"I love you," Blaise says, peering over me.

My heart skips a thousand beats. "I love you, too."

I never planned on this. Never thought the man of my dreams was living two stories beneath the bedroom he taunted me in. I fell for the most unexpected person and at the most unexpected time. That's the beauty of this thing between us, it never stops surprising us.

I met the devil when I was fourteen years old. By the time I was eighteen, I was madly in love with him.

The End.

THANK YOU FOR READING! If you enjoyed Devil Heir, be sure to check out my Redwood Rebels Series. Bad boys, strong girls, and so many twists you won't see coming.

NOTE FROM THE AUTHOR

Thank you so much for reading Devil Heir. I hope you loved Penny and Blaise as much as I do. If you'd be so kind and leave an honest review, I'd be forever grateful!

I'd also like to thank everyone who helped bring this baby to life—Carolina, Amanda, Sara, Rebecca, Rumi, and Kirsty. Thank you for the support, alpha/beta reading, edits, proof-reading, graphics, and cover.

A big thank you to my amazing Street Team, The Rebel Readers! You're support means so much to me!

Thanks to the members of my readers group, The Ramblers, I'm so grateful to have found you all!

ALSO BY RACHEL LEIGH

BOOK LIST

Redwood Rebels Series

Book One: Striker

Book Two: Heathen

Book Three: Vandal

Book Four: Reaper

Redwood High Series

Book One: Like Gravity

Book Two: Like You

Book Three: Like Hate

Fallen Kingdom Duet

His Hollow Heart

Her Broken Pieces: Coming February 2022

Standalones

Guarded

Four

Claim your FREE copy of Her Undoing

ABOUT THE AUTHOR

Rachel Leigh is a USA Today bestselling author of new adult and contemporary romance with a twist. You can expect bad boys, strong heroines, and an HEA.

Rachel lives in leggings, overuses emojis, and survives on books and coffee. Writing is her passion. Her goal is to take readers on an adventure with her words, while showing them that even on the darkest days, love conquers all.

www.rachelleighauthor.com
Rachel's Ramblers Readers Group

Printed in Great Britain
by Amazon